To Andrea.
Lots of lo
Grace Xx

TWO MOMENTS OF MADNESS

2ND IN THE HILARIOUS ANYTHING FOR LOVE
SERIES.

GRACIE BOND

TWO MOMENTS

of

MADNESS

© Gracie Bond, 2022

No part of this publication may be replaced, stored in a retrieval system, or transmitted, in any form or by any means, without the prior permission of the publisher, nor be otherwise circulated in any form of binding or cover other than that in which it is published and without a similar condition including this condition being imposed on the subsequent purchaser.

This book is a work of fiction. Names, characters, places and incidents are either a product of the author's imagination or are used fictitiously.

Cover design © 2022 Gracie Bond - Published by Gracie Bond

✸ Created with Vellum

I dedicate this novel to Jeff Poole, a man who touched my soul with his gentleness and wit, kindness, and laughter. And I know if I said, 'Say hello to my heavenly friends.' You'd have been into it once you'd picked up your heavenly souls, first. You were that kind of person. A true gem.

We will remember your patience when taking endless photos of outstanding quality of the animals and flora you loved so much. Those images, we know, will be seen lifetimes from now. We are all proud to have known you, Jeff. Our loss is heaven's gain.

We miss you.

True love never dies, it rekindles when we meet our soulmate again and rest assured, we do.

OTHER TITLES IN THIS SERIES.

Anything for Love
Book One

Romantic Comedy: Leah, desperate to raise money for her grandad's operation, bungee jumps into her first and *only* date as a paid hooker, almost knocking her client Dan Ryan out cold, then she makes up to him by being amazing; but neither knows his condoms have been pricked! Almost nine years on, her son Tom wants to meet his dad, and he wants to meet him now. Yikes! Leah performs crazy attention-seeking antics to get Dan to listen to her, but this unconventional, bumpy journey is crossed with Dan's jealous PA, Chelsea and everything her devious mind connives. Can true love survive?

GRACIE'S NOVEL ANYTHING FOR LOVE IS BASED ON HER AWARD-WINNING SCREENPLAY.

Anything for Love received the accolade of:

The Emerging Artist's Award for Best Comedy Script 2015/6 Filmmakers

An award Gracie is truly grateful for and very proud of. Her dream would be to get it on screen. And who knows maybe the whole trilogy, one day. She keeps asking the Cosmos in hope they are listening and is grateful they are listening now.

1

THE PRINCESS

hitby, north-east England

W Dan Ryan walked through into his wife's café - the Amazing Dog Friendly Café - wearing khaki shorts and a simple white T-shirt emblazoned with *Pilates Pays Off* across his well-muscled chest. He spared a look to the view of the North Sea, a seascape he cherished. On his head, Dan wore a baseball cap with a Newfoundland dog's image on it, specifically *his* dog,

Hero. Despite his informal clothes, Dan looked as distinguished as ever.

The May Day holiday was almost upon them, and tourists were flocking to the seaside, but many were caught out without a coat or umbrella as the strong coastal breeze and the occasional cloud-burst often hampered the sunshine.

Joey, Leah's cousin, popped his head around the kitchen doorjamb. He was as camp as ever in his own white T-shirt with the image of a pink flamingo on it, holding its hand on its hip and rolling its eyes. Beneath it was printed *Gay and Proud of It*.

'You've got a whole week off work, and you're in here,' he said to Dan. 'Are you crazy, man?'

Dan grinned. 'Leah is having a ride on the beach, and I need to get back to reality. I'm on the school run too.'

'Gosh, she's got you wrapped round her little finger,' Joey sniped, knowing it would wind him up.

'No, Joey, I offered,' said Dan with a quirk of his brow. 'Actually, she looks a bit tired, and I was worried about her.'

'Can't you handle our Leah? Or is she the one who handles you?' asked Joey with a straight face.

'Not sure what you mean,' Dan said, looking a bit cross. 'Leah and I are a team.'

Joey burst into laughter. 'I get you every time. You're just so easy to wind up. Five years on, after you met up again, do you still love her? And do you still fancy her?'

'What do you think?' Dan responded with a smug smile.

'Wait a minute, you're not answering my question,' Joey said. 'Is there a reason for that, Danny boy?'

'Yes, of course I am still in love with her, and I fancy her too - not that my sex-life is any of your business. I don't ask you what you get up to in your bedroom with Ben, do I? Perish the thought,' Dan said.

'Well, that's typical. I said nothing about sex, Dan Ryan-Savidis!' Joey gave an enormous sigh. 'What would your mother say to that?'

'My mother would say it is our private business, Joey. Leah loves all of us, without losing her own identity, and as her husband I support her wholeheartedly.' Dan wished Joey had not mentioned the word 'mother' because he knew Joey was missing his own mum very badly. His parents Robbie and Susan had been away overseas travelling around Australia and were only very rarely in touch. The last he'd heard they were on their way through Hay and on to Wagga Wagga for a few days before making their way to Canberra. Dan could tell that Joey was annoyed with him because that was the only time Joey called him by his full name.

'Well, you're lucky. I wish someone would tell that mother of mine how to be a good mother like yours, and come back for her only son's wedding! She'd rather be in Wagga flippin' Wagga!' Joey stomped back into the kitchen, but not before Dan had seen the shimmer of tears in his eyes. He could hardly blame the young man, knowing how Joey would have loved to have his mum and dad around to get him through his pre-wedding jitters before marrying Ben. Oh well, if anyone could find Joey's parents in the outback, Sisco would do it - and unbeknownst to Joey, Dan had already assigned him the job; in fact, Sisco had been in Wollongong only the day before yesterday, arranging for Dan's jet to be available to bring the three of them home – once he found the couple. Only Dan and Leah knew of his mission.

Dan wanted to confide in Scotty, the bodyguard and driver who had always been close to him, but couldn't trust him not to blab. The fellow was incapable of keeping a secret. At the moment, Scotty was nodding off in a comfy chair with Hero laid on the floor by his side doing the same. Hero raised his tired head and Dan winked at his boy. No matter what people had said to him over the years, he sensed that his canine friend understood a lot of what he was saying to him. Not that long ago, Hero had saved his life. The Newfoundland had pushed him out of harm's way when a loose tile had blown off the stable roof; its sharp edge missed Hero by centimetres. It was the next job Dan had to get done on Scarthingdale Hall.

He pondered about the Hall. It had been very run down when they'd first bought it, and thanks to Leah's local knowledge he'd managed to acquire it for a song. Dan had been so busy over the past few years with his business empire that he had let Leah deal with all the renovations - and what a fabulous job she had done. While the work was ongoing they'd lived on the land in two caravan-style/mobile homes joined together, purchased from the campsite on the hill overlooking the harbour. Dan's mum Sophie and her best friend Ruby had stayed on at Leah's grandad's house in Whitby until their own wing at Scarthingdale Hall had been finished a few weeks ago, just in time for Joey's and Ben's wedding. The old gentleman Thomas was only too happy for the company, delighted to let the two women lodge with him until the big house was ready for them. Who would have thought a billionaire and his family would be as happy as pigs in mud in a mobile home! It must surely be poky for a tall man like Dan, but Dan didn't mind, as long as he could cuddle up with Leah. He had insisted that the builders worked on the master bedroom suite and the kids' rooms before anything else. Their first Christmas had seen Leah and Dan gathering around a large dining table at Thomas's house.

Dan remembered the day when his mother and Thomas had asked them all to run away with them to Gretna Green and get married there, with the children in attendance. It was a lovely idea. Gretna Green was historically romantic for runaway couples. The old blacksmith's smithy there had been charming and close to one of their favourite hotels. They'd all had a great time. Alice, the daughter of Leah and Dan born after their reunion following eight years of separation, was too young to remember the occasion, although she was very intelligent for her age, and would always say she did recall it.

Leah, 'my wife' - it still felt good to say those words, Dan thought. Since the day she'd walked back into his life, she had turned his world on a spinning axis and it was only just slowing down, but he knew she would speed it up again with her next great idea. In the past five years, those ideas had made them millions. Now, standing at the coffee machine in the café, he frothed up some milk, added a double shot of coffee and walked over to place the cup in front of the sleeping man.

'Scotty, mate, wakey wakey. Hero needs a walk after you've drunk this coffee.' Dan shook the little fellow's shoulder. 'Didn't you sleep last night?'

Scotty opened his eyes and said rudely, 'Bugger off, will you. I was just in the middle of a pleasant dream. Don't you forget I'm retired - you can't order me about now.' He eyed his coffee. 'Give us it here.'

Dan did so, saying, 'Yes, you are *semi*-retired but you can walk Hero when we ask, just as long as you feel well enough. You can still take him for a stroll on the beach, but be careful to keep away from the west side of the harbour. I was speaking to the Dog Warden this morning, and he told me we're not allowed on some parts of the beach now, particularly down by the quayside. However, we can go for walks on the east-side beaches below the Abbey, or further up here towards Sandsend. I've checked the tide, you'll be safe. So, if you want to drive him down there, the keys are at the back of the counter or you can walk from here.'

'You mean Mr Grumpy Britches the Dog Warden? He's a jobsworth if ever I saw one,' Scotty griped, taking a big slurp of coffee and knowing it would annoy Dan.

'Yes, and he's doing a job, Scotty. A paid job, like I pay you to walk Hero.' Dan marched back to the counter. Several customers were watching and listening, some even chuckling as Dan's words were like water off a duck's back.

Joey placed a set of perfectly decorated ginger-bread policemen and women in the cabinet. He was a brilliant and inventive baker, and always added a bit of humour to his creations. 'Hark at the kettle calling the pot black,' he sang out.

Scotty chuckled to himself. Although Dan Ryan was a wealthy businessman, the men who worked for him and shared his life with Leah treated him like an equal. It was all in good fun.

'I'll take Hero as soon as I've had my coffee and a gingerbread copper,' Scotty said. 'By the way,' he went on after snapping a WPC in two and dipping her lower half in his drink, 'that

Sergeant Warke was asking if we'd seen any flying bungee jumpers or Fabergé eggs recently.

Thinks he's being so clever, doesn't he. I don't know how the bloke ever got to be Sergeant.

He'd be much better off in the dungeons in York – that way he could frighten the ghosts. They

wouldn't haunt anything with his ugly mug around.'

Swigging the rest of the policewoman down with a gulp of his coffee, Scotty glanced up and caught sight of a bent old woman dragging a little dog along the West Cliff, jerking at its collar in a cruel way. The woman then disappeared from view, but he could swear he'd seen her before – probably in this beautiful seaside town he now called home.

The woman was soon forgotten, however, when Joey placed a second gingerbread police officer in front of him. 'Thank you, lad,' Scotty said. 'Don't mind if I do.' He could just see Sergeant Warke's face in the little ginger fellow as he bit off its head. Then he noisily crunched it up, annoying Dan even more.

LEAH WAS RUBBING Ebby down until the horse's black coat shone when she heard a vehicle pull up into the yard. It was Great-aunt Penny who had arrived with some home-made savoury treats.

'I'm over here!' Leah shouted.

'I'm coming. Ooh, I could do with some help with these bags of carrots. Thank you, young man,' the woman said to Quinn, who was in charge of the stables. 'Now, come and take your bacon butty, or are you the vegetarian?'

'A bacon butty would be lovely, thank you,' replied Quinn, licking his lips.

Looking forward to her own butty, Leah stroked Ebony's face. They had become firm friends, the big Friesian mare and Leah.

Aunt Penny was an older woman who loved to care for people and animals, and as of late, she'd been a godsend, helping with feeding this family bunch when the cook had fallen and broken her ankle. Leah was very pleased that her Great-aunt Penny and her grandad had made friends again. Brother and sister shouldn't be estranged over trivial matters. In the grand scheme of things it just wasn't worth it. Joey was Leah's cousin, and she knew she would be heart-broken if she and Joey were ever to become strangers to each other.

Penny came over to say hello properly. She was larger than life, with grey hair just showing hints of the blonde she used to be. Admiring Leah's slim figure, she said for the umpteenth time, 'I'm so

pleased you didn't take after the two fat ladies that
were way back in our ancestry. I often wished I'd
been the slim one. Alas, no.'

'No, Aunt Penny, you needed somewhere to house
that huge heart you have,' said Leah honestly.

'Well, your heart is just as big,' Penny returned.
She loved Leah as if she was the daughter she'd never
had - and despite her fall-out with Thomas, Leah had
always been kind and loving towards her.

'There you go then. I've inherited a part of you,
and that makes me proud.' Leah turned away from
Ebby and caught Penny wiping her eyes. She was
such a soft soul, but Leah knew she would fight to the
death for someone she loved or something she
passionately believed in.

'I was just telling your grandad on the phone last
night that someone's moved into that ramshackle
place they call Sledborough House, up by me on the
moors. You know the one,' announced Penny, trying
to change the subject. Most folks thrived off a bit of
gossip, and she was no different, only these days she
had to rely on phone calls to her friends in the local
villages or the few she had left in Whitby. She'd been
amused to hear that the Australians called such catch-
ups 'the Galah sessions'. For many years, her usual
source of tittle-tattle and information had come from
being Headmistress at a local primary school. Gossip

spread like wildfire there, but alas now it was all down to the coffee mornings or the telephone.

'Oh. I thought it was completely derelict?' Leah said and pulled a face. 'Surely it's in a worse state than this place was.'

'Well, I saw the chimneys billowing out smoke the other day. I dare say they could do with the chimney sweep. I might call in on the new owners, see if I can be neighbourly, bake them a cake or just welcome them. Tell them how far the nearest shop is. Ha! They'll be shocked to know it is miles away.' Penny stroked Ebby and then went and petted Ivy, another horse in the stables of Scarthingdale Hall. 'When are you moving these two into the new American barn, Leah?'

'In two days. I just want to get the cherry picker out and check the guttering. I've got a feeling those lazy builders left some rubbish up there.'

'Yes, well, you could be right. I don't trust them when their trousers are so low you can see their cracks,' Penny tutted.

Leah laughed out loud. 'You mean a builder's bum? Most show them these days, you know.'

The twinkle in Penny's eyes was purely wicked. 'I'd rather *not* see them.'

'And that's an out-and-out lie, sister dear.' It was Thomas. He winked at Leah from the doorway.

'You've always ogled the bums of the opposite sex, my girl, in any and every situation, so don't fib.'

Leah flung herself at the old fellow. 'Grandad, you're back. Oh, Tom will be ecstatic. He wants to show you some new foals that have made an appearance since you went gallivanting on your holidays.'

'I'll look forward to that then. And what about my little granddaughter? I hope she's missed Sophie and me.' Thomas looked around.

Sophie sauntered in. 'She'll be at school, darling,' she told her husband. 'Where's Dan, Leah?'

Leah hugged Sophie. 'It's good to see you back home. Dan's gone off to do the school run to collect Tom and Alice. He was keen to get back to normality.'

Sophie looked at Thomas before going on: 'Um, I understand your grandfather has something to tell you. We don't want you alarmed or anything like that . . .'

Leah looked at her grandad with concern, but then he put as warm an expression as he could on his face before saying gently, 'I'll tell you what it is, my pet. We've heard that the Chelsea woman is out of jail. Come up for parole, apparently.'

'I was going to ask Sisco to check the facts and monitor her movements.' Sophie motioned towards Ebby. 'Would that horse carry me, Leah?'

'Yes, I am sure she would. Why?' Leah answered,

still mulling over her grandfather's shock announcement.

'Because my "tundra" is frozen rock-solid from roaming around Shetland looking for the Northern Lights, and I thought that getting my arse, sorry my bottom, on her warm back might defrost me quicker, so to speak.' Sophie was trying to lighten the mood, and Leah was grateful for her efforts.

'Well, Dan looked it up, and the best time to see the Northern Lights up there is in November or December. Maybe we can all go next time?'

Leah sensed the tension in the air between, Penny, Sophie and Thomas and she knew it had nothing to do with Northern Lights.

'Sisco had a family emergency, so he's away - but you know what? I don't think Chelsea will find us up here,' Leah told them. 'After all, why would she? I'm sure she's made her peace with us. Surely a person can't hold a grudge for all this long time. It's been years!' Leah stroked Ivy. 'What say you, Ivy?' and the horse whinnied her reply.

'There you go - even Ivy agrees she's not a threat,' Thomas confirmed.

DAN OPENED his arms as his little princess ran to him, her long blonde ponytail bobbing around and her hair almost slugging him in the face once he'd lifted her into his arms. She smacked a kiss on his cheek.

'Daddy, can we have Aunt Penny's cookies after tea?' Alice looked into his eyes, and he almost melted. 'I've been weally, *weally* good.'

'So, you're hungry, are you?'

Alice nodded.

'Well, maybe you can have half because Auntie Penny does not know portion control. Come on, let's pick up Tom from the bus stop,' Dan said as he tickled his daughter before putting her back on the ground. He held his hand out, and she tucked her small hand in his.

After fastening Alice into the child seat of the Range Rover, he drove out of the schoolyard and onto the road. As he pottered down the winding lane, he glanced in the rear-view mirror and still the white van was following him; annoyingly, the dark blonde female driver had tried to pass him several times, but it had been too dangerous. As Dan moved towards the town, however, the van veered off and he soon forgot about it.

'Look, Daddy, Tom is waiting for us.' Alice pointed.

'I know, darling. Hey, buddy, how's your day been?' Dan asked his son through the open side window.

Tom climbed into the front of the vehicle and quickly fastened his seat belt. Dan drove out of town.

'I've had a great day, Dad. How was your day in the café?' Tom turned to greet his sister. 'Hiya, Alice.'

'We can have a cookie to share when we get home,' the little girl told him with an excited giggle.

Tom laughed, 'Before or after tea?'

Alice shrugged. 'I don't know. Before or after tea, Daddy?'

'Probably after,' confirmed Dan. He glanced in the mirror at Alice because he knew she would want it before. Her little brow was puckered; she would be thinking of ways she could wangle getting the cookie earlier.

'But if we are good all the way home . . .' she said in a sorrowful voice.

Dan tried to smother his laughter. She was at it again, always pushing boundaries without even knowing.

Tom too glanced across at his dad and licked his lips.

'You may get it before, if - and I mean if - you do something amazing,' Dan confirmed.

Alice whooped with joy then settled down to watch the countryside go by.

Driving on, Dan chuckled at his princess until she burst out: 'Daddy, my arse has been hurting me all day today, because the chairs are very hard at school.'

'It will hurt, if you were sitting on it all day, Alice. Now tell me where you got that naughty name from. Remember we call it your bottom. So, who taught you that word?' Dan looked across at Tom.

'It wasn't Tom!' the little girl said immediately. 'It was you, Daddy. You.'

Dan tried his best to recall when his daughter might have heard him say that. 'When did I mention that word?'

'When I came downstairs on Thursday night, you were playing a game with Mummy and you said, "I've missed this arse." And then you slapped her bottom, and you jumped on my mummy. She's my mummy, not yours.'

Dan bit his lip. 'And did you see or hear anything else?'

'No, because I went back to bed. You were squashing mummy on the couch. She's my mummy, and she shouldn't be squashed!' Alice folded her arms, and adamantly nodded her head.

Dan threw a look across at Tom, who was grinning. 'And that told me, didn't it?'

'As Mum says, Alice is always listening and repeating things she hears, so better "arse" than anything worse,' Tom declared to his dad with a laugh.

'I suppose,' Dan replied, throwing a glance in the mirror at his princess. He'd not had to deal with this kind of thing before, because Tom had been eight when he came into Dan's life.

'Can I still have my cookie, Daddy?' Alice asked.

'Yes, if you forget that word.' Dan couldn't keep a straight face.

'Huh, Grandma Sophie says it too. Is it a Greek word, Daddy? Will Uncle Eros say it when he comes to Joey and Ben's wedding?' Alice asked again. Eros was Dan's cousin.

'No. It isn't a Greek word. My understanding is it's a British word. Enough about this word, if you want your cookie don't say it again.' Dan glanced in his rear-view mirror and saw the same white van with the same dark blonde-haired woman driving it. Indicating, he turned off down the back road, but he noticed her staring after them.

LEAH GOT Penny to hoist the basket on the cherry picker, with herself standing inside it, and direct it towards the guttering. She'd gone through the knobs and levers several times, instructing Penny what to do and when.

'OK, you can stop now, Aunt Penny, just as I showed you,' called Leah as the basket juddered to a halt. Getting to work, she quickly scooped some sand and rubble out of the guttering and scooped it into the bucket. The cherry picker suddenly lurched, and it almost threw Leah onto the roof. The hand bucket went flying into mid-air, depositing its contents all over Aunt Penny, who spluttered and spat the grit out of her face.

'Whoops! Did you hit a knob just then? Can you lower me down a little, but very gently,' Leah shouted loudly as she remembered that Penny often forgot to put her hearing aids in.

Penny looked down at the controls, muttering, 'I hate knobs with a vengeance! Which one was it, Leah? Ah, hang on, Dan is back, he's just pulled up into the yard.' She leaned over the controls to wave at Dan, and as she did so, her ample bosom hit a knob. The cherry-picker basket swung to the right. Leah held on frantically, her arms wrapping around the basket's safety rail.

Dan parked up quickly. 'Kids,' he ordered, 'get out and stand clear of the cherry picker. A lunatic is at the controls.'

'That's not a lunarticky. That's my Gweat-aunt Penny,' Alice said indignantly to her dad as he pointed a safe distance for the kids to be. Alice stomped away to the area with Tom holding her hand.

'Penny, turn the key to stop,' Dan said, carefully approaching her.

Penny looked down at the knobs and shrieked out, 'I don't see Stop! Where is Stop?' She pressed another button, and the bucket flung to the left, but this time Leah was prepared. She hung on for dear life.

'No, no, Penny. Listen to me. Listen carefully. Can you see the handbrake? Touch nothing yet. Just tell me if you can see the handbrake.' Dan held his hands out in a calming gesture and strode towards the vehicle, aware that it could decapitate him at any moment with this demented woman at the controls.

'Where's the sign?' Penny inspected the instrument board; her eyes were darting from one thing to another.

'What sign?'

'For the handbrake, duh,' Penny said dryly.

Tom called from the sidelines, 'I think it's got a red knob on the end of it.'

'Oh Tom, dear, they all have red knobs on the end, son, but not all are used to being handled. I think this one must be shy,' murmured Penny, looking at the instrument panel.

'They don't like being handled?' asked Tom, quite confused.

'All the ones I've seen do, yes they do, and I've seen a few. Sorry - what are we talking about? I see no handbrake sign nor a red knob.'

'You can touch the one that looks like a joystick,' said Dan.

'A joystick? It's like no other joystick I've ever seen or used, and I have a PS4.'

Dan grinned to himself as he realised he was confusing her; it didn't take a lot.

Alice watched on, shrugged her shoulders, then said as calm as a cucumber, 'It has a pwace where your fingers go.'

Penny looked down, sighed, and pulled on the handbrake.

'Thank God,' Dan said. 'Leah, are you OK, sweetheart?' He leaned across and lowered the cherry-picker basket.

Penny put her hands on her hips. 'Don't thank him, thank your four-year-old daughter. Go, girl.'

Leah breathed a sigh of relief as she got out of the basket with trembling knees and into the safety of her husband's arms. As she kissed him, she thought the guttering would have to wait, although a decent amount of rubble was still on Aunt Penny's face.

Dan whispered, 'Is that a new make-up, Penny?'

'Ha-ha, funny-funny,' Penny retorted, still trying to get the bits out of her hair.

2

CHRISTENING THE NEW POOL

Dan let go of Leah and turned to help Penny off the cherry picker.

Penny pointed to the instrument panel. 'Look, nowhere does it say On or Off. Nor does it say handbrake, nor joystick for that matter.'

'I know, I was panicking,' Dan admitted, then he whispered to Penny as Leah walked towards them. 'She's precious to me.'

'Who's precious?' Leah asked. She looked up at the guttering. 'You know the builders have left rubbish up there.'

'And you remember that I said I would call the builder and get them to clear it,' Dan said.

The kids ran up to Leah, Alice wrapping her arms around her mum's leg.

'You OK, Mum?' Tom asked and Leah nodded to reassure him.

'Daddy said we could have a cookie before tea and I've been ever so good, Mummy, and I was amazing just then,' Alice said.

'Yes, you saved us all from disaster, Alice,' Penny agreed. 'So, I'm definitely in favour of you having a cookie before our main meal.'

'I suppose I shouldn't have asked her to use that machine. It wasn't fair of me. She's deaf, doesn't know a joystick from a handbrake or anything else,' Leah said to Dan. 'A long time ago, Aunt Penny had a local motor dealership in panic as her brand-new car kept stopping. Grandad said she'd been using the choke as a handbag holder.' Leah couldn't stop giggling.

Dan took hold of Alice's hand. 'I think you deserve a whole cookie for saving the day and as you say, Princess, you have been so amazing. You too, Tom.'

Alice beamed at Tom and said to her brother, 'You get a whole one too, even though I was the gweat one.'

Leah nodded, 'Yes, but not every day, you understand.'

Alice frowned, saying, 'Why not, Mummy?'

'Because you want to keep your teeth nice, don't

you? We've discussed this, Alice,' Leah reminded her daughter.

'Yes, but Jessica said our baby teeth fall out when we get older, so I don't understand why we need to look after them.' Alice turned to Dan. 'Did your teeth fall out, Daddy, when you were little?'

Dan ruffled her hair. 'Don't worry about it, Princess, just listen to what your mummy is saying; Mummy knows best.'

Dan and Leah shared a look and linked hands. They'd been trying for their third baby a while but wanted to keep it a secret, so now they had decided they were going to up their game in the bedroom and other exciting places. Leah giggled. Life was so different to the way it had been when she'd first met him. If it were possible, he'd become more handsome with age, and she felt more connected to him now than ever before because they were sharing a wonderful secret.

'How about we use the new swimming pool tonight as it's the weekend.' Dan lifted Alice onto his shoulders. He pointed to the extension which was built onto the side of the old house. The entire place was being reborn with all the sympathetic décor and renovations, extensions and so on that he and Leah had put into place. As they reached the back entrance of the house, he warned his daughter: 'Watch your head, Princess. And Leah, are my mother and Thomas home today?'

Leah nodded. 'Yes, they arrived home about an hour ago. Sophie was complaining about it being cold up in Shetland.'

'I told her it would be chilly at night, but she insisted they wanted to go. On another subject, when is Ruby back from the Caribbean?' They all trooped into the house and Dan switched on the coffee machine in the kitchen.

'Tomorrow, I believe.'

'Is Uncle Joey coming over today, Mum?' Tom asked as he walked into the massive kitchen.

'Yes, darling, he's on his way and should be appearing in the driveway very soon. You know Joey - he wouldn't want to miss christening the new pool.' Leah looked up at Tom. 'And as for you, stop growing! You make me appear small and I'm not.'

Tom had grown taller than Leah now, much to his amusement.

'I hope Joey is coming,' replied Penny to Tom. 'I want to discuss his wedding plans.'

'It's all we've discussed all year, don't encourage him, Aunt Penny.' Leah went to wash her hands. 'Kids, wash your hands, please, if you want a taste of cookie.'

Dan took Alice down from his shoulders. 'There you go, do as your mum says, Princess.'

Alice washed her hands and took her seat with her booster cushion at the enormous wooden kitchen table. 'When can I have a whole cookie?' the little girl whined.

'Maybe after the christening of the pool,' replied Leah. She watched Dan open the Aga door, and a whiff of kleftiko came out.

'Shut that door. This lamb needs gentle cooking,' scolded Penny. 'I may not know much about cherry pickers, but I do know how to cook.'

Dan quickly closed the oven door. 'Penny, we are going to christen the pool. Are you game?'

'I can't swim, Dan, but I've always wanted to try, and since the lamb is going to be a while yet . . .'

'Then let me get you a swimming costume from Ruby's collection because she won't miss one. We have noodles and we'll look after you, so you won't drown,' Dan promised.

'I'll get the swimsuit, Dan, you'd be out of your depth in Ruby's drawers. Literally they're so deep we could lose Alice in them,' Leah giggled.

'Noodles? We don't need Chinese noodles, Dan, I can assure you I've made enough food to feed a light infantry,' Penny said, somewhat nonplussed.

'You're hilarious, Aunt Penny,' Dan kissed her cheek. 'Hilarious.'

Penny looked confused. What was funny about

Chinese noodles with Greek Kleftiko? She didn't get the joke.

PENNY ARRIVED at the swimming pool in a bright orange longline two-piece swimsuit, with her more than ample bosom spilling out over the top of the bikini. 'My puddings are boiling over,' she joked to herself.

Dan swam over to the gentle slope and held out his hand to help Penny into the water.

'Oh, this feels rather strange.' Penny had an amazed expression on her face. 'Wow, I like this, Dan.'

'Good, the warm water might help your bones. I have it at a pleasant temperature for my mother and Thomas,' Dan told her.

Penny held onto the side rail, her eyes rolling because the only time she'd tried to go in water was at the bay in Whitby. That experience had been horrendous, for a rogue wave had wet her up to her waist, and then knocked her backwards, leaving her floundering, all in front of the school kids. It had been so embarrassing.

Dan reached for the bright yellow noodle from the baby pool and handed it to Penny. 'Just put it under your arms and across your chest, like this. You might as well christen the yellow one. *This* is what we call a noodle.' Dan set off swimming.

Penny's eyes opened wide. 'I don't have to move my arms and my legs like that, do I? I don't know how.' She put the long noodle across her chest and under her arms and lurched forward, loving the sensation of weightlessness.

'What? I don't believe it,' cried Joey from the doorway as he walked in, sporting his red swim shorts. 'Be careful, Dan. Aunt Penny can be *very, very* clumsy.'

No sooner had Joey said it than Penny swung around in the water and the edge of the noodle slugged Dan on the side of the head as he swam past.

'Ouch, you weren't kidding.' Dan ducked as she spun around the other way.

'Noodle-Ninja, watch where you're spinning,' Joey said as he slid into the water.

Penny put a hand to her ear. 'Pardon?'

Joey tucked Penny's noodle under her arms, fitting it snugly around her. 'There, you shouldn't be quite so lethal. Should you?'

Penny grinned. 'I like water. I might just let the Newfoundlands rescue me on your fun day.'

'Don't get carried away, old girl. We don't want you keeling over of heart failure when you get into the cold water,' countered Joey with a little twinkle in his eyes.

'You will not get a hold of my worldly goods yet!' Penny said and plunged forward, beaming. 'Amazing. I love it. I love the way I keep afloat.'

'You know, Penny, you might be better with a dry suit for the Water Trials; that way you can keep your clothes on underneath,' Dan said; then he caught his breath as Leah walked in with their kids. How could it be that after five years she could still make him breathless? She was more beautiful than ever in the light blue one-piece with high-cut legs.

Leah waved at them all and said, 'Aunt Penny, I'm shocked you actually got in. I thought you always hated water.'

'Not now that she's the Noodle-Ninja - and Lee-Lee, guess what?' said Joey, seriously this time.

'What?'

'She's going to let the dogs rescue her when the Newfoundlands come at Bank Holiday.' Joey leaned over when Leah lowered herself into the pool. 'And she doesn't want us to have her worldly goods yet.' He sniffed. 'A load of old tat if you ask me.'

'Aunt Penny's possessions are not old tat,' Leah said indignantly. 'They are her family heirlooms.'

But Penny was making her way through the water towards them and was now within earshot.

'Rubbish or not, it's my treasure,' Penny said, and she struck Joey with the foam noodle, then overbalanced and came up spluttering. Her Great-great-niece

Alice and young Tom came to her aid. Alice, she thought as she tried to get her breath, looked as pretty as a picture donned in armbands and a pink costume.

'I'm surprised you went under like that when you have natural water-wings in the shape of big boobies,' said Joey as he ducked away from another onslaught from the Noodle-Ninja basher.

Alice thought it was fun as she bobbed up and down, clapping her hands. She whispered to Tom, 'Aunty Penny's a Ninja-Noodle. Cool.'

'No, Alice, she's a Noodle-Ninja,' corrected Tom. On seeing Hero pushing his nose at the glass-panelled door, the lad turned to his dad and asked, 'Can Hero come in? The vet said he needs to swim for his arthritis.'

Dan indicated the door, where all three dogs now had their noses pinned to the glass. 'I think they're all waiting. Let them in, son.'

And that's when Alice's giggles went into overdrive.

As the family all sat around the dining table, Dan watched Leah as she traced her finger over the heavy glass top. The design had captured a part of the lightning tree, and he knew what she was thinking. She was remembering the awful night when the car in which she was travelling with her parents had been crushed by a tree, felled by a lightning strike. Cruelly, her mother and father had died instantly, while Leah, aged just eight, was left alive and orphaned.

'This table is stunning, isn't it?' Leah said quietly. She was pleased she'd seen Greg Biggs and had counselling and clinical hypnosis with him. It had helped her move forward, and she wasn't so scared of the lightning now, but there was a sadness in her eyes and Dan knew why. She often told him she would have liked her parents to have met Tom and Alice and Dan himself, the love of her life.

Dan had commissioned the table and chairs to be made from wood salvaged from a lightning tree in the valley that was part of the 3000 acres they now owned. He had suggested that they use the one nearer to home, but Leah was adamant that the tree on the hill was there to represent her parents looking over their land.

Joey broke the silence to say, 'There was a maggot of an old woman in the café this afternoon. I'm sure she kicked her little dog under the table, and she glared at me as if I was the devil himself.'

'Joey, I'm sure she was just an arthritic older woman whose legs are sore when she moves. Maybe she just caught the little dog by accident,' Grandad Thomas suggested.

'That's doubtful, Grandad, because she did the

same thing yesterday and the day before that. The poor little mite looked scared to death of the old trout, and when I offered it a biscuit, she scowled at me. I thought her make-up would crack, it was so thick, but I dropped two of my best chicken doggy biscuits, and the poor creature walloped them down. Did you notice her, Dan?' Joey asked.

'I can't say I did.' Dan tried to think which old lady he meant.

'Well, she couldn't get enough of *you*,' Joey told him. 'Gawping, she was, blatantly so and muttering like crazy.' Then Joey attacked the lamb on his plate with a, 'Mmm, this is gorgeous,' and was busy with his dinner for a while.

Penny looked at Dan and studied his features, saying cheekily, 'Just because some ladies are old doesn't mean they can't appreciate a good thing when they see it.'

'Here, here,' said Sophie, wagging a finger at her son.

WHEN DAN HAD PUT the kids to bed, he went in search of Leah and found her busy loading the dishwasher. He put his arms around her waist and kissed her neck. She giggled and squirmed in the most delightful way then turned in his arms.

'Are you away again next week?' she asked, looking up into his handsome face, and breathed a sigh of relief when he shook his head.

'What – go away and miss the first Goth Week of the year? No way. Why, do you need me in the café?'

'No, I've got several people coming over from Scarborough to cover. I hired two caravans for the week for them to stay in, so they don't have to commute. They are looking forward to it, but I'm looking forward to you being here the whole week too.'

'I'm all yours,' he said, dropping his head to capture a kiss that meant the world to her. He whispered, 'Shall we have an early night?'

'I think we need to.' Leah's eyes shone with a promise of what was to come.

PENNY HAD GONE HOME; she was looking on ePay for a dry suit to wear in the water. The darn internet kept on dipping in and out and was frustrating her, but it didn't stop her from smiling. She was so much happier these days, ever since she'd mended her rift with her brother Thomas. As always, it had been about sommat and nowt. They'd often quarrelled as kids, and he would disown her for a while, but once Sophie came on the scene, she had made him see sense. They were all getting older and didn't need the aggro. Sophie had also told Thomas that Penny was alone now and needed her family at her side.

'Ah, this is just the right size.' Penny pressed the *Buy it Now* button before the internet signal went down again - and the dry suit was hers. She'd show Joey, but as she put the iPad down, she was so thankful she had her family, or at least her brother's family, back in the fold. Tomorrow she would investigate the house on the moors. No one could stop her: those moors were as much hers as anyone born in this grand county of Yorkshire, and besides, she felt she had a right.

As Penny switched off the light, her mind was all of a buzz. She hadn't been able to confide in anyone yet. The postman had caught her that morning with a Special Delivery envelope, and as she had opened it, she couldn't believe her eyes.

A friend she had known had died and left her the whole of his estate at Sledborough House. He'd never married, but he had been her and her late husband's best friend. The letter had gone into little detail but had asked her to travel down to London to see the solicitors. Penny was a little apprehensive about taking this step all on her own, so she had asked the family to accompany her. At the same time she was full of curiosity; she had always thought she knew everything there was to know about Gerard, and both she and her husband had been fascinated by the house on the moors.

A lady called Kitty Babbinger had lived there until she was ninety-five years old. A legendary figure, Kitty had been a bit of an old battle-axe. She was the only spinster Penny knew who still pumice-stoned her front doorstep, and even at her age she still made herself a home-made roast dinner every single day. Gerard and David had once or twice knocked for permission to go inside the house just to take a look around, but Kitty always saw them off with threats and her double-barrelled shotgun.

First, Penny needed to check that the people who had recently moved into Sledborough House after Kitty's death were kosher tenants. It had long been an obsession of hers to take a peek inside as she could see the place with her binoculars and her telescope, and as she was Kitty's only neighbour, she liked to make sure the lights went on and off. It was a good sign that the elderly neighbour was OK and it had been a sad night when the bedroom light did not go on to illuminate the moor.

Penny knew there was a right of way through the land, because it was where she Penny and David had often walked 'Bertie Bassett' as they called their beloved Basset Hound, named after the Bassett's Licorice Allsorts sweets that the couple loved. First it was David who died then Bertie had left her too. Both deaths had left Penny devastated, but when Bertie Bassett died of old age, it was awful because he was the last link she had with her beloved husband. Strangely, since Bertie's passing, she had often felt his head on her knee as she was drifting off to sleep and she would reach out in the dark to stroke his soft ears and could swear she felt them. And, with a tear in her eye for her missing menfolk, she would close her eyes and was soon snoring rather loudly.

PENNY PUT her walking shoes on, her chequered skirt and clean white blouse. She dragged her coat off the rail and set out with a lemon drizzle cake in a tin. It wasn't a long walk to the house if she went over the short-cut. She checked her pockets to ensure she had treats for Brian the Bull who she was now friendly with, but he could be very naughty and many a time she'd seen people running down the lane away from him. Having always been an animal-lover, Penny had read up on the bovine species. In theory, Herefords were quiet, docile creatures, but she reckoned Brian the Bull had not read the manual. What she mustn't do was let him smell the cake, or she would never get rid of him. And there he was, eyeing her up as she fastened the five-bar gate. Striding towards him, she showed no fear. Brian could be a force to be reckoned with, but she knew at fifty paces he could smell the horse treats and the ginger biscuits she had in her pocket.

'OK, Brian, are you hungry for a treat?' Penny asked, dropping the broken treats on the ground beside him, but for the first time ever, he showed no interest. Today, Brian had other things on his mind. 'You can forget that, Brian,' Penny told him firmly. 'Eric said you are not going in with the girls until next week, so just eat your treats and don't be a prat.'

Heaving a sigh of relief, Penny was thankful the pile of treats caught his attention and kept him busy as she trod past him.

Five minutes later, after knocking on the front door and getting no reply, Penny realised there wasn't a car in the drive so they must be out. She walked around the back and peered through the window into the kitchen. It was a mess. Pots and pans were strewn across the draining board. Rubbish was stacked up high too. Going back around the front, she saw that the fire was lit in the front sitting room so the tenants couldn't be too far away. She'd thought there was a good possibility that they would be out, and had written a note in the cake box saying she'd call again. She left her telephone number, signing it *Penny Barker*, and leaving the cake box on the front doorstep.

On the way back, she was free to pass by as Brian

had run across the paddock to shout at his ladies in the adjoining field. Brian would be pleased when Eric put him in with the heifers because the poor animal had got wire cuts from where he'd tried to get into their field. Maybe next time she'd fetch some antiseptic spray.

DAN AND LEAH were up early, riding in the new flood-lit indoor arena. Over five years both had improved their equine dancing to music on their respective mounts, and as they floated across the sand it was evident that they excelled at the art. The couple didn't go to all of the competitions, but they tried to get to a few a year.

Leah now rode her young Friesian mare, Diamond, and could tell she would soon be ready for competition. Dan knew that before long he would have to let Sir Galahad retire just to do his stud work, but he had his son King Arthur waiting in the wings, so he would always have a part of him. Galahad always seemed to pass on his gentle temperament to his progeny, for which Dan was grateful. They'd had a famous 'horse-whisperer' staying with them at one time, and the fellow had given all the family an alternative way to communicate with their equine best friends.

Grandad Thomas's friend Cyril knew a lot about horses, but some of the demonstrations he'd watched had amazed him - and he even admitted he was never too old to learn!

Dan had given Quinn the manager's role at the stables, and all aspects of that upgrading had been finished to a high standard, especially considering that parts of the house were still building sites. Fortunately, these areas were around the back of Scarthingdale Hall and not seen by anyone apart from the family and staff. Things were slotting nicely into place. Now all he had to do was stop Alice using her favourite new word of 'arse'. No doubt she would find another unsuitable phrase soon.

3

MUD-LARKING ON THE THAMES

The family climbed out of their taxis at the Belleville, a grand hotel on The Strand that Dan had chosen for its far-reaching views of the Thames and the South Bank complex. Once inside the entrance, Penny looked around with her eyes out on stalks. It was spectacular - something which Ruby seemed to take for granted when she waved Penny in as if it was her own London home.

'Flippin' 'eck, this is impressive,' Penny breathed, looking around in awe and noting the smart concierge and staff in their uniforms, including their top hats. 'Wow.'

'Wait until you see the rest of the hotel, Penny. It is unbelievable,' Ruby promised.

'I am totally gob-smacked,' Penny gulped.

Dan and Ruby shared a look of amusement as the latter announced, 'Oh, this is nothing. Just wait until you see the view from our room. You did know we are sharing a suite, didn't you?'

'Yup. Wherever I lay my hat and all that . . .' Penny was still gazing around, eyes wide like Dorothy in *The Wizard of Oz*.

Leah shot a glance at Dan, enquiring, 'We do have adjoining suites, us lot? We do, dote we?'

'Us lot, dote we?' asked Dan in his best Yorkshire accent.

'Didn't you know it is addictive, our Yorkshire accent?' said Leah to her husband in perfect English.

Dan grinned and leaned into her to murmur, 'You're addictive too.' He kissed her cheek and surreptitiously squeezed her bum cheek.

'Ugh,' said little Alice. 'Old people kissin', tung down throat.'

Tom nudged his sister. 'Shush, Alice. They'll be wanting to know who taught it to you.'

'Come on then, who did?' asked Dan with a mock sternness on his face. 'But no, don't tell me - I believe I already know.'

Both kids shared a panicked look, and Tom added, 'We're sworn to secrecy.'

Leah laughed. 'That'll be Joey then. Speak of the devil, and he will appear. Exactly what are you teaching our kids, cousin dear? Tongue down throat - hmm?'

Joey wore a bright pink spotted open-neck shirt, pink chinos and white pumps. He looked over his sunglasses. 'Who, me? As if I would dare do anything like that, and you know Lee-Lee, I'd never say a thing as rude or as common as "tongue down throat".'

Dan studied Joey. 'I thought you were working?'

'What? Oh no, I delegated just as you taught me to do. Besides, I need a designer shirt for my wedding day.' Joey planted a kiss on Dan's cheek, much to the surprise of Aunt Penny.

'Joey! Behave! We are in one of the best hotels in the capital,' she scolded.

'Sorry. Dan knows I do it to tease him – and besides, we're in London, I feel liberated.' Joey's eyes sparkled with humour.

'Are you staying here, Joey?' Ruby asked once they'd reached reception. She plopped herself down, examining her highly manicured nails.

Joey shook his head. 'I haven't booked anywhere yet.'

Dan magnanimously offered, 'I'll sort it, Joey.'

'Oh Dan, how generous.' The young man was thrilled. He looked around the hotel foyer, and said naughtily, 'I hear the lavvies are ever so posh too.'

The kids giggled, even though Alice had to ask, 'What's a lavvy?'

'It's a toilet, darling,' Joey clarified. 'Never mind, Alice, your mum will show you it later.'

Dan bit his lip then replied, casting a glance at Joey, 'Remember, she's at the copying age, Joey, so we have to watch what we say these days.'

AS IT WORKED OUT, the hotel staff had an extra bed put into one of the suite's bedrooms for Joey, which meant Ruby and Penny were sharing a bedroom. They really were all one big happy family.

Leah arranged for Penny to go to the solicitors by Rolls Royce since it was at their disposal.

'Would you like me to go with you?' Leah asked as she opened the adjoining door between the two suites and watched the kids immediately run into a bedroom, giggling and jumping onto the bed. 'I don't mind.' Then she called out, 'Be careful, you two. You are not at home now.'

'No, Leah, I'll be all right now we're here. I reckon it's all going to be a fuss about nowt,' said Penny, staring out over the Thames and Westminster Bridge. 'This is a beautiful view, but I've never seen so many people! Why, they're like ants. Thousands, if not millions of them. Mind you, I'm still dead keen to hear how you get on, down on the shore with your mud-larking while I head over to the solicitor's. I checked the tide chart and it's low tide right now.' She rubbed her hands together. 'I've read about the fascinating things people pick up as the tide flows in and out from the sea. The Thames is full of history, and objects get washed up that have been in the water for hundreds and hundreds of years.'

'I could go with you to the solicitor's office, Aunt Penny. I'm not bothered about getting up to my knees in mud,' Joey said, but then he saw Alice's face crumple.

'You can't disappoint little Alice. After all, it was your idea to bring the kids for this mud-larking.' Aunt Penny was adamant. 'I will meet you all back here.' When the children started playing again she took an envelope out of her bag and passed it to Dan surreptitiously.

He looked at the name on the embossed paper. Howard Levinson was well known in the city, so Dan knew instinctively Penny might be in for a shock, a good one at that. Putting an arm around the older woman's shoulder, he whispered in her ear, 'It's only a short drive, and your car will be here in fifteen minutes. Tell Howard you are a relative of mine - he'll get his best brandy out for you.'

Penny perked up. 'Now you're talking. I'll just get my jacket.' She reached for her favourite tweed.

WITH THE SUN shining above them, and ready for their mud-larking excursion, the party left the hotel and strolled over Waterloo Bridge to their destination. Unable to talk for the roar of the traffic on the road beside them and on the Victoria Embankment beneath them, they had to content themselves with the wonderful views of London to both sides of the bridge. When they reached two steep flights of steps, strewn with rubbish and unpleasant-looking stains, Dan urged everyone to hold on to the rail. He took Alice's hand and helped her safely down.

'Dad, is that the National Theatre?' Tom asked when they reached the bottom. 'The kids who are doing A-level English at school are coming here to see a play in the autumn.'

'Yes, son, that is the National Theatre,' Dan answered, so proud of his son. Tom was a good-looking boy and Dan felt sure he would break a few hearts before he met the right girl. As long as Tom recognised when he met The One, instead of wasting years as he himself had done after that one, passionate night with Leah.

'Whose daft idea was this?' asked Joey as they walked along towards, ducking as a pigeon flew by, far too close, and spattered the ground.

'Yours,' everyone said in unison.

'Another reason why you, Joey, had to come too if you remember?' Dan remarked. 'Plus, you promised my princess here.'

'Yes, I did, didn't I, Alice,' Joey confirmed and watched her nod emphatically. He squirmed as yet another pigeon flew past him. 'Are we anywhere near Trafalgar Square? Or have these pigeons migrated from Whitby to be with Alice, seeing as she feeds everything on your property.'

Ruby pointed over the water. 'You just turn left out of the hotel and it's two minutes away.'

'The pigeons like Uncle Joey,' Alice said, smiling up at her daddy.

'Yes, I think they do, but we are *not* taking any home.' He grinned as he heard her sigh.

They had arrived at a short flight of steps with its gate open, ready to allow passers-by to walk down to the beach. The tide was out, thanks to Dan having checked the tide tables for London Bridge.

Walking by the Thames was reminding Leah of the kiss she and Dan had shared while walking across the Millennium Bridge, a few years ago when she was heavily pregnant with Alice.

Dan caught the dreamy expression in her eyes, and winked.

He secretly didn't hold much hope of them

finding anything at all, only maybe a few old oyster shells, which he'd read had been a poor man's meal, hundreds of years ago. Leah and Tom followed him down the steps, with Joey and Ruby gingerly bringing up the rear.

'It's muckier than I thought it might be and the water is grey, not blue,' Joey moaned as Dan handed out disposable gloves to wear. The Thames water could hold some nasty germs, so it was better to be safe than sorry.

'The Thames was used as the main shipping port for hundreds of years, it's bound to be grimy,' Leah called back.

'Don't fall, Joey, because I can't afford to get a bruised behind.' Ruby grabbed hold of his shoulder.

Joey grinned. 'Well, at least you'll be cushioned, so to speak.'

'Cheeky. I didn't expect it to be so muddy, either.' Ruby tiptoed off the steps and onto the shale.

Alice was jumping near the water's edge, excited by a couple of swans who were drifting by. Dan smiled as he watched his daughter's blonde hair blowing in the breeze, just like her mum's. She was so pretty.

'Look, Daddy, I found a shell,' Alice announced.

'Let me see, darling.'

'OK, Alice, if you like the shell, I will put it in the

carrier bag to wash later.' Leah knew even before she saw Alice nodding her head that the shell would be going in the bag. On the many walks they had taken, Alice always came back with a pocket full of stones and 'diamonds'. At least in her book, they were diamonds and not pieces of coloured glass. It was the magic of childhood.

As Leah put the shell into the carrier bag, she saw Dan bending over the shoreline with Tom.

'Look what I've found, Mum. It's part of a white pipe. Did someone smoke it once in the olden days?' asked Tom, holding it up and looking at it carefully.

It was Ruby who answered, much to Dan's amazement. 'Well, you see, Tom, the boatmen and passengers - anyone on the river, in fact - would buy these pipes already made up with tobacco in them. They were sold that way, so the men would just smoke 'em and chuck 'em in the river. You can find bits of pipe stems everywhere on the riverbank, but you were really lucky to find most of a pipe, with some of its bowl intact. Well done, young man.'

Then Joey screamed, and Ruby shouted at him, 'Drama Queen, what's wrong?'

Joey's white shoes had sunk into a patch of mud. 'Oh *no!*' he wailed. 'My lovely Chilean pink-flamingo designer chinos are ruined. Ruined!'

Dan caught Leah stifling a giggle beside him, and

he burst out laughing too. It was catching. Tom also found it funny, but Alice ran towards Joey to help him.

'Oh no, Princess, you're not going in the mud.' Dan went to catch her in his arms, but she evaded him. 'Or you will be in it up to your elbows.'

'No, Alice, please don't! Do as your daddy says and stay away. I'm sinking into this, and you are too tiny,' said Joey, really serious by now.

Alice began to cry, and Leah scowled at Joey. 'Don't frighten her.'

'I didn't mean to. Look, I really am sinking.' Joey tried to pull his foot free and there was a slurping noise. He reached out to grab Dan's arm and was hauled bodily out onto the stony, safe part of the foreshore.

'Oh look – I've been rescued, thanks to my hero.' Joey managed to get onto terra firma and looked down at his chinos and his one, pump-less foot. 'Oh dear, my shoe has sunk, never to be seen again. The Thames has taken my treasure.' But he was a little shaken up and genuinely relieved to be back on dry land.

Even Dan had to admit it had been challenging to haul Joey out of the mud.

'Come on, gang,' he urged, 'let's find a new location to search.'

But Alice dug her heels in. 'Look, Daddy, look there.' She pointed into the middle of the pebbles.

Dan looked but couldn't see what she was gazing at. 'Where, Princess?'

'There, Daddy,' said Alice firmly, reaching out to point to a specific area.

Finally spotting the glint of something, Dan bent down and moved the grit away. 'Well, well, well, you are a clever girl.'

'What is it?' Joey asked with interest. 'The Crown Jewels?'

'Yes, you could say that. This young lady has struck gold.' Dan examined the old gold ring with what looked like an amber stone. He wiped it clean with a paper hanky. 'Look, Alice, you've found an amber and diamond ring. You're a real mudlark now. Congratulations. Well done.'

'Holy cow!' said Joey. 'A gold ring, with diamonds and amber? Ruby, can you keep searching? We could be millionaires if we are diligent.'

'I am a millionaire,' stated Alice proudly, as they all laughed.

PENNY WAS SHOWN into Howard Levinson's office. It was a plush room with cream leather chairs and a soft pale carpet, with panelled walls and oil paintings of Victorian influence hung over the grand fireplace. Penny picked up one of the glossy magazines and nearly dropped it as she saw the price of it. Gosh, she looked again, she could buy a fish and chip supper in Whitby for the cost of this magazine. Her face was a picture, and she was continually drawing her brows together at the shock of the prices she saw on the pages.

The kindly receptionist was amused behind her large iMac screen as she observed Penny's facial expressions and was disappointed when the visitor was called into Howard's office so soon.

As Penny walked into the heavily panelled office, she realised that much like herself, Howard enjoyed his food, since his rotund belly stood out proudly before him. Perhaps he had enjoyed far too many puddings – although Penny herself knew all too well that looks were deceiving. For instance, it wasn't for want of staying on a diet that she hadn't lost weight. She'd tried every damn one of them with no success, and she was sure that Howard had tried many of them too.

'Ah, Mrs Barker, how are you?' Howard held his hand out, and they shook; his hands were warm and gentle and his eyes were a beautiful shade of blue. 'Please, take a seat.'

'I'm well, thank you, Mr Levinson, and, yes, I will park me bum if you don't mind. My nephew by marriage said if I mentioned his name, you might get the good brandy out,' Penny said with a smile to her face. 'His name is Dan Ryan.'

Howard raised a brow in amusement at her straight-speaking: one of the things he missed about Yorkshire was the colloquialisms. 'In that case, let's have a quick snifter now, and please call me Howard.' He looked Penny up and down, appreciating her glorious bosom and her shapely bum; he'd noticed that when she'd walked in. He just loved curvy women, especially when they had an attractive face as Penny had. 'Do take a seat, my dear. You may need a drink.'

'Why do you say that, Howard? Gerard was known for his thriftiness, but he was only a Headmaster so he surely wasn't worth that much, poor man.' Penny parked her rear end in the comfy seat.

Howard handed Penny a glass of brandy, and it was a good measure. He reckoned she might need it. He cleared his throat.

'Well, Mrs Barker, or may I call you Penny? You do know you've inherited the whole kit and caboodle, and I think maybe this letter will tell you why.' Howard passed her the sealed envelope and watched her shaking hands take a good hold of it. 'Why not have your snifter first,' he said gently. 'Let's just say that my client Gerard was a dark horse. Headmaster he might have been, but he was outstanding on the

Stock Exchange. Your friend had an exceptional talent for stocks and shares dealing, and his intuition was absolutely second to none.'

Penny swallowed nervously. 'I see. Thank you, Howard. I will just have a little taste, then whatever he has to say, let's get it out into the open.' She sipped the brandy then took the antique silver letter-opener that Howard was holding out to her. She slit the envelope and carefully pulled out the embossed pieces of paper inside. 'He always did like nice stationery,' she said, and tears unexpectedly filled her eyes. Blinking them away, she unfolded the pages.

Penny was familiar with Gerard's handwriting, but the first line caught her attention good and proper. Her mouth dropped open. It went:

My dearest, loveliest Penny, if you are reading this letter, then I must have gone into the ether or as you believe to heaven. Or to the place where David is, and we'll be taking a drink by the stream near your house by now. I hope I haven't gone into the underworld or, as your friend Marigold often called it, 'the underground'.

Well, on with this. You must know by now that I was jealous that David had your affections and your heart, but I knew I could never make a play for you while he was around because your heart truly belonged to no one else. You two were a pleasure to be with, and your love for each other was the most beautiful thing to see. And, when he died, you were a woman without solace. Oh, I tried to cheer you, and in many ways I did, but your heart still belonged to David, and so I was happy to be your friend. We were friends, all three of us, and you and David were so kind to me, which leads me to tell you this.

I bequeath my whole estate to you, dear Penelope.

PENNY LOOKED UP AT HOWARD, a tear falling down her cheek. 'Poor man, he had no family to speak of. They'd all popped their clogs.'

'Yes, but in your own words you said to me, "Gerard was known for his thriftiness." So, read on.'

Howard loved this part of his job when someone he liked was in for a marvellous surprise.

Penny turned the page then looked hopelessly across at Howard. 'Exactly how big was Gerard's estate? There are so many pages here that I can't cope. I mean, there are four properties here on this page alone.' She didn't know whether to laugh or cry.

Howard rubbed his hands together, his brown eyes sparkling with mischief. 'This is where it gets interesting. His portfolio is substantial. His numerous building society accounts and bank accounts are full to the limit the government will guarantee. He was a brilliant, shrewd man and I'm happy to say a good friend of mine too. He certainly made me quite a lot of money on the Stock Exchange.'

Penny took a sip of the brandy. 'How substantial is the portfolio?' she managed to say. 'How many accounts are there?'

'Well, maybe we should talk about it over lunch.' Howard looked down at his notes. 'Now, Gerard said you might like to go to Harrods, but I think we can do better than that.'

'Fish and chips are my favourite, but I've heard they're not as good as up in Yorkshire.' Penny finished off her brandy. 'I don't like the skin on my fish, and I hate bones!'

'I take that as a challenge, but I have to say there was an excellent fish and chip shop not far from where I worked in Leeds when I was employed in my uncle's business. You know that old saying, Penny - may I call you Penny?'

Penny nodded.

'You can take the boy out of Yorkshire, but you can never take Yorkshire out of the boy. I knew Gerard. I knew him well, so to see his wishes fulfilled is marvellous, and an honour, and I don't know how he got my services so cheap.' Howard laughed. 'Come on, Penny, let's go to the Mandarin Oriental

Hotel. I think you may like the puddings there.' He blushed a little as he eyed her chest, then hastily said, 'I certainly do.'

They both burst out laughing as Howard rubbed his rotund stomach, with Penny telling him: 'As it happens, I do like puddings too.'

LEAH WATCHED Joey limping around on the shore of the Thames with a wicked gleam in her eyes.

'I doubt they will let you into the Rolls Royce with only one pump and muddied up to your knobbly knees,' she teased him.

'Oh no - how will I get back?' Joey was really worried, then he saw his cousin's expression and said crossly, 'Oh, that's right. Laugh your socks off.'

'Maybe we need to find a taxi?' Ruby could barely suppress her own giggles too. Then something made her glance at a woman away down on the shore-line who was holding a long-range camera – and Ruby saw that it was aimed directly at them. The woman pulled the camera away from her face, and Ruby gasped. Was she seeing things? When she looked again, the woman had her back to her and was moving swiftly towards a set of steps leading up to the walkway above the shore. Ruby pointed but couldn't utter the words. She'd know that walk anywhere.

Joey had spotted her too and he gulped: 'Is that who I think it is? It's - '

Ruby broke him off. 'Come on, you and me ought to get a cab. Sharpish.'

Leah had moved further down near the shoreline with the kids. Dan flitted his gaze up from studying a medieval red rooftile that he'd unearthed and was coming over to show it to Ruby and Joey. 'Are you two leaving already?' he asked, surprised.

'Might as well, Danny boy. I need to get to the shops or I'll have trouble being allowed back into the Belleville, the state I'm in,' said Joey while being dragged away by Ruby.

'See you both later,' called Dan after their retreating backs. Then he turned to walk down to Leah and the kids.

'COULD IT HAVE BEEN HER? She looked like she had dark hair, and we know that Chelsea was a brunette. Wasn't she?' Joey was limping as fast as he could but it was painful due to the pebbles and stones he kept stepping on. 'Hold on, Ruby,' he panted. 'My foot is hurting.'

'I don't care, and you'll live. We need to see if

that was Chelsea. And for your information she used to get her hair cut and coloured on expenses. It's a wonder it is isn't sky-blue pink with yellow dots!' Ruby ran up the steps as best she could whilst dragging Joey by the arm, and they entered the small shopping area in Gabriel's Wharf. The woman sped on and jumped into a passing black cab without a backward glance. Ruby mentally noted the cab number and kept repeating it until she could write it down.

'Well, what did you think? Was it our old friend Chelsea?' Joey asked.

'Seventy to thirty it was her,' Ruby said grimly.

'Not exactly good odds, are they?' Joey leaned against the wall and looked at the sole of his bare foot. 'Quick, get me a taxi, woman.'

'It's more than even odds,' Ruby went on. 'I just know it was her, Joey, I just know. I worked with her for a lot of years. Too many, if truth be told. I know that scuttle of hers.' Ruby kept on reciting, 'Seven seven seven one.' Thankfully it was a manageable number to remember, an Angel number plus a one.

They reached the street after a few minutes and Joey hailed a cab, but it went straight past even though the light was on. 'Huh.'

'Well, if you looked at yourself, who'd want to stop? Let me try.' Ruby hailed the next available cab, jutting out her chest and plastering a big smile on her face. The cabbie braked and drew in beside them.

'Hello, darling, can you take us to the Belleville Hotel.' Ruby climbed in. 'Sorry about my friend here. He had a row with his girlfriend, and she pushed him in the mud.' Ruby ignored Joey's gasp. 'I don't suppose you can find out where she went, as he's heartbroken. She jumped into cab number seven seven seven one. We'd be grateful as they're supposed to be getting married soon.'

'I'M HUNGRY, DADDY,' whined Alice for the third time. She kicked at the shale, then pulled at his sleeve.

'The car will be picking us up soon. Besides, I've just given you a little biscuit,' said Leah as they walked towards the steps. She had collected up the plastic gloves and given everyone a special wipe to clean their hands, just in case. She stopped to put on her padded gilet. 'And by the time we get up these steps and down to the street through there, I think we should look for the Rolls.'

'Cool.' Tom smiled at his dad. 'Are you carrying all the spoils, Dad?'

Dan nodded. 'I am, Tom. I think your mum has got enough to deal with, don't you?'

'I was just wondering if we could stop at the shops,' Tom asked.

Leah called back over her shoulder, 'Why not. Oh look - there's a cute café with sand outside, where you can sit and pretend you're in the Caribbean. And I think Alice would like to have a look at the carved animals and other things just there.'

They were peering into an art gallery near the café when it happened. Dan heard a clattering sound and looked up to see a moped only fit for the scrapyard twisting through the gates at the end of the tiny shopping centre. His senses came on full alert as he saw someone thrust something into the rider's hand - even though the latter tried to bat them away. The scooter lurched and wobbled, heading directly at Leah and Alice while the rider struggled to control it, nearly falling off. 'Leah, move, move!' Dan shouted in panic. Other people were screaming and jumping out of the way.

Leah was bending down to lift Alice out of danger, but the rider was already alongside her. As his front wheel hit a crack in the ground, the knife he had been forced to take slipped in his hand, cutting his palm and catching Leah on her right shoulder. She cried out in shock, for the blade had caught in her gilet and sliced a cut in her skin.

As he stared in horror, unable to get to her side quickly enough, Dan saw Leah fight the maniac off before he accelerated away, back through the rear gates, narrowly escaping horrified members of the public who ran after him in pursuit.

The scooter raced onwards, its engine popping, drowning out the sound of its rider as he recited in a panic, 'I'm sorry, I'm sorry, I didn't mean to hurt anyone.'

Dan had dropped the bags and was chasing after the man within seconds, leaving other pursuers behind in his rage. Dan was quite fit, but couldn't catch up; however, he managed to get a partial number-plate. Panting heavily, he walked back to see Leah holding onto her shoulder; he could see the blood dripping from her hand.

'Oh, Lord, please let her be OK,' he whispered as he ran to help his wife.

Alice was crying and screaming, clinging onto Tom's hand. The white-faced young lad had kept his cool and was calling an ambulance and the police on his iPhone. The crowd melted away after offering to help.

Dan gathered his wife in his arms, cuddling her, then staring down at the damaged gilet and the wound underneath. Instinct told him that if the man had wanted to truly hurt her, she would be dead by now.

Leah had gone pale with shock and she was shaking, but she smiled reassuringly at her children.

'The ambulance and the police will be here shortly, Dad,' Tom said, taking his mum's other hand.

'Will you die, Mummy, with you being so old?' asked Alice, who by now was tasting her tears as they ran down her cheeks.

Leah managed a small smile. 'No, darling, it's just a scratch. Besides, we Yorkshire women are made of tough stuff - even the old ones like me.'

Dan grinned at her resilience and her humour in such a difficult situation. He was relieved when they heard the sirens of the ambulance and the police heading towards them.

'I don't need all the dramatics, a few sterile strips would've sufficed,' moaned Leah.

'Mum, you do need the hospital,' insisted Tom. 'The wound needs to be cleaned and checked.'

'Can I go in the am-bu-lance, Mummy?' Alice asked with her puppy-dog eyes.

'OK, I will go to the hospital,' Leah agreed, knowing she was outnumbered.

RUBY AND JOEY HAD SHOWERED, changed and were down in the foyer when Ruby took a call from Dan.

'What's wrong?' Ruby knew Dan as if he was her own son, and she picked up immediately on the concern in his voice. 'What? . . . My God, is she OK?

. . . Have the police caught anyone? . . . Just a minute, I'll ask Joey.'

'What's going on?' Joey asked as panic spread across his face.

'Leah was attacked by one of the moped thieves that roam around London, but she's OK, she's getting checked over at St Thomas's Hospital. Dan wants to know if you saw anything.'

'Come to think of it, I did see a tall guy on a Suzuki scooter - yes, it was definitely a Suzuki. To me he looked a bit like Lurch in *The Addams Family*, just sitting further up the road as if he was waiting for someone. It struck me that he was too tall and broad for the machine he was sat on. And his legs were far too long for the scooter.'

As Ruby hung up, she said to Joey, 'I hope the taxi man will get back to us because when he does, we can find out if it was Chelsea trying to stir up trouble.'

'Stirring up trouble is an understatement, but what I can't understand is why they would target a woman who has been mud-larking. She's hardly going to find buried treasure in the Thames, nor is she likely to be carrying much money on her person. This all stinks a bit if you ask me, just like the Thames mud. Look, we'd better not mention anything to Dan and Leah unless we know for definite that it was that horrible woman. I think I need to hit the shops now.' Joey turned. 'Leah is going to be all right, isn't she?'

Ruby patted his arm and said kindly, 'Don't fret, Joey. Dan seems to think they should be back for dinner, and as we have our very own chef and butler, we will make sure we are there too. Right, come on, Joey, get a move on. You'll need a second opinion on your shirt colour. Besides, I'm good at haggling and I know how you Yorkshire folk like a bargain.' Ruby linked arms with Joey as they walked outside to get into one of the taxis that waited there.

'And you don't?' quipped Joey, feeling much better now. Just then, he spotted the woman who was just alighting from a taxi that had pulled in close by. A dumpy man had got out first and was holding her hand in his before he kissed it lightly. He certainly seemed to be flirting with her.

'The old fox,' breathed Ruby, whose eyes had nearly popped out of her head.

'You know him?' Joey asked, then shouted: 'Unhand her, my good fellow. That's no lady, that's my aunt.'

Penny smiled over at Joey, her voice slurring. 'It's all right, dear. Howard is going to get changed and come back for cocktails.' She kissed him goodbye and he climbed back into the taxi, which moved off. 'See you when you return from your shopping trip.' She then flung her arm out, almost decking a man walking past.

Joey gasped. 'She's kaylied. Off her friggin' rocker.'

'I shall go and get another cocktail,' Penny announced in a kind of mumble, then tripped and would have fallen on her face had a concierge not caught her. She could have easily flattened him had she fallen upon him, as he was a lighter build than most.

With great dignity, Penny said, 'Thank you, young man. I see you could do with a good dinner. Come to Yorkshire and I will feed you up.'

'You need to sleep it off, Aunt Penny, by the looks of it. Watch you don't hurt someone or yourself,' grunted Joey in disgust. 'Who did you say that man was?'

Ruby replied for her, since Penny was beyond rational thought by now.

'Apart from being one of the wealthiest lawyers in the City, he's a nice man, Joey. No harm will come to Aunt Penny with Howard looking after her.' Ruby had a smile on her face, knowing too well that these days, Howard was as safe as houses. He hadn't always been that safe - he used to like the ladies but now preferred a good dinner. Together, she and Joey helped Penny upstairs to her suite, ordered a tray of tea for her, and made sure she was safe and comfortable before they headed out once more for their favourite activity - shopping.

LEAH LOOKED A BETTER colour after her wound had been cleaned and dressed, and she'd had a second cup of tea. The police interview was thorough, as it was in their words 'a bit of a strange location for the scooter heists'. The attacker hadn't robbed Leah and had also put himself in a vulnerable position, swooping where there were lots of people. Also, moped thieves usually worked in pairs, with the one on the back wielding a stick to frighten people away. The officers were going to check the CCTV from the shops at Gabriel's Wharf and from several other sources like the pub down the road.

'Are we going back to the hotel, Mum?' Tom asked when the hospital administrator discharged Leah. 'I think Alice is hungry.'

'Yes, of course, Tom, I'm feeling back to normal now. In fact, why don't we all get a chocolate bar from the machine over there,' Leah suggested, knowing it would be a while before they ate dinner.

Alice's eyes lit up, and her infectious smile was so cute as she pointed to her favourite – a milk chocolate coconut Bounty.

Dan didn't want anything. His appetite had been

swept away by anger at what had happened. He would need to look into some kind of security while they were down here in London.

Leah forced down a little chocolate to try and calm Dan. If he thought she was eating, she knew he would be happier. However, each square almost stuck in her throat, and she only managed two squares before putting the rest in the bin in the screwed-up wrapper.

'Right, let's go back to the hotel. I, for one, want a bath and a change of clothes,' said Leah, as chirpily as she could muster under the circumstances, but feeling a little faint from shock.

'The car is waiting downstairs, darling. And you can't get your dressing wet. Now, do we need a wheelchair?' Dan asked, trying to be helpful, then he saw Leah's chin jut out, and he knew the answer without her uttering a single word. Sweeping her up into his arms, he and his family made their way to the hospital lift.

JOEY WAS ENTHRALLED with Ruby taking him to the poshest shirt shop in Jermyn Street, and he didn't even flinch at the prices – well, only once or twice, maybe. It was, after all, his wedding shirt, so it was super-duper special. He'd decided on long sleeves because he knew that on a hot day in Whitby his bare skin could burn to a crisp, but in reality, it was more likely to be blustery even in May. Several times in the past, he had laid out on the beach believing that he would stay out in the sun only a few minutes and then he had fallen asleep with his sunglasses on. Big mistake, he looked like a lobster with puffy cloud-white eyes. So now, he was always careful.

Joey looked at the pink tailored shirt. It was perfect. Just like the flamingos at a particular zoo he frequented that was named after them. His fiancé Ben had loved the zoo too when they'd visited. As they'd fed the orphaned lamb, they'd called it Louis after their favourite outrageous celebrity.

'Is that the colour you want?' asked Ruby, knowing only too well by the look of adoration Joey had on his face, as he twirled in front of the full-length mirror, that it was precisely what he wanted.

'Oh yes, I think it's fabulous. Don't you?'

Ruby took a sly look at the clock. She needed to get back and see how Leah was, and besides, she was starving. 'If you feel happy in it for your wedding day, then it's got to be the one, darling. Don't you agree?' Ruby added to the shop assistant.

The young, immaculately dressed assistant smiled, then added in an East London accent: 'I just 'ope I can find the perfect shirt for me own wedding. The gentleman looks a right old toff in it.'

Ruby saw Joey's ego take a boost as he twittered, 'Less of the old. Now, I think I'd better look at the ties while I'm here.'

Ruby sucked in her breath as if it were her last. Couldn't he hear her stomach gurgling? 'You liked the one in the window,' she said. 'How about that?' She then turned to the shop assistant and smiled. 'Maybe a cup of tea and a biscuit would be in order?'

'That tie costs a bomb, more than the shirt,' Joey complained, 'but it would go superbly with this shirt. Oh, but can I afford it? And then we still need to walk up to Selfridges in Marble Arch. They have a luxury pet accessories department and I must get my cat basket before it shuts.'

'Can you afford to be *wivvout* the tie, that's the question, innit?' the assistant asked.

Ruby's tummy grumbled again. 'Oh, I'll buy it for you. A wedding present from me. Now, *is that all*?'

IT WASN'T long before Joey was looking at the expensive but stylish cat travelling baskets, weighing up his options on which was the best one to purchase.

'But, darling, they all look the same. So, which one? And are you getting a kitten?' Ruby asked, feeling ravenous by now. She was a big lady and needed sustenance. 'I'm sorry, Joey, but we will have to stop and have a sit-down and a cup of tea. I was hoping to go straight back to the Belleville, but I feel a little faint from the lack of food.'

Joey nodded. 'I've decided, Ruby This beautiful turquoise and pink one with a pink fluffy cushion is perfect. The kitten is a present and it's a secret so say nothing. I will ask the salesman to put it behind the counter until we've had our cuppa.'

He went to the counter, where he was in for a shock. After paying for his purchases, he looked up into the eyes of the cashier and instantly recognised him. Joey gasped. Surely it couldn't be? 'Oh, hello,' he whispered, darting a look around to check that no one could hear. 'Fancy meeting you here. Would you be a darling and look after my cat basket for me? My friend and I are off to have some tea and can hardly take it in there with us, can we?'

'Of course I will look after it, sir. It would be my pleasure,' said the man whom Joey knew as Kim from the famous gay night club called Heaven. It had been many years ago when Joey and Kim had met on his weekends off back down in London, but of course, this was long before Ben. 'My pleasure entirely,' Kim repeated.

'Come on, Joey, I'm desperate to sit down. We will come back later for the cat basket, young man,' Ruby promised.

As they seated themselves in the closest of the

many restaurants within the huge store, Joey said wistfully, 'Maybe we could pop into the menswear department?' Then on seeing Ruby's face, he quickly backed off. 'Or maybe not.'

Just then, Kim, who had followed them, played a trick on the pair. With a cheeky grin on his face and flirtatious eyes and body language, he hoisted the cat basket high in the air and waved it around, calling, 'Oh madam, oh madam, you have forgotten your pussy.'

Everyone turned to see Kim holding the cat basket in the air. Some tittered, and others tutted.

'Oh no,' said Ruby with a huge sigh, 'not another of your conquests. Really, Joey. Go and get the basket from him and let's get out of here. We can pick up a few sneaky cans of gin and tonic on our way back to the taxi, and we will drink them secretly.'

'But I thought you wanted tea, and I thought you had never drunk in a black cab, let alone had a gin and tonic,' said Joey indignantly. Snatching the basket, and shouting to all and any customers: 'Ger-rout o' me way,' he ran off to the entrance of the café, looking like a frilled lizard with his legs akimbo and his mouth open wide. Ruby wondered at that moment if he'd been one of those creatures in a previous life. She flinched and covered her eyes, afraid that there would soon be a pile-up of customers in Joey's wake.

Under normal circumstances, Ruby tried not to

carry her own bags, but in this situation the sooner she got out of Selfridges the better. What if anyone saw her and recognised her? So, loaded up with more bags than she thought was possible, she struggled off to join Joey and got them out of the store. A cabbie helped them both with their purchases. As Ruby got in the taxi for the short journey to the hotel, she slid off her shoes. 'If the pink shirt is the one, why have you bought seven different colours?' she grumbled to Joey. 'There's no way I'm paying for all of them.'

'I know you're not. I got them because I might change my mind and that would be disastrous. Besides, I have squirrelled away my tips for the past nine years, just for this occasion. Oh, I shudder at the thought of me being in a quandary on my wedding day.' Joey physically trembled.

Ruby patted his hand. 'There, there, you have enough shirts for seven weddings.' As she looked through the cab windows at the people thronging Oxford Street, her thoughts went back to the woman on the beach and she blurted out, 'I *know* that was Chelsea down by the Thames earlier.'

Joey too had been thinking back to what had happened. 'I agree. It was Chelsea all right. I recognised her walk, the way she totters - even though she wasn't in heels.'

'But how do we convince Dan?'

Joey, who was no fool, already knew the answer to that.

'On some level he still believes that Chelsea was innocent of trying to frame Leah all those years ago for the theft of his precious Fabergé egg. And that's even when he could see Chelsea handling the egg *after* it had gone missing. So good luck with convincing him she was involved in the attack on Leah. I reckon he's blinded by guilt at ending their relationship, so it's up to us to be vigilant.'

4

THE BUFFOON AND THE
MADWOMAN

In a sleazy bed and breakfast place near Victoria railway station, Chelsea stood in front of her Cousin Brioche, her fists balling at her sides. For his part, he was nursing a wound on his hand. What a twerp her aunt was, calling her son after a French bread bun. Perhaps it was because he was full of hot air and puffed up and out. This idiot of a cousin stood a foot and a half higher than her and was as broad too, and yet he was shaking in his boots. He reminded her of Herman Munster, her grandmother's favourite TV character.

By contrast, the woman at his side was different again. With pale, intelligent green eyes and dark blonde hair, Pepper was nothing like her brother Brioche. But then she'd always claimed that her real brother had been swapped at birth. However, it wasn't the looks that Chelsea wanted from Pepper, although they would come in handy to lure Dan; it was her very special talents.

'So, do we think he maimed her for life?' Pepper asked Chelsea.

Brioche shuffled uncomfortably under their stares. When he'd seen the victim's pretty face and her little girl in her arms, he'd gone to jelly, and even though he'd accidentally struck out at her, he knew the knife had barely connected. He had never wanted to hurt anyone. 'Better luck next time, eh?' he said weakly.

'So, what's your excuse?' prompted Pepper, jabbing him in the stomach.

'The scooter was too small - I was losing my balance. And anyway, it was a ludicrous idea in the first place,' said Brioche, defending his actions. Besides, he thought to himself, they had looked a nice family unit.

'Stop going all soft on us,' snarled Pepper, knowing what that sentimental look on his face was all about. 'What have we told you about her? She stole Dan Ryan from our Chelsea, and she is wicked. She deserves everything she is going to get, and you are going to give it to her.'

Chelsea put on her hurt look, which she had mastered to a fine art over the years when she had worked for Dan. 'She was awful to me,' she said now, trying to summon a tear or two. 'She threw me in the muck pile and then broke my Jimmy Choos.'

'Jimmy who?' Brioche looked blank.

Pepper jabbed him again. 'Stop being a smart-alec. You know damn-well who Jimmy Choo is.'

'I dare say she beats the kids up too,' murmured Chelsea.

'What?' Brioche thought about this for a while; he wasn't the brightest button in the box, but he hated cruelty to animals and kids. Just the thought of it made him angry. Reluctantly, he agreed, although the woman he'd attacked hadn't seemed the kind. 'OK, I'm in on one condition: that I get to stay in the same hotel as you two. This place is the pits.'

Chelsea nodded, albeit reluctant to give in to Pepper's brother. 'Pack your case, and we'll move you now,' she said, 'although tomorrow we will travel back to Whitby. Thanks to you bungling the job here, Dan will now increase his security in London and we won't get a second chance to act. We have lost the element of surprise.'

PENNY LOOKED out of the floor-to-ceiling windows in the main Royal Suite, a cup of tea in her hand. The view was spectacular, looking over Westminster and then downriver towards St Paul's Cathedral and the

City. As she tried to shake off her hangover and the
dizzy feeling that went with it, she reflected on what
Howard had said about Gerard's will. Gosh, she'd not
drunk on a lunchtime like that in years, and now
whilst she waited for everyone to arrive, she had time
to think on exactly what she'd been told.

Gerard's worth - in cash alone - had been
£9,740,000 plus all the properties, and they were
numerous.

It was apparent to Penny now that their dear
friend had been in love with her for many years. He'd
invited himself so often to Sunday lunch and tea with
her and David that it had become a private joke
between the couple. However, in all those years
Gerard had never made his feelings clear to her - not
that she would have left David, who had been her
soulmate. Gerard had been happy to be included in
their family; ecstatic to go on holiday with them once
a year and share the odd weekend away. He'd made
as much of David as he did of Penny: as a matter of
fact, he often referred to her husband as the brother
he'd never had. So maybe he'd just fallen in love with
their lifestyle and was grateful to have been a part
of it.

Wiping a tear from her eye, Penny wondered what
she would do with her newfound wealth. She would
definitely get in touch with the Basset Hound Rescue
but first, now that she owned the house on the moor,

she would visit it. Although Howard said it had recently been let, it was still much too tempting not to call by. After all, she was now their landlady, wasn't she - so she had every right to arrive for an inspection.

Just then, Joey and Ruby marched into the suite, followed by a bellboy with more shopping bags in his arms than Penny had ever seen in one shopping spree. She rushed to help him, tutting, 'You poor boy, struggling with all those bags. Joey, how could you let him carry all of these!'

The bellboy moved away from Penny, keeping a good hold of the bags. No way was this lady taking his tip. 'I'm fine, thank you, madam.'

Ruby handed the bellboy a note. 'Put the bags there, sunshine,' she directed him and waited until he had left to say: 'It's his job, Penny. Besides, we've had an awful shock. I take it Dan and Leah aren't back yet, so you've not heard about Leah being hurt. It was one of the moped attacks, it would seem - a question of being in the wrong place at the wrong time.'

'Is she all right?' Penny asked, shaken. How could anyone hurt her beautiful niece deliberately?

The door was opened at that moment, and Leah walked in, looking a little pale and overhearing Penny's last words. 'I'm fine. Honestly, there is no problem. I just needed a stitch or two.'

'But who on earth would do that?' asked Penny, ushering Leah to sit where she could see the river. 'I will make a cup of tea whilst you watch the world go by.'

Joey said immediately, 'Darling Aunt Penny, one does *not* make a cuppa at the Belleville. You ask, they make. I will ring down for refreshments to be sent up.'

The kids then came in looking rather solemn, and Dan followed. 'Maybe something stronger than tea for me, please, Joey,' he said. 'This has been a shocker for us all. Then after dinner, I will arrange some security.'

'Oh, surely there's no need for that, Dan,' Leah objected, but as she saw everyone turn and stare at her, she knew she was being overruled.

'At this point it might be prudent to tell you, Dan, that earlier, Ruby and I thought we'd seen Chelsea Saffer hanging around down by the Thames,' Joey announced. 'Although why she would be there I can't imagine - and why it couldn't be her lovely pumps sinking into the mud instead of mine I will never know, but it certainly looked like her. When she left we tried to follow her, but she got away in taxi number 7771.'

Dan looked questioningly at Ruby. 'Did you think it was Chelsea?'

'Yes. Although as soon as she saw that I'd spotted

her, she scampered up off the shore.' Ruby accepted a drink from Dan. 'Thank you, darling. I'm positive it was her.'

'And how did she know we were going to be here? This trip was spontaneous, and I agree we knew we were coming to London months ago, but we hadn't planned mud-larking until last week when we were in the café in Whitby,' Leah said.'

Dan furrowed his brow. So, was someone spying for Chelsea in their café?

Leah accepted a very small brandy from Dan and then looked over to Penny. 'How did you get on at the solicitors?

'Well, it seems Gerard left me a few things in his will. No, thank you, Dan.' She refused the proffered brandy with a tiny shudder.

'Well, that can't be much. He was a tight-fisted old get,' interrupted Joey. 'Tight as a duck's . . .'

Dan cut Joey off in mid-sentence. 'We have children present, Joey.'

'I'm just stating the obvious,' Joey complained, but he could appreciate what Dan was saying as Alice was at the age where she picked up everything and repeated it. Little did they know that Alice already knew that expression. He peeked a look at her, but she was closing her eyes. Thank goodness she wasn't going to say anything. And then she did.

'Duck's ar . . . bottom,' said the little girl, and her eyes closed again.

Dan threw a look of disgust at Joey. 'I see I'm too late.'

Leah was biting her lip. It was the only funny thing that had happened all day and then she couldn't help herself; she burst out laughing.

Joey grinned, then ducked as Dan playfully tried to slug him, saying, 'We secretly have high hopes for Alice. So the last thing we want is for her to know rude expressions like that.'

Alice was a kind little girl. She rushed in with: 'I overheard Uncle Joey on the phone. Don't blame him, Daddy. It's my fault.'

'OK, Princess, I believe you, but I do not want to hear that word again, understood?'

'But what is it, Daddy?' Alice frowned as she had seen Dan do.

'Don't give me that innocent look, young lady. You know full well what it is. Why, you said it just a moment ago.'

'Duck's bottom. Hahaha!' screamed Alice as she legged it to her mummy and hid behind her.

Ruby diplomatically changed the subject, addressing Penny. 'Did you manage to buy yourself a dry suit?'

'Oh yes, thank you. They had Extra-Extra-Extra Large size, so I can fit my woolly drawers under it to keep me warm until I will be able to be rescued by Hero,' said Penny with pride. 'It's the first on-line purchase I've ever made. I think it was too easy. Press a button, and you've bought it when the internet works.'

Over the sound of the kids giggling at the words *woolly drawers*, Dan said loudly, 'I'm proud of you, Pen. Very proud indeed.'

She smiled back at him, thinking that yes, her great-niece had caught the best fish in the sea this side of the world, and that was a fact.

OVER A RELAXED DINNER, Dan wore smart trousers and an open-necked shirt. He sat next to Penny, who by her standards was quite dolled-up with a sparkly top and skirt. Howard was sat opposite her. Ruby and Joey were across from Leah and Dan, and the kids were facing each other. Dan touched Leah's foot under the table, and she raised her eyes at him.

'Penny for your thoughts,' Dan whispered to Leah.

She winced. 'I just can't imagine why Chelsea would be here in London nor how she would know where to find us. I'm baffled.'

'I can't see it either. It was probably nothing to do with her, but just an opportunist trying to steal an easy buck.' Dan reached across and squeezed Leah's hand, but his grim expression was telling a different story.

'So, Leah, are you recovered, my dear?' asked Howard, sipping the delicious wine that the hotel butler had poured.

'I am, thank you, Mr Levinson. I feel much better, but I would like to know why anyone would target a person who had been mud-larking.' It was the only thing that was strange about the whole incident. 'I mean, our bounty was hardly worth robbing: a few clay pipe stems and a pretty ring.'

'Please call me Howard.' The man cleared his throat. 'Indeed. What a very sad state of affairs. These moped robbers seem have appeared out of nowhere over the past few years and they are practically impossible to catch. However, I hear you weren't even carrying a handbag. Were you using a smartphone?'

Leah shook her head. 'I had a small rucksack but no phone visible.'

'Well, all I can say, dear, is that if they catch him. I will represent you in court for free,' promised Howard, who now fully appreciated why Dan had fallen hook, line and sinker for this beautiful York-shire girl. He didn't know all the details but the stories that were flying around the City at the time about their romantic history were almost too bizarre to be believed.

'So, come on, Aunt Penny, what did Gerard leave you?' Joey asked nonchalantly.

Penny looked over her glasses at him. 'He left me everything, Joey.'

'Yes, but what does *everything* mean?'

'Joey, don't speak to Penny like that,' Leah remonstrated, quite appalled at his rudeness.

But Penny didn't mind. 'It's fine, love. Let's put it this way: I will be asking Dan how to invest a few million.'

'Bloody hellfire. The old goat!' Joey exclaimed. 'But then he could save, couldn't he, as he ate almost every meal with you and Great-uncle David and from all accounts, he never paid his share.'

'You're being very unfair, Joey. Gerard often paid for our meals out,' Penny corrected him. There was no way the young man would find out about Gerard's fondness of her yet. She was still trying to get used to it herself. She pinched her own thigh under the table and then smiled. Maybe Joey was right and Gerard had been an 'old goat' - but an intelligent one at that.

'What I want to know is how he saved that much on a Headmaster's salary.' Joey wouldn't let it drop.

It was Howard who replied. 'I've known Gerard for a long time, young man. He could have worked the stock markets as a professional. He had intuition, and expert knowledge of how the stocks and shares worked. He studied the Fibonacci rules, and he made himself a rich man. Of course, he came from a good background and was left a small fortune too.'

'Wow, I'd have been extra nice to him if I'd known he was loaded,' muttered Joey into his wine.

DAN WATCHED Leah walk from the en-suite bathroom as he lay on top of the stately four-poster bed in his boxer shorts. Leah had her head down and was touching her shoulder gently. He saw her bite her lip.

'I've arranged for a plainclothes security guard to be with us for the rest of the stay,' Dan said with determination in his voice. 'And before you object, please don't, Leah.'

'Well, I hope your security man likes *Toy Story*, the fifth or fourth in the series or whatever it is because that's where we are going tomorrow. To the cinema. We promised, and I'm not letting the kids down.' Leah caught Dan smiling at her.

'Even after everything that has happened to you today, you're still prepared to go to the cinema. You're amazing.' Dan patted the bed next to him.

'That's *my* word, amazing.'

'I don't think you can copyright that word. Amazing, amazing, amazing,' Dan had lust in his eyes. 'Come here.'

'Are you sure you're not talking to Hero?'

Dan shook his head. 'My big boy is at home. As well you know.'

'And when is our baby coming?'

'Come over here, and I will whisper in your ear exactly when our baby will arrive.' He patted the bed again.

'In that case, I'm on my way. Ouch!' Leah cried out as by mistake she grabbed the four-poster with her bad arm. 'This is so painful.'

'Then let me just cuddle you and know you are safe,' Dan replied genuinely.

'You daft bugger. It's my shoulder, not anything else.' Leah moved onto the bed. 'Besides, would you ration me, husband?'

'I wouldn't dare.'

Just then, the door burst open and Alice ran in; she leaped on to the bed, cuddling up to them both. 'I think there's a spider in my bed.'

Leah looked across at Dan, while stroking Alice's hair. 'Shall I go or you? I doubt there will be a spider, but if there is it will be a Royal Spider in these rooms.'

'I want Daddy to come and shake my bedcovers and read me another story,' Alice announced.

Dan shrugged his shoulders and gave Leah a

quick kiss. 'Come on, Princess, let's go and drive him out.'

BY THE TIME Dan had banished the so-called 'spider' out of Alice's bed, read her a story which he thought was far scarier than any measly old spider that had turned out to be a piece of chocolate she'd hidden, he went back into the sitting room to switch off the lamps before returning to their bedroom. He saw his queen lying fast asleep, all skew-whiff over the bed, wearing a cute matching underwear set. Watching her whilst she slept like this made him realise just how precious she was to him and as he climbed onto the bed, she moaned, and her arms came slowly around his neck.

'I just wanted to say you were my hero today,' she said dreamily.

Dan chuckled. 'And what do heroes get?'

'Why rewards, of course, my knight in shining armour,' replied Leah, still half-asleep.

'Oh good, my damsel in distress,' Dan murmured in her ear. 'Because I want to undress you very, very slowly.' He started nibbling on her ear, breathing so close to her neck she shuddered with desire. His lips traversed across her cheekbones, moving lower over her mouth. He simply loved kissing her.

Suddenly Leah jumped up, pushed Dan back on the bed and straddled him. He reached up to the lace of her top and felt her nipples as he worked his hands over her silk- and lace-covered flesh.

'I see you were waiting for me,' he said with a smile.

'I've been waiting for you all my life, Dan.' Her voice was husky as he worked his magic around the silk and lace. She reached up and was careful of her shoulder as she shrugged out of her top.

'Wench.' He flipped her onto her back, careful of her wound. Then with a dark, sensual look in his eyes, the one that secretly thrilled his wife, he claimed her.

'Is it good?' he said harshly.

'Oh, yes, yes!' cried out Leah as he reached her g-spot again. He ploughed into her while he reached his own goal. Falling from the precipice, they embraced each other until their breathing had subsided.

Dan moved.

Leah yelled, 'Watch my shoulder, you big oaf.'

'Oh, sorry, sweetheart.' He settled himself more carefully. 'I think Alice likes the Belleville,' Dan went on. 'She said she wants to come again. I reckon she takes after her mum - enjoys the finer things in life.' He reached for a glass of water, grinning to himself, knowing that his wife would react to this provocation.

'You mean she's like *you*,' Leah said immediately, as Dan had predicted.

He laughed, then kissed her. 'I mean that I love you for bringing our Princess and our Prince into this world and I love you for being funny and special, and today for one moment I thought I was going to lose you. Lose the woman I love.' Dan put his forehead on hers. 'Please be gracious about the extra security.'

'All right, I'll be good. But he'd better like animation films, hadn't he?' Leah kissed her husband. 'I love you, Dan. Without you, my clock doesn't tick. My heart doesn't beat, and my world would be a sad place without you. Now let's go to sleep, it's been a long day.' As she closed her eyes, Leah honestly thought things would be fine. She just hoped Chelsea wasn't watching from the side-lines.

THE FOLLOWING day was eventful in a fun way. Dan, Leah, minder and kids had gone to the cinema and returned to find that Joey and Ruby were out shopping, again.

'Isn't seven shirts enough for any man on his wedding day?' Dan asked Leah.

She shrugged. 'He goes over the top. You should know him by now, and since he took over as manager and his wages have increased, he saved up and now he has to spend, spend, spend.'

'Well, he's not a canny Yorkshireman then, is he?'

'Not when he's acting like that, he isn't.' She giggled, then became sombre. 'I've been thinking, Dan. Do *you* believe it was Chelsea that Ruby and Joey saw down by the Thames?' Leah herself didn't want to believe that Chelsea would be so foolish. Surely she wouldn't jeopardise her freedom like this, end up back in prison? It had been five years since Dan and Leah had got back together and were now married with a young daughter to join their son Tom – their family was solid, so Chelsea must be mad to still bear a grudge against them. Whatever she did, Dan's former secretary and one-time lover would *never* split them up. Why couldn't she accept that and just be happy and find a man and a life of her own?

Leah took in the beautiful scenery before her; the London Eye rearing up in all its glory over the Thames. She waved at the people quite a distance from her.

Dan came up behind Leah and encircled her in his arms. 'I'm not sure they can see you, darling.'

'Oh, I just thought I'd wave. It's such a glorious day.' Then Leah froze as she saw a tall, broad man standing far away on the prow of a Clipper boat – the water taxis that take Londoners along the Thames to avoid the traffic on the busy roads. Seeing him, the hair on the back of her neck stood up. She pointed to the vessel. 'Dan, you'll never believe it! That looks like the one on the scooter yesterday!'

The security man who was stood inside the room ran to the window. 'Which man, madam?' He picked up his binoculars.

'The very tall man, down there, with his back to us.'

The security man took a quick photo on his phone and Dan did the same.

'I can count ten tall men without even trying,' Dan said to calm his wife, slipping a hand around her waist, gently stroking her back.

'I will check their CCTV and get back to you,' the security man said.

'Thank you, Michael. You can go and do that now if you like. We'll be fine.' Dan studied the grainy photo on his phone. 'What do you think, Leah? Could it be him?' Dan personally was sceptical.

Leah watched closely as Dan tried to make the photo more prominent, but it was just a blurred image.

'I agree he is a very tall man - but how many of those are there in London?' Dan asked, feeling this was a hopeless case. With all these tourists and the commuters around, it was an impossible task to find the man they sought. Surely the assailant who had attacked Leah would lie low for a few days if he had any sense. Dan put a comforting arm around his wife. 'Let's just wait to see what our security guard has to say. How about we have afternoon tea, Belleville-style.'

'Yes, that would be nice. Then you need to go to the office, right?' Leah had seen it on the calendar which they shared.

'Yes. What time did you say I'm due there, babe?'

She reached up to kiss him. 'Not until teatime. I think the meeting is around five p.m.'

'Well, I've arranged for Eros to take it in my absence. I've briefed him, and I may have to have a conference call here, but I'm staying put with my family. So, let's tell the kids. Or shall we leave the Princess for another hour. I mean she's asleep, and Tom is listening to music.'

'Maybe we could forget about afternoon tea, Belleville-style?' Leah suggested.

'Or maybe we just delay it a while . . .' Dan gathered her to him.

5

RUDE, RUDE, RUDE

Soon, the brief respite in London was over, and the children were back at school in Whitby. The café was full; visitors from all corners of the county had been served and were busy chatting while watching the surf of the North Sea. Joey had been taking a well-earned break in the kitchen. Now, picking up his oven gloves, he took out the last batch of scones.

Leah dropped by the café to see him while the youngsters were in school.

'Coo-ee, Leah, I will be out in a tick.' Joey popped his head around the kitchen door, and again he examined the slight elderly woman with the poor mite of a hound as she ordered another coffee with an imperious shake of her purse. Old cow, thought Joey. Some days he felt he could throttle the unwelcome customer because of her rude tone and the way the sad little dog which accompanied her cowered and flinched from her umbrella or stick. Joey was convinced she was unkind to the little creature.

Joey came over and hissed in Leah's ear: 'I'll just serve that nasty old bully in the corner. I want to take her poor little doggie home and snuggle him.'

'I know - you've spoken about her before. Well, if she is cruel, then report her, but only if you have proof, mind.' Leah then added, 'I can't stay. Just came in to say hi.'

'Is there anyone working, anybody at all?' declared the scratchy old voice coming from the corner of the café.

'Yes, I will be with you in a mo,' Joey said loudly. 'I am just taking my buns out of the oven. Keep your friggin' clouts on,' he added in a whisper. 'A girl can only do so much.' Then to Leah, 'She's been in hours, and it seems like years.'

'She's probably lonely,' Leah offered. 'I shall make her a cappuccino. You take care of your baking. Pass me a pinny, Joey, please.'

Leah grabbed the apron from Joey to protect her outfit and made the coffee just as she always had. As she set the cup in front of the lady, she inhaled her perfume. 'Sorry for your wait, madam.'

'At last. A woman my age could drop down dead before she got her second cuppa here.'

'As I said, I have apologised about that. Joey is busy with his buns,' said Leah politely.

'I bet he is,' came the cryptic response.

Leah frowned as she caught the scent again. She noticed the woman now as she rose to her feet to visit the Ladies toilet. She returned as Leah was clearing and wiping down the next table. Her make-up looked very thick, and her double chin seemed out of character with her slim arms and big breasts. Her jam-jar glasses were the finishing touch to an odd appearance. Then Leah glanced down at the pup at her feet, cocking its head to one side and looking up at her.

'May I give your dog a treat?' she asked, already reaching into her pocket.

The woman gave a stern reply. 'Very well. Just one.'

Leah gave the little dog a stroke and put the treat on the floor. She normally decided on people as she found them, but this rather unpleasant old woman was not easily readable, she surmised as she moved back to the kitchen.

'I'm positive I know the perfume she's wearing; I've smelled it before, but for the life of me, I can't think where. What's more, it's too fashionable and too young for someone like her,' mused Leah.

'Ooh. Well, I try not to get close enough to smell her,' Joey said, wrinkling his nose. 'She may be a nasty piece of work, but she keeps an eye on what everyone is doing, I've noticed that. She watches us all like a flippin' hawk.'

'What do you mean exactly?' Leah poured herself some water from the fridge.

'Well, she leans back in her chair if I am talking on the phone, almost like she's earwigging. At first, I thought nothing of it, but as the weeks have gone on, I sometimes hear her talking to the staff, questioning them about various things.' Joey was frowning. 'I hope I don't get like that. A nosy old cow!'

'What do you mean - you already are. Hahaha,' Leah ducked as Joey threw the oven gloves at her.

'Leah Jensen-Ryan-Savidis - phew, what a gobful that is - you're skating on thin ice over Whitby harbour.' Then Joey stopped messing about and pointed surreptitiously to the horrible customer and mouthed, 'Look.'

Sure enough, when Leah took a sneaky peek, she could see the elderly woman craning forward and trying to listen in. Teasing Joey, she said, 'Maybe she is just an old washerwoman, like you. It takes one to know one.'

A dog treat flew across the kitchen aimed at Leah by Joey, but she easily dodged it, hiding her laughter. Joey and she often became like children when they got together.

A few minutes later, the strange woman suddenly got up, yanked the little dog from under the table and marched out. Leah could ignore her uneasy feeling no longer. There was something about her that she couldn't quite put her finger on; what's more, she'd left behind the coffee Leah had just made her and about which she'd made such a fuss.

Joey came over and watched with Leah as the woman got into a taxi outside the café, almost throwing the little dog inside the footwell of the cab none too gently. 'See what she's like,' he said disgustedly.

'Well, let's monitor her. But this is under your remit now. You are the manager. Right. I'm off to run some errands for Dan.' Leah took the pinny off. 'But remember, Joey, you could open a can of worms or one of caviar.'

'Do you mind? That is one of *my* sayings.' Joey walked back into the scullery with a tray of used crockery, asking over his shoulder, 'Where are you going? Or is it some kind of top-secret mission?'

'No mystery, I'm just going to search for some jet cufflinks for my wonderful husband to wear at your wedding,' said Leah with a wave. 'See you, Joey!' As she walked up the steps and across the cliffs, thinking about the woman, the dog and the perfume, the sight of a very tall man a few feet behind her sent shudders down her spine. She patted her shoulder in an involuntary move. Taking a nifty shortcut that only a local would know about, she hastened down towards the harbour where she disappeared in the crowds.

BRIOCHE HAD LOST HER, much to his disappointment, because he knew that scary Chelsea would be annoyed with him. She had ordered him to abduct Leah and take her to Sledborough House to lock her up. It was a stupid plan – they'd never get away with it. And kidnapping was a serious crime. His heart turned over at the thought of ending up in prison for years. Knowing Chelsea, she would throw away the key just so she could have another chance with Daniel Ryan. Brioche's heart sank. Why couldn't she see sense? The affair with Dan was over years ago, but the silly woman couldn't let go.

As luck would have it, he did actually spot Leah in one of the small jewellers' shops up the cobble-stoned streets. All he wanted to do was shadow her for a while; he would never do what his cousin and his sister wanted him to do. He observed Leah chatting to the jeweller, and the more he saw of her, the more he disbelieved what Chelsea and Pepper had told him. She seemed lovely, and kind too - and that made him feel bad. He'd never meant to hurt her in London - and yet he'd heard that he'd cut her and she'd had to go to hospital. He shuddered at the thought.

Brioche moved around the square out of sight as he saw the jeweller wrapping up her parcel and Leah paying for the purchase. With a huge smile, she made her way to the door then strolled down the hill away from him and towards the swing-bridge. He saw how she stopped to stroke several dogs and talked to them as they sat and waited for a biscuit. She spent time with the fishermen on the harbour wall, joining in their jokes, and it was apparent they liked her very much. No way could he believe that this woman could possibly hit her children. Chelsea had said so, and it had made him angry at first, but Brioche had no proof and without evidence he wasn't going to kidnap anyone.

Carefully, he followed her back to the café, leaving quite a distance between them. By now she was on the beach, and he was walking along the path on the cliff tops. He'd seen her buy carrots and watched her feed the donkeys on the sands. She petted each one and had a conversation with the man who led them up and down on the beach. Leah had then helped with the rides whilst the donkey-owner went for a quick cup of tea and a sandwich. Each donkey's saddle-blanket matched their bridle colour, and each noseband had a brass nameplate. When the donkey-owner came back, Brioche saw her kiss each donkey on its nose, then wave to their keeper, and walk on towards the café.

Brioche let out an exasperated breath. He'd had enough. This woman was no child-beater, and he would find out for sure as he was going to follow her to the school.

JOEY WAS FAGGED; he went to the doorway for a breath of air and saw Leah coming back from her errand, kicking at the sand as she approached. He thought about his cousin and Dan. It was like they had known each other a lifetime. They were so comfortable with their life together. It wasn't so long ago that they'd been across to Ireland with the horses and the kids. They'd been going to an equestrian dancing competition, and they'd got lost. Dan had climbed out of his Range Rover outside a church, and Leah being Leah, she had checked the horses then made her way to the oldest part of the small churchyard with Alice in tow, holding her daughter's hand in hers. Tom had walked into the village with Dan to find out where the Castle Hotel was. They were going to be staying there as it was next door to the event.

He could hardly believe it when, that same evening, Leah had shown him the photo she had taken of a particular tombstone. Dan and Tom had

returned from the village, armed with directions, to
see Leah and Alice walking around the churchyard.
Tom started a game of hide and seek with Alice while
their parents had walked towards the church hand-in-
hand. Running her fingers over the wall of the small
building, which was made of flint with a grey slate
roof, Leah sighed contentedly. But once they'd
walked inside, they quickly realised that half the roof
was missing. Church pews stood damp and damaged
from the weather; the ornate font was still in place, as
were the mouldy hymn books. There was a space
where the organ was missing, and the chancel where
the choir sang was no longer there. Leah had told
Joey repeatedly that she had thought somehow, at
some time, she had been there *before* – but how could
that have been possible, because it was her first visit
to Ireland?

They walked back out of the church, and that was
when Leah saw the tombstone. She stopped dead in
her tracks and pointed to the weatherworn tribute to a
local couple. The words were simple and yet
profound. *Here lieth Dan and Leah, 1818*. Most of the
other inscriptions were weatherworn and had become
indecipherable, but the inscription underneath said
clearly, *Our love till eternity*. Both Dan and Leah had
felt the massive impact. Tears filled Leah's eyes. Why
had they stopped here? Why had they walked around
this churchyard and why had she insisted she must go

into the church? For they would never have seen the gravestone nor the inscription.

Now, as he recalled the incident, Joey secretly prayed that he and Ben could love to eternity too.

As Leah walked up from the beach, she glanced up at the cliff, and once again she saw a tall man staring down towards her. She ran to the café as fast as she could.

'What on earth's the matter, Lee-Lee?' Joey was shocked by his cousin's ashen face.

'I think the man from London is here to attack me again. Come and check the cliff near the Whale Bone Arch. Quick!' Leah looked so shaken that Joey stepped outside to peer around.

'I can't see anyone, Lee-Lee. Come and look.' Joey delivered his answer gently.

Leah came to the door. True enough, there was not a single person on the clifftop. Shrugging, she gave a deep sigh. Perhaps she had been mistaken. 'I have to pick Alice up soon,' she told Joey. 'Tom is going to see his pal Troy tonight and will be staying over there.'

'Would you like me to get Olly in to help and I will come with you?' Joey said, genuinely concerned about her.

Leah shook her head. 'No. I will be fine. Maybe this London incident has got to me more than I thought. Or maybe I'm thinking of the Dracula legend here.' She tried to laugh.

'Well, if you're sure.' Joey cuddled Leah before he went back into the kitchen. 'I will come and have dinner with you tonight, as we have so much to arrange, and with Dan being away I don't want you to be frightened.'

'Thanks, Joey, I would appreciate that. Look, I don't want you to tell Dan about this. It's probably my over-active imagination. I'll get off now. See you later.' Leah walked out. She ran to her vehicle and jumped in and drove off. When she had disappeared, Joey went to the door just to check again for any sighting of a tall man. It wasn't like Leah to get spooked.

DAN COULD SEE the house coming into view as the helicopter prepared to land. It was great that he could fly onto his front lawn, well, on the landing pad next to their lawn. He heaved a sigh of relief as he did so. He couldn't wait to see Leah and the kids. Then, after he'd had a cuppa, he would ring around his co-ordinators for the Newfoundland Water Display which was due to take place this weekend. He hoped it would run like clockwork, but first, he wanted to kiss his wife, and he didn't have long to wait as she came out to the helipad and waited for the rotor blades to stop before she ran into his arms.

'This is a pleasant welcome,' Dan murmured into her ear. He looked down into her face and saw she had tears in her eyes. 'Hey, what're the tears for?' He kissed her on the lips, then took her arm and walked her away from the helicopter.

'Oh, just ignore me. I've missed you,' said Leah, feeling such a relief that he was home now for a while. She wanted to feel him next to her in bed, to have his arms around her. 'Did you miss me?'

'Stop fishing for compliments.' Then he scooped her up into his arms. 'Not quite school-run time, is it?'

Leah wriggled and giggled as he carried her into the house and up the stairs.

Dan stopped at the edge of their bed. He tossed his wife on top of the quilt and smiled down into her beautiful face. And with that, he joined her on the bed, where he proved just how much he'd missed her.

Sledborough House, North Yorkshire Moors.

Chelsea marched about in the bedroom she'd chosen, faffing around with two little speakers she had surreptitiously carried just into the doorway of the darkened rooms where Brioche and Pepper were sleeping. The sea air had made them all tired as they'd walked on the beach plotting. She went back to her room and sat on the bed talking into a small device, while relaxing music drifted into the rooms.

'I would like you to look up to the ceiling and stay there for say five seconds, maybe six or seven. Now I will count you slowly down a flight of steps into a full hypnotic state.' She flicked the page of the hypnosis book. Damn, she thought angrily. I spilled coffee on this page, and it's faded. Hoping she was going to be able to recall the text, she carried on, 'You will now walk down thirty steps . . . into a beautiful rose garden . . .' at the same time thinking to herself: What's this, a frigging skyscraper with so many freaking steps?

Taking a deep breath in, she murmured, 'Now I want you to take the first step down slowly, one, two, deeper and deeper, three.' Oh, stuff this for a lark. 'Four, six, eight, eleven.' She reeled the rest of the numbers off so quickly it was like watching a film reel at the end of the cinema spinning out of control as she missed many of the numbers out and finished off with. 'Twenty-one, twenty-six, thirty!' She almost screeched the last number, not realising she'd been counting up not down as the manual stated. What she also didn't realise was how powerful it was, to swap the numbers around, helping her patients to go deeper into hypnosis.

The little dog chose that moment to creak her door open, scaring the living daylights out of her as it simply stood there and stared at her.

'Argh. Shoo! Shoo!' she hissed then went back to the hypnosis. 'Now you will do what I say, and *every-thing* I say, Pepper and Brioche. *Everything* I say. You will follow my orders to the letter where Dan Ryan and his cheap hooker wife Leah are concerned. Now, when I click my fingers - *once* - you will drift off into a deep slumber, remembering everything when you awake. So here we go . . .' She clicked her fingers into the microphone.

The dog, disgusted with the horrible woman, had trotted back to Brioche's room where the big kindly fellow was laid fast asleep in bed. The little dog jumped on the bed beside him to cuddle up in his neck, next to the ear plugs and earmuffs he was wearing, because if nowt else, Brioche knew it was cold out on the moors tonight.

Scarthingdale Hall. *Same night.*

Dan walked down to the stables with Leah that night to see Galahad. Quinn the stable manager had called up earlier to say that the horse didn't seem himself, so the couple made haste there. When they arrived, Galahad's head was down, and he hadn't touched the rack full of haylage or his spring-meadow hay. Quinn had taken his temperature, but it was OK.

'Why don't we just get the vet out? It's not late and I'm sure he wouldn't mind,' Leah said, knowing she'd feel better if the vet came over. He didn't live too far away.

'I noticed that something had unsettled him earlier, boss, and he hasn't gotten any better,' Quinn reported.

'I see. Well, maybe Leah is right and you should call the vet in, Quinn,' Dan said. He looked across at Leah. 'I may have to stay up with Galahad.'

'We can both keep him company. He might be your boy, but I love him too. I'm sure Sophie and Grandad Thomas won't mind. It's so handy, now they've moved most of their stuff from Abbot's Bridge Road to the wing we had built for them here. I know they couldn't wait to join us here, and I'm sure they won't mind sleeping in the bedroom next to the kids' rooms. Grandad phoned earlier to say they were coming up in time for a nightcap.'

Leah stroked Galahad's velvety nose. 'Has he been near the beach?' she asked suddenly.

'Yes, Davey took him down there,' said Quinn.

'Why do you ask that, darling?' questioned Dan, searching her face for answers.

'Just hang on with the vet,' Leah said, and grabbed her phone out of her pocket. 'I'll just be a moment.' She walked outside and pressed the number bearing the name *Cyril*.

Dan could hear Leah talking, and then she appeared back into the stables some five minutes later.

'Quinn, did you get the psyllium husk powder remedy I asked you to order?' she asked.

Quinn nodded, but added sceptically, 'I did, although I think it's an old wives' tale.'

'An old wives' tale?' Dan echoed, stroking Galahad's sad face.

Quinn explained, 'I believe Leah thinks he has sand colic.'

'What?' Dan stopped stroking, but Galahad nudged his hand.

'Yes, I do think it's sand colic and I reckon the psyllium husk remedy will help him. It helped my old horse on one occasion, so let's see if he will eat it first.' Leah looked for approval from Dan, and when he nodded, she said, 'I will make it then.'

Dan watched her go towards the feed store. 'So, you're on the fence with this?' he asked Quinn.

The young man told him, 'I am, but having said that I've not lived by the sea until I came here, and Thomas's old friend Cyril mentioned it to Leah. He knows his stuff, and no doubt that was who Leah phoned just now. So, it's worth a try.'

Dan watched Leah coming back with a bucket. She popped it into Galahad's trough, and he immediately put his head into it and looked interested. He soon started munching.

Leah smiled. 'He likes it, that's a start.'

'He does indeed.' Dan was pleased. 'Let me know how he goes on, Quinn. We'll pop in later.' He took Leah's hand. 'Let's go back to the house and return in an hour or so. We can curl up on the sofa and watch some TV.'

AROUND 10 P.M. the doorbell rang. Leah looked up from her mug of hot chocolate.

'I wonder who that could be?' Dan asked, then he set off to the front door. 'Ah, Cyril, good to see you. Come on in.'

Leah joined them in the hall.

'I've come to see how t'owd hoss is goin' on. Leah said he 'ad stomach-ache,' said Cyril. He grinned, showing gaps where his teeth were missing. He wore the same battered tweed trilby which looked as old as he was and was always stuck on his head.

'We're just going down to the stables, why don't

we all go? It was kind of you to come.' The older man's concern touched Dan.

'Where's Thomas, Leah?' Cyril asked.

'He's just going to join you,' said a voice coming from the staircase as Thomas walked down the steps.

Cyril greeted his old pal, and they all walked out of the back door down the path to the stables, the dogs following one by one.

Dan held the door open for them all to get in. Quinn popped his head over Galahad's stable door.

'How is he?' Leah asked, noting that Galahad looked less stressed and more comfortable in himself.

'He's fine. He ate the whole mash and then he started on his meadow hay about half an hour ago.' Quinn fondled Galahad's head.

'Wurks every time for my hosses,' Cyril said. The old fellow patted the horse's head. 'I thought I'd better come across because yon Fletcher over t'valley lost his old pony not so long ago, wit' same thing too, so I thought I'd check.'

'Which old pony, Cyril?' Leah wanted to know.

'Not little Smokey?' Thomas asked.

'Aye, but I reckon he were forty-four if he were a day. He's had a good old innings. I went to every birthday party, as did you, Thomas, and I got smashed out o' me skull each time.'

'Oh, I'm so sad. *She* was an adorable *girl* pony, Cyril,' Leah said with emphasis.

Cyril laughed. 'Aye, mebbe she were a mare, but they're all the same to me - unless I am grooming as you have to treat sum o' the ladies with a bit o' respect, or they'll kick you in the balls.'

Thomas heaved a sigh. 'Thank you for sparing my Leah from the worst of your language. That's the politest expression you have, I guess.'

Cyril grinned.

Thomas didn't see Leah's face as she bit her lip to stop laughing and shared a cheeky look at Cyril. Many a time she and Joey had sat with Cyril on his wooden bench, with the old fellow telling all the naughty tales he could think of. But Leah would never enlighten her grandfather on that score. Some things were best kept a secret.

GALAHAD WAS fine the following morning and Quinn had to bow to Cyril's knowledge of sand colic. Quinn had made a reference to it in the book he kept of ailments and cures.

Dan was grooming Galahad and talking to him when Leah crept up. She loved listening to him whisper to the old stallion.

'I know you're there.' Dan bobbed his head around the stable door. 'Galahad knew too. Quinn's making coffee. If you call him, he'll make you one.'

Leah sighed. 'I drink too much coffee. Why didn't you wake me?'

'Because you didn't get to sleep until the early hours and when I woke, you looked so peaceful,' Dan replied with a smile.

'Something kept me awake.'

'Something I should know about?' Dan asked straight away.

Leah shrugged. 'I suppose I ought to tell you. It's this: I thought I saw the same man who attacked me near the Thames - and I know that sounds crazy. He was on the cliff in Whitby, and I recognised him, but the more I think about it, the more I wonder if I could be mistaken.'

Dan walked out of the stable and took her in his arms. 'So, you saw a tall man in Whitby?'

'That's what Joey said,' Leah murmured, her hands resting on his tanned muscular forearms.

'And the likelihood of that chancer being here is very, very minimal. Would you like me to go into the probability factor?' he asked, trying to settle her nerves.

Leah shook her head. 'I know I'm being stupid.'

'Never stupid, darling. That creep scared you. He frightened the life out of me, and he didn't slice me with a blade.' Dan tightened his hold. 'If it helps, I will get security stepped up here as well.'

'No, no, Dan,' Leah said immediately. 'I am overreacting.'

'If you change your mind, just say the word. Promise?'

Leah nodded. 'I have to pop into the café. I will be back at lunch.'

'Fancy a siesta after lunch?' he whispered cheekily.

'Dan Ryan, didn't you get enough of me last night?'

'I could never have enough of you.'

Leah reached up and kissed him. 'See you for an exciting siesta.'

'You bet, wifey.'

KNOWING SHE WAS ON A PROMISE, Leah dashed upstairs to put on her black stockings and suspenders and her pink underwear under a short skirt. Taking the cerise-coloured jumper which was hanging on the chair arm, she put it on and glided it over her breasts. Her make-up was already on, but she renewed her lipstick.

Looking into the mirror, she smiled at herself. Even without all the trappings of Dan's wealth, she knew he would always make her happy. She was more than capable of making her own money, but his fortune made any financial problems disappear. She knew how lucky she was, and she was always very grateful for her love and her life.

Picking up the new photo frame on her dressing table, she could see the top of Striding Edge in the Lake District with herself, Dan, and Tom posing beneath it. She had loved that weekend away, and she'd always be grateful for Sophie and Grandad Thomas looking after Alice in the hotel while they'd walked the length of Striding Edge. They'd asked another walker if he would take a photo of the three of them, which he kindly did. It had been so special.

Leah stood for a short while at the café doorway looking over Whitby's west bay, watching the waves tripping over themselves as the tide rolled in. Soon she would have to ride on the beach with Dan and the kids as she could feel the cobwebs building up. Even Tom had noticed that she hadn't ridden since the attack on her in London, and he'd mentioned his concern to her. Bless him, thought Leah, he was growing up into a lovely young man. She was very proud of the person he was becoming.

'Hi, cousin,' said Joey, coming to join her. 'I just wanted you to know there is a tall man in the café. He seems harmless enough. Ooh, look at you, all dressed up. Am I allowed to know why?'

'No.' Leah peeped in and saw the man reading the morning paper. 'OK. I'm not sure it's him, but I think I can cope. I told Dan about the man from yesterday, and he thought I was overreacting too.'

'We don't think you're . . . We think it's very hard coping with that kind of thing.' Joey sighed; he wasn't handling this very well.

Leah moved past Joey and walked into the café, saying, 'Hello, everyone.'

Brioche looked around and caught Leah's eye. She looked like a rabbit caught in the headlights, he thought guiltily. 'Hello,' he said. 'I saw you with the donkeys on the beach. You were very kind feeding them. I like donkeys.'

Leah heaved a sigh of relief. He seemed like a nice, somewhat simple guy. 'Me too, I love all animals. Would you like another coffee?'

Brioche nodded.

Joey leaned over and murmured, 'You see? That wasn't too hard, was it?'

Leah nodded. 'You're right. OK, I'm going down to the harbour for the things we need. Is there anything else you want?'

Joey put his hands on his hips. 'Well, if I dare ask Gypsy Mizelli for another reading, I would come with you in a flash. But . . .'

'She's banned you again?'

'Yup. Leah, you haven't forgotten we have Stanley's funeral, have you? We will have to work it into the rota.'

'Of course not. Stanley and his beautiful Australian Shepherd dog Halley were excellent customers and besides, he was a fascinating old chap.' Leah smiled in memory of the older man.

'Did I mention I'm taking on Halley?' Joey asked. 'She seems well trained and as soon as I knew she was named after the comet I knew it was kismet. Do you remember when she took a customer's cigarettes out of her handbag? And it appalled the woman when she saw that Halley had the packet open between her front paws and two cigarettes in her mouth, one broken.' Joey couldn't help laughing at the picture in his mind of the tri-coloured Australian Shepherd with her black back and brown edging, pips above her eyes and a stunning white chest and legs, holding two cigarettes in her mouth as if she was having a sneaky fag. When Stanley had said, 'You naughty girl,' she had looked so innocent and spat them out as if to say, 'Who, me? It wasn't me. I've no idea how those ciggies got there.'

'She didn't want to give the fag packet back either. It was in between her paws and it was hers.' Leah looked at Joey, and they burst out in a fit of giggles at such a wonderful funny memory. The whole place had been in uproar, except for the woman whose cigarettes they were. 'I think it's a lovely idea,

Joey, she's so used to you, but right now I have to dash.

'Why? And might I ask why you've got a skirt on?'

'I'm on a promise,' Leah's eyebrows raised up, 'and I can't wait.'

'You naughty girl! I wish I were on a promise. Ben's gone home to make sure his parents and his brother know how to find us.' Joey smiled. 'It will be here before we know it, the wedding, won't it?'

'I hope so.' With that, Leah kissed Joey on the cheek. 'Don't forget his coffee, the tall man.' Then she left, giving a little wave to the tall customer in the café.

When Joey handed over the cup of steaming coffee Brioche looked up and gestured at Leah. 'Is she OK?' he asked.

'I'll say so. She's on a blummen promise, which is more than I am. Lucky sod.' Joey stomped away, leaving Brioche to watch the Land-Rover drive towards town.

So, she was 'on a promise' - but what kind of a promise would that be? Brioche had never heard that saying before. Stirring four sugars into his coffee, he wished he could get an invite to the dog weekend which he'd heard wasn't open to the general public.

'Excuse me, can you tell me if I need a ticket for

the dog displays on the poster over there?' he asked Joey.

'Oh, you pay on the gate, and the proceeds are shared between dog and horse charities. They also give to children's charities too,' said Joey proudly, since he knew lots of people had said they were coming. 'I hear the weather could be lovely.'

DRIVING INTO TOWN, Leah kept thinking about her promise. Would Dan be in a demonstrative mood, or a kinky mood? Or, best of all, a masterful mood . . .

She just needed a few odds and sods from the town and maybe some fish from the harbour. It was handy knowing lots of the fishermen because she could buy the fish direct from them as fresh as if she'd caught them herself. Running from one shop to the other and coping with the excitement that was building up inside her, she was almost coming to a thundering climax by the time she got back into the vehicle, and that was just at the thought of her and Dan together in a clinch. What on earth was the matter with her? But she knew why she was feeling like this: it was her hormones and that fact excited her.

LEAH PULLED up outside the house and jumped out of her vehicle. She ran into the house. 'Dan, Dan,' she called, but there was no sign of him. She looked out of the window and saw him on the patio pouring wine and setting out sandwiches. Sensing he was being watched, he glanced up at her. The smile Leah received was enough to send her running out to greet him.

As she burst onto the patio, Dan caught her in his arms, saying tenderly, 'I've made you lunch.'

'So I see, how kind, darling.' Leah touched his face. 'There's just one problem.'

'What's that?'

'I am hungry but not for food.'

Dan nuzzled her neck. 'If not for food, then for what?'

'You, you daft ape.'

Dan swept her into his arms. 'I'll come back for the sandwiches.'

'You're hungry?' Leah asked incredulously.

He laughed and nuzzled into her hair. 'For you first, then maybe a sandwich.'

'Well, I'm pleased I come before your stomach,' said Leah as she tugged her fingers through his hair. 'Mm, salt 'n' pepper temples.'

Dan playfully slapped her bottom, making her squeal and giggle. As he slid his hand down her thighs, he felt the suspenders, and his body reacted accordingly. He tightened his hold. 'Are you feeling sporty?'

'Sporty?'

Dan moved into the snooker room and deposited Leah on the snooker table. He looked into her eyes and she told him, 'I must admit I've been waiting to christen this baby for ages but be a love and turn that key.'

He went and locked the door, asking, 'Who are you expecting?'

'Nobody, but you never know.' Leah hitched up onto her elbows.

Dan pushed her gently back, then seemingly pulled a cushion from nowhere. He placed it under her bottom, then dragged her closer to him and kissed her deeply. Responding, she moaned against his lips. But just as Dan's hand moved towards her thighs, there was a shrill voice.

'Leah? Leah, where are you, dear? I've come for a coffee and a chat. It's Great-aunt Penny.'

'Oh, no. Can we pretend we've not heard her?' Dan said breathlessly. He ran a hand through his hair.

Leah heaved herself up and slid off the snooker table then tried to fix her clothes. 'Dan, go upstairs and get in the shower,' she said softly. 'I will sort Aunt Penny out and join you.' She unlocked the door and pushed Dan out then she went into the hallway, calling, 'Aunt Penny, I was just getting in the shower.

Come out onto the patio - there's sandwiches and wine.'

Aunt Penny took in Leah's flushed face. 'Is everything OK?'

'Yes, but I'm all hot and bothered from a run around town and need to jump in the shower. As I say, there's sandwiches and a nice glass of expensive wine. I will be as quick as I can,' Leah said as calmly as possible. Please go and get a sandwich as I'm in the middle of something that can't wait, thought Leah.

'Very well, I'll go on the patio and amuse myself whilst you join Dan in the shower.' The older woman winked at Leah. 'I remember when I was young. Now go. Go!'

Leah smiled sheepishly. 'I won't be long.'

'Take your time - I would. A sandwich satisfies me these days, but it never used to.' Aunt Penny walked towards the patio. 'I was quite a game headmistress. Hahaha.'

Leah ran upstairs with a smile on her face. She loved Penny so much and was so happy that she and Grandad Thomas were friends again. Leah didn't like discord in the family. She knew only too well how precious her family were to her.

Entering the master suite, Leah could hear the shower beating down and Dan serenading himself with 'You're the one . . .' from *Grease* the movie. She ran across the room and met him in the shower, and he did not disappoint.

AUNT PENNY THOUGHT the wine was lovely as she tucked into the sandwiches with her usual enthusiasm. The diet she'd started yesterday would just have to wait. Stanley, the late owner of Halley the Australian Shepherd dog was with her in spirit, and she knew he would need his fair share of food and drink to fuel his way into the next world - or so Ethel had told her this morning during their 'galah session'. Penny paused for a moment, thinking about the house on the moors and wondering why every time she went up there, the tenants from Sledborough House were out. There seemed to be no answer even though the fires were burning. She wasn't sure at this stage whether or not she would be able to get access soon, but she did want to meet the people who were renting the place just to see if they had everything they needed. Taking another sip of wine, she shrugged. No doubt if they needed anything they would get in touch with the agent, but still, she would like to meet them.

Looking across the patio into the gardens, she was pleased with the way Dan had set out this house and its grounds. He had taken a big wall out of the field that lay in front of her on the slope down towards the sea and instead he had put in a ha-ha to give them an uninterrupted view of the ocean. It was stunning. The couple had so much land with this house and stables that could accommodate all his horses, which made a perfect situation almost like in a fairy-tale.

Time passed very pleasantly, sipping at the ice cold white wine. Staring at the now empty bottle of wine, Aunt Penny thought it looked a little hazy. She squinted. Was the bottle moving, or was it her head? Maybe she should open another bottle just to clarify.

DAN AND LEAH let the warm spray cascade over their naked bodies; both were breathless and spent. Leah looked up at him.

'I love you,' she said.

Dan smiled. 'I love you too.'

'I suppose we ought to go down to the patio and see Aunt Penny,' whispered Leah.

Dan disagreed. 'Would it be so rude of us to leave Aunt Penny to her own devices? I did leave the morning papers down there, and Hero was laid on the patio to keep her company. She's got my lunch to eat; I think she can keep herself amused, don't you?' He was already feeling 'sporty' again and needed another shower with his wife.

'You have an insatiable appetite, Dan Ryan,' Leah

said happily.

WHEN LEAH HAD DRESSED, she went down to the patio and found Aunt Penny sitting with her head lolling. Then Leah saw the empty bottle and the other bottle half empty. 'Oh, no,' she sighed. 'Aunt Penny, do you want a coffee?'

The older woman looked up, her eyes focusing in opposite directions. She tried to shift herself upright on the chair and nearly fell off. 'No dear, this wine will do fine.'

Leah reached the bottle just before her aunt did.

Dan came striding onto the patio. 'Is everything OK? Oh, I see.' He saw Aunt Penny all boss-eyed.

Aunt Penny stared blearily at him. 'Dan, Leah tells me you've been riding. She said you have a special magic wand. Is it possible to see it?'

'No!'

Leah giggled. 'I think she means your father's magic wand. Your riding crop, Dan.'

'Oh, *that* magic wand. Yes, of course, Penny I'd be happy to show it to you. It is awe-inspiring,' Dan said, clearly proud of the crop his father had bequeathed to him.

As he walked away, Penny shook her finger at Leah, saying, 'Did you have a good old shag?'

'Aunt Penny, watch your language. What if the ladies from the Women's Institute could hear you now?'

'Huh, Leah, some of them if not most are worse than me!' Penny laughed and hiccupped.

'Please stay there while I go and make black coffee, but maybe you need a nap?' Leah said as she rushed into the kitchen to fill a cafetière of strong black coffee.

Dan strode back to the patio and offered the crop to Aunt Penny. She took it in her hands and ran her fingers the length of it.

'My, that's impressive. It's beautiful, Dan,' she smirked. 'Leah said you both ride bareback.'

Dan looked for Leah to rescue him from this grilling. 'Well, yes, we do. We ride from the field down there sometimes up to the stables.'

Aunt Penny hit the crop on the table, making Dan jump. 'I bet it's nice feeling that warm back against your inner thighs.'

Dan breathed a sigh of relief and his shoulders relaxed as he saw his saviour appear with coffee.

'I've just been talking to Dan here,' said Aunt Penny, scowling at the coffee arriving and aiming the crop in Dan's direction.

'I heard, Aunt Penny. Now, let's change the subject. Are you ready to be rescued by Hero at the weekend?' Leah enquired tactfully.

'I am, and I can tell you both, I can't wait. I think Fred's coming to watch it.' Ignoring the coffee, Penny slurped the rest of her wine.

'Fred?' queried Dan. 'Who's Fred?'

'Fred the solicitor in London. The one with the nice brandy.'

'You mean Howard Levinson,' Dan corrected with a smile.

'I do mean Howard, so who's Fred?' Penny scowled at the cup of coffee which was placed in front of her. 'I don't want that muck.'

'What do you want?' Leah asked, feeling a little frustrated.

'An Earl Grey, please. I don't think I know a Fred, do I?' replied Penny.

'There's Fred down at the Amusement Arcade. You accosted him the last time you drank wine,' Leah reminded her.

Dan looked wistfully at the empty plate that had held their sandwiches, and he offered, 'I'll make the tea, and I'll make some more sandwiches too.'

'That was very thoughtful of you, Dan, you are such a treasure. This man is so lovely, our Leah. I can see why you fell for his magic wand.' And then Penny couldn't stop herself from laughing.

Leah was biting her lip but then burst out laughing, and even Dan walked away, joining in with their laughter.

FOR THE FUNERAL, Leah was dressed in smart black slacks and a white silk shirt with a black linen jacket, the outfit completed with black patent sandals. On a hot day like this she'd usually be wearing shorts, but as a mark of respect to Stanley she wore the proper outfit. How she'd drive the Land Rover togged up like this, she wasn't sure. Joey, in comparison, wore a gaily coloured striped jacket over his white shirt and black tie; he called it his Joseph jacket.

Leah decided she would have to drive as Joey was experimenting with his phone and swearing at it, and he was getting on her nerves.

'I don't know what the heck is going on with this. I've got a new ringtone, downloaded it this morning and it just won't work,' moaned Joey, shaking the iPhone in frustration.

'Well, just switch it off, Joey, we are at the church.' Leah swerved to miss a female pheasant that ran across the road in front of her in a frenzy. She knew full well that the birds had a terrible habit of changing their minds in the middle of the road and then running back to where they had come from. She also remembered the time when she saw two male pheasants: one was lying dead at the side of the road, and the other one was in panic mode and running around like a headless chicken. Leah was sure that the birds were brothers. It was such a shame.

As she approached the church in Gravescliff, she slowed for the barriers at the level-crossing; they were just coming down.

'Huh, you never see a train coming through here, not in a million years, then just when we need to get a move on, along comes one. Trust it to be a flipping goods train an' all,' Joey huffed.

'Sod's law, I guess.'

'Suppose so,' Joey agreed.

Leah felt sadness encompass her. She knew that the churchyard just a few yards away was home to some Commonwealth War Graves as she'd looked at them before, and it came home to her that she would never see Stanley again. He'd been such a nice old chap and very talkative. Leah wasn't too sure how Stanley had got an Australian Shepherd at his age, from the rescue place, but then he hardly looked his own age and he had been as fit as they come.

His death was the result of a sad accident. Whilst hiking across the moors he'd tripped over a bramble, they'd assumed, and banged his head badly on an outcrop of rock. Halley had barked and barked at his side until another rambler up on the moors had heard her. By the time Stanley was rescued, and due to the severity of the fall he'd taken, this had been his end game. He'd often talked about death being the age he was, but he was so confident that heaven existed it didn't faze him at all. The only thing he'd put in place was someone to look after his beloved Halley, and that was Joey; he'd even left money for her insurance and food, but right now Joey was unaware of that. Stanley had spoken to Leah about it, and Leah had assured him that if Joey couldn't have Halley, there was always a home with her, Dan and the kids. As the barriers came up, Leah set off only to pull up a little way away at the church.

Joey, seemingly satisfied at last with the phone, put it on silent and placed it in the top breast pocket of his colourful jacket, confessing, 'The reason I got myself in a state about this phone was because Stanley always promised he'd send me a sign. You know - from the other side - to let me know he was OK. I wondered if it might show up on the phone.

'That's nice; look for a white feather then,' Leah said absentmindedly. 'I believe they are signs from the other side.' She tapped Joey's shoulder; he jumped out of his skin.

'Arrggghhh!'

'Come on, let's get into the church, we can get a good seat. Aren't you taking Halley today? Look, someone from the kennels has brought her. Oh, bless.' Leah jumped out of the Land Rover and walked up to Halley. The Aussie Shepherd wagged her natural little stump fifty to the dozen. 'Hello, sweetie.'

Joey flounced up. 'Hi, poppet. Come and cuddle Daddy.' The dog looked around for Stanley.

'Joey, stop being this insensitive, she's looking for Stan.' Leah stroked Halley. 'It's OK, baby. Joey'll get used to his role as your papa. Look sharp, Joey, the hearse is here.'

'Sorry, Halley and Leah, I'm all of a quandary and now, well, I'm hunting for feathers and mysterious text messages and white ghostly apparitions. Oh dear, I don't even know what I'm saying.' Joey took the dog lead from the kennel maid. 'I'll take her from here. Thank you.' Then he was pulled off his feet as Halley, sensing Stanley was in the hearse, dragged Joey towards the black vehicle.

'Oh, I'm so sorry, she's missing her daddy,' he whispered to the undertaker. 'I can't say it too loud because she knows he's in there.' He pointed to the hearse.

'Yes, lad, I understand. Animals are so wise.' The undertaker made to unlock the hearse boot, whilst the pallbearers moved towards the hearse, and other people started mingling around the church entrance.

'Budge over, Ethel,' Joey was saying fussily to a frail little woman in the queue. 'I need to get a good seat at the front because this lovely dog knows that Stanley is in the coffin and besides, I need to keep my wits about me. Stanley said he was going to send a message from the Other Side. And I know that for a fact because he told me so the day before his accident. So please, Ethel, if you see a white feather or hear a voice that sounds heavenly, because Stanley was heavenly, then don't try to talk to it or remove it if it's a feather. I will get it, or I will reply to it, and yes, I know you think you can talk to everyone, including the dearly departed, but the message is for *me*. Understood, Ethel?'

The little woman put her hand to her ear and said, 'Speak up, Joey lad, my hearing aid batteries have gone.'

Joey stormed in past Ethel and went to the front left-hand seats with Halley at his side; Leah followed and let Joey sit near the aisle with Halley; it was as if she knew her owner was in the coffin. Joey stroked her head as she cried, and shed a tear with her.

THE WHINING of poor Halley mourning her master's passing interrupted much of the service. Joey seemed in a world of his own. His eyes were darting all over the place. And when the prayers began, that was when it happened, and every single person's head came up in open astonishment. Into the eerie silence, a voice shouted, 'Help, help! I'm in here.' With a crackle and a hiss of 'white noise', in a softer tone that only the front row and a shocked vicar could hear, the words came out of Joey's top pocket. 'Nah then, get me out o' this pile o' grass cuttings. I said eco-friendly not Reedco, because the CEO stole my ingenious idea!'

Joey's eyes darted from the coffin to the funeral memorial and in tiny letters it said *Reedco eco-friendly caskets.* The voice came again.

'Bloody hell. For God's sake, will somebody *help me!*'

But all the congregation could hear was, *'Help me!'* coming from Joey's top pocket.

Joey screamed, and Halley barked deafeningly.

A loud voice shouted from the back of the church: 'That's your message, Joey, from Stanley. Or should I say from Joseph 'cos you're wearing his coat!'

Then again, the voice - much fainter now: 'Oh bloody hell, get me out of this pile of grass-cuttings. This isn't proper reed; he's done it on the cheap!'

Joey's head was a mush as he dashed over to the coffin, white in the face. With Halley twisting the lead around his legs, he tripped and crash-landed spreadeagled over the coffin. There was a gasp. Then: 'Has anyone got a screwdriver? Anyone?' Joey asked feverishly. He pushed himself up from the coffin. 'We need to get Stan out of here.'

The undertaker looked at the eco-friendly reed coffin and gave Joey a black look. 'It's not Stanley talking to you, lad. It's coming from your flaming top pocket. It's your frigging phone!'

Joey's mouth opened wide; he stood in shock with his hand on his hip. He glanced back at Leah and said, 'Oh, that's right - it's my new ringtone. At least I know it works.'

Leah put her head in her hands and groaned, but she'd heard *all* the words coming from the phone too and now she knew without a shadow of a doubt that Stanley had indeed gone to heaven, for the extra words had definitely come from him.

AT THE GRAVESIDE, Joey had transformed into what he often called his fairy-mode; he was moving around the burial plot like a dancing circus horse searching for white feathers because he didn't believe Stanley had given him the sign yet. Little did he know that the sign was staring him right in the face because at his side Halley was looking into the distance just down the grassy slope under the oak tree and she was wagging her tail - at nothing, seemingly - but with a look in her eyes that brought Leah to tears.

Leah glanced across just in time to see a white feather as it fell towards the ground from the mighty oak. She nudged Joey and whispered, 'I think that's your message over there.' And then she wiped her eyes.

Joey looked up just in time to see a snow-white

feather land over by the oak tree's gnarled-up roots, and he went with Halley by his side to pick up the said mystic sign. Eyes heavenward, he whispered, 'Thank you, Stanley, I can rest assured you are still around.' Then, just as he was picking up the feather, a bird pooped on his shoulder. 'Aw, Stanley,' Joey grumbled, 'that's unfair. Sorry about the ringtone. I guess this is payback, but you have to admit it shook the buggers up, didn't it?' As he set off back to the graveside, he tripped over one of the gnarled roots.

Ethel smiled as Joey fought to stay upright. The sprightly old lady said, 'I think your trip might have been the message that Stanley had for you. He always was a trickster.'

'Ethel, you crack me up,' Joey said, taking a sod of earth from the graveside. 'Ashes to ashes, dust to dust, the devil don't like tricksters and so God must.'

Leah elbowed him. 'It wasn't Stanley who tripped you up. Watch where you are going - you've always been clumsy.'

'Sorry, Stanley,' mumbled Joey.

Ethel linked arms with Joey. 'Where is the funeral tea?' she asked.

'You tell me, Ethel, you go to every one of them in a thirty miles radius of Whitby. I'm sure it's a vocation with you. What is it, you want to see who's got the best grub in and if anyone will supply you with a drink or two?'

'I know many people, that's why, you young whippersnapper know-it-all,' Ethel said, looking wounded, but knowing he was right on the money, she blushed. Why would you pay for lunch or tea when you could get one free at every funeral?

A tear came to her eye. She hoped neither Joey nor kind Leah ever, *ever* experienced the loneliness she often felt since her cat Katkins had died. Every day had been the same after that, with no one to purr around your feet when it was feed time. And in the mornings, getting out of bed and wondering why God had spared you again to the loneliness. After meeting Leah, all that had changed. The young woman had a kinder heart than her cousin and had said that if Ethel needed to call in at the café or the farm for a chat she could. So, in return, Ethel wiped the tables in the café or dog-sat at the farm. She knew there was no reason for the dogs to have a sitter as there were always people coming and going, but she loved doing it. Leah was even teaching her how to brush old Hero.

Giving a happy sigh, Ethel turned her hearing aids up a tad. She didn't want to miss the gossip. It had been a ruse, telling Joey her batteries had gone.

But he had noticed. 'I thought your hearing aids had died?' he said suspiciously. Then: 'I suppose you want a lift back with us to the wake too?'

'Well, thank you, lad. I wouldn't say no.' Ethel turned her hearing aids down again, just so she could enjoy the silence and watch the silvery figure walk away from the graveside. Hah. Joey had missed Stanley's wispy appearance - but then, not everyone had the gift of second sight as Ethel did. She wondered whether Joey had heard the message about Reedco, and nearly giggled out loud thinking about the vicar's shocked expression. She had definitely heard Stanley talking in the café about the way he'd been cheated, saying he'd approached the company with the idea and they had sent him away with a flea in his ear. He knew the CEO was a crook and that his coffin wasn't made with proper reed even from beyond the grave. Ethel wiped her eyes and blew her nose. Many youngsters knew nothing about the afterlife, but some believed, like Leah. Often Ethel had felt and seen proof - and she would never forget that first day, the first time it happened.

She'd been working in an old hospital just down the coast. On that particular day, Ethel and another woman called Clara had been assigned the task of cleaning the mortuary. Ethel kept on having this feeling that she was being watched and Clare seemed terrified and jerked round at every little noise. That was when Ethel felt someone, or something, walk straight through her. She grabbed the other woman and they ran for dear life, although afterwards, she couldn't explain to Clara precisely what had happened, because she didn't know herself then.

Clara never returned. Ethel was subsequently trans-
ferred onto a ward where she felt safe, but from that
day on, she knew that what had touched her had been
an angel and nothing to be afraid of. Joey would
never take her seriously, although she had often hoped
he would since he believed in the psychics, but it was
Leah who listened to her and Ethel knew Leah was
happy to think her parents were together in heaven.

'Joey, help Ethel into the front seat,' Leah urged
as they reached the Land Rover. 'You must sit in the
back with Halley.'

'Oh, I'm all right in the back, Leah duck,' Ethel
told her. 'I don't mind sitting with Halley. Stanley
used to call round to bring me his paper on a morning
after he'd read it and Halley was always with him.
She was good with Katkins too,' she added softly as
Joey helped her into the back. Life, the old lady
thought. Sometimes it swept you up and sometimes,
like today, it brought you face to face with the divine
mystery that lay behind everything. But she knew
while ever there were stars in the sky the mysteries of
the Universe were safe and there was more to this
world than the eye could see. As the Land Rover
engine started up, she whispered a last prayer to her
old friend, Stanley.

6

OH, WHAT A MONSTER!

I t was the day of the dog trials. Cook was running around in her wheelchair like a headless chicken, banging into cupboards and getting into everyone's way until Leah told her to go and rest. Besides, Leah had arranged outside catering for the lunch, with a self-cook barbecue for the evening meal, which was why she couldn't understand the woman getting herself in a pickle. However, there was still breakfast to prepare for Dan's list of coordinators, stewards and judges, so Leah found herself busy. At long last there was a temporary pause as the last of the butties disappeared, with no more orders.

It was time to think about the grooming demonstration. Leah knew whose dogs they were getting people involved in bathing and grooming. Dan looked

across at his wife and winked; he would thank her
when they were alone tonight because they had a plan
that no one else knew about. He was always grateful
to Leah's army of friends who were willing to roll up
their sleeves and muck-in, whereas some of Dan's
'friends' were only here because of his wealth and
status, not to mention the free booze later in the
evening. He did have a few real friends he could rely
upon, but nothing like Leah's group of pals: she was a
magnet to people, himself included. The Newfoundland gang of dogs he could rely on too, and he called
them his friends. The magnificent animals were wide-
spread all over the globe and many of this noble breed
had come to Scarthingdale Hall specifically for this
weekend.

Leah had so many genuine people who loved her
for who she was, and Dan blessed the day she had
literally flown into his life from a bungee rope on the
roof of the Mayfair hotel he was staying in. She'd
come zooming in out of the sky to crash-land on his
balcony and nearly knocked him dead – literally.

As he grinned at the memory, Ruby walked into
the kitchen with her arms full of boxes of chocolates.
'The cavalry has arrived!' she sang out. 'What can I
do to help? I brought these to go with the awards.'

'Hi Ruby, and thanks.' Dan passed her the clip-
boards. 'These need to go to the stewards. All the
canvas dog retrieves and the tables, et cetera, were out

by yesterday evening. Here's the list. Thomas and my mother are down there, getting the tables sorted with the stable hands doing the heavy lifting.'

Great-aunt Penny walked into the kitchen. 'Am I the star turn?' she trilled. 'You said Hero could pull me in from the lake, didn't you?'

Dan put his arm around her shoulder comfortingly. 'The thing is, Penny, we need one fitter, younger dog to rescue you. Hero is getting too long in the tooth. However, we have a lovely dog named Trooper who will do the job. He's only two years old.'

Penny sighed. 'That's all right, Dan. Hero is going grey around the chops now, isn't he?'

'Oh, he'll always be our Hero, and he will get a swim, but we need it to be a gentle one. Maybe he can pull Alice in.' Dan hugged Penny. 'Thank you for understanding.'

'When the time comes, Aunt Penny, let me know and I will help you get into your dry suit. They can be a tad awkward,' Leah offered with a smile.

'Oh, I will, dear. I will,' replied Penny, looking for a drink to quench her thirst. She found a bottle of water. 'I brought some gin and tonics for later around the campfire and a few bags of marshmallows. They're so tasty when roasted. I will borrow one of your lovely stable hands to get the bottles out of the car.'

'Talking about cars, Joey's new - well, refurbished second-hand - Beetle should arrive soon. Dan's had it resprayed, and the photos they sent are wonderful. I'd be happy to drive it into Whitby myself. He'll be so pleased, bless him,' Leah said in a calm voice then looked up as the man himself walked in. Hoping he'd not heard her, she nodded a greeting.

'Who'll be pleased?' Joey asked, looking from Leah to Dan.

'I will be pleased when I can relax this evening. It's a busy day for us, Joey,' Dan put in, with a smile of reassurance to his wife.

'I'll bet. I bought an old jacket potato oven at the local auction. I'm going to set it up so we can all have jacket potatoes this evening,' Joey said merrily. 'I'm glad I don't have your job, Dan. No wonder your temples are sneaking a little silver in them. The stress of organising this lot must be horrendous.' He opened the door of the enormous American fridge. 'Is there anything to nibble on? I'm famished.'

'Ben hasn't arrived yet then, I take it,' said Penny, so deadpan that both Dan and Leah stemmed their laughter. 'Or was that him setting up a pink thingam-abob? I saw a pink tent, I believe.'

'Take what you want, Joey,' Dan said, 'Right, I'm off down ta lake. You, munchkin, are with me and Tom.' He held his hand out to Alice who slotted her small fingers in his.

'Hark at him. "I'm off down *ta* lake" - anyone would think you were Yorkshire born and bred, Daniel,' Joey teased.

'My wife is a beautiful Yorkshire woman, and I have Yorkshire children. I'm staking my claim.' With a grin, Dan walked out with Alice running to keep up with him, until he swept her up into his arms, swung her around, then put her back onto her feet.

Through the kitchen window, Leah saw both Dan and Tom holding Alice's hands; they were swinging her to and fro as they walked. Her little daughter's squeals of enjoyment made Leah feel so happy, and she hoped nothing could ever take that away from her.

Joey opened his mouth to question Aunt Penny. 'Do you mean a pink gazebo? So is my Ben here?'

And when she nodded, he shot out of the kitchen like an emu on a rampage, his head bobbing up and down as he ran around outside looking for his man.

CHELSEA WAS JUST GETTING her hairpiece on and the finishing touches to her disguise from Pepper, who was a make-up artist extraordinaire. Who would have guessed her little cousin's occupation would have come in handy like this? Chelsea was confident that she could stand next to Dan - and that dull smug wife of his - and neither would know.

'Why on earth you gave up that lucrative job as a make-up artist for that thriller theatrical company I will never know. You seemed to have been happy enough there. Then, when you agreed to use your skill to help out with a little . . . er . . . little stunt, in other words to help with that robbery, I knew that one day I would hire you to work with me. Remind me – what was it you did again?'

'I made the Bond Street bank robbers look like little old men when they were only in their twenties.' Pepper preened herself. 'I did my part just fine, but then those wankers made a mess of the job, and they gave my name to the police. One day I will get my revenge, you just wait and see. Oh well.' She sighed. 'If it wasn't for me ending up in jail, we two might never have found each other again. Remind me, what was *your* sin?' Pepper asked as she carefully fixed the grey wig onto Chelsea, which made her look like an eighty-year-old grandma.

Chelsea reared up. 'My charge was a travesty. It should never have come about.' She stuck her nose in the air. 'If that Yorkshire witch hadn't had a sprog by Dan - a child, I might add, that should have been mine - I would have been well in with him by now, and his billions would all be mine.'

Pepper wasn't having that. She said impatiently, 'I

thought you tried for ten years, Chelsea, and he was having none of it. Not everyone is tempted with the candy counter just because it's on display. Face it once and for all – the bloke wasn't interested in you. There's plenty more fish in the sea even if they are filthy flipping rich like Dan. And don't frown like that or your make-up will crack.' Pepper gave the finishing tweaks to her cousin's wig. 'There, they'll think you're that miserable git with the pup. Where is the puppy?'

'It was in its cage, but Brioche has taken the horrid thing for a walk. I hate dogs! You do know it sleeps with him, don't you? Ugh! Hairy, smelly thing! However, it is a necessary evil if I am to get any information from that loudmouth, Joey. Thanks to you we've even wangled our way into the wedding party and Brioche has made pals with Joey, so he's going to the evening do. By the time that wedding is over, they won't know what's hit them - and their family.' Chelsea had an awful smirk on her face.

'So, the famous plan is what, exactly?' Pepper asked, then listened as her cousin began in a whisper.

'I will have to wait for the right time to get Dan by himself and persuade him to come back to me - once I have acquired certain powers of persuasion,' Chelsea purred.

Just then, Brioche walked in with the little dog and overheard her last words. 'That won't work, cousin. He's all over Leah. I showed you the video I took of them - under your instructions, I might add. To me, it's sacrilege to make me spy on and film a couple who are so in love. It disgusted me to do it.'

'He'll come back to me when he knows I'm out of prison - and as I say, I have my little secret weapon,' Chelsea snapped.

'I reckon you are well out of order, and I don't think your plans will work,' Brioche said stolidly. 'They're a waste of time! It's obvious Dan Ryan still loves Mrs Ryan – his lawful wedded *wife*,' Brioche said in a last attempt to make his cousin see sense before he shambled off into the kitchen to feed the dog.

Chelsea scowled at his retreating back. 'Huh, I'll show him. I'll show all of you!'

'So, what gives with this little secret? Is it some kind of love potion, and if so, can I have some?' asked Pepper, now somewhat intrigued.

'I met this character in prison before you appeared on the scene. Let's say she had the guards wrapped around her little finger, and she taught me that hypnotic skill.' Chelsea stood up and looked at herself in the full-length mirror. 'He'll never recognise me now, and Joey and the bitch didn't either, even close up. Although you can be a pain in the arse with your nagging, you are very talented at this game.' She high-fived with her cousin.

Chelsea was thankful Pepper could be herself without needing a disguise. All her cousin had to do was to get close to Leah and Dan and then tape their conversations and find out something about their movements and the arrangements for the wedding. Whereas Brioche, well, he could join Joey and see if he could get any information from him.

'Right, let's get your dumb-ass brother out of the kitchen with the dog, and I'll brief you both when we're in the car about what I want us all to do today,' ordered Chelsea. 'Me, I shall cause chaos while you two keep your ears to the ground.'

Chelsea knew what she was going to do, and that was to get into the house and see if there was anything of use in the couple's papers or jewellery. She would look for Leah's engagement ring in partic-ular as she could always pick-up a cheapo wedding band in town. As Pepper drove and Brioche cuddled the dog, Chelsea sat in the back of the car and schemed.

RUBY STOOD LOOKING at the lake, thinking how cold it might be if anyone fell in without a wet suit. Sophie walked up and linked arms with her.

'How are you, girlfriend?' Ruby asked. 'I love this place, don't you? I've never felt as if I belonged somewhere before, but Whitby and the moors are home for me now.'

'I know, it's beautiful, but right now I've got other things on my mind. I'll be honest with you, I'm worried about Chelsea turning up like a bad penny. I just get this gut feeling. It's like a premonition.'

Ruby looked into Sophie's concerned face and said, 'I hear you. We both know what a devious bitch she is, and we both also know we haven't seen the last of that woman.'

'Thomas and I were saying the same thing, even though Dan seems relaxed about it all when he should be on his guard, and Leah is the same. Well, I'm like you, Ruby. I can feel danger in my bones. Well, at least Sisco should be back soon. I don't know where the heck he has gone to, but I heard Dan saying he was coming home this weekend. I reckon it's got something to do with the wedding, but my son has not kept me in the loop which I am miffed about, I have to be honest.'

Sophie shivered, even though it was a pleasant morning. Then, changing the subject she pulled at Ruby's arm and chuckled, 'I reckon it's going to be a right laugh when Penny gets in the water. She's a game old bird. I can understand where Leah gets it from.'

'I should say, as a comfortably built woman myself, the waves will part when that bottom of hers descends into the water. I've heard it's what they call round here "a robust bottom" or a "right arse"!' Ruby laughed heartily. 'I also believe that Howard is coming up to see this - this spectacle.'

'Oh, Howard will enjoy it, dear, and speak of the devil - there's his brand new Gold Range Rover now,' Sophie declared, pointing to the vehicle with private number plates in the gateway. 'I believe he has a bit of a thing about our Penny. Let's watch this space where those two old codgers are concerned.'

The friends trudged back up to the 'Flamingo tent' as Penny called it, but Joey would swear that it wasn't a tent, it was a very stylish gazebo, in a lovely shade of pink, and they had christened it Priscilla.

'Don't mind us,' said Ruby as she and Sophie caught Ben and Joey in a clinch.

'Sorry, ladies,' Joey said. 'It's a while since I've seen this handsome buck and as I'm sure you'll understand only too well, it's nice to have a cuddle. Which reminds me - when are you going to find yourself a chap, Ruby?' he asked, untangling himself from Ben.

'I'm in no rush. Mr Right will come into my life one day soon.' Ruby turned to Ben. 'How are you, sweetheart?' she asked.

'I'm fine, thank you, Ruby, and I will be even better once they marry us. Right, Joey, I'd better get the sound system ready.' And he busied himself with his task.

'Shall we go to the catering marquee and get some coffee? I know for a fact Leah has put some nice cakes and fancies on,' Joey said. 'I'll fetch you a drink and a nice bun, darling.'

'Thanks, sweetie-pie,' Ben said, testing the microphone by tapping it several times.

LEAH AND DAN were down by the lake with the kids, checking that the first water trial tests of the morning were going well. They confirmed that all the judges and stewards had score cards and the other things they needed.

When Tom spotted his friends, he said, 'Dad, can I leave Alice with you and join Harry and Troy?'

Dan looked up and could see the two boys walking down towards the lake. 'Yes, off you go, mate.'

'Why can't I go?' scowled Alice as she stamped her foot.

'Because, munchkin, you're with me.' Dan put her on his shoulders. 'Now sit up there where I can keep my eye on you.'

'Silly billy, you can't see me up here,' Alice giggled.

'Ah, but *I* can see you,' replied Leah, reaching up to give her a little tickle. 'I'll just start the grooming demonstration. It's so important for all the visitors to know that these dogs need dedication and grooming expertise. Some people buy them for the wrong reasons and get rid of them when they grow too big, and their hair becomes unruly.'

'Yes, let's get this event on the road as quite a few people are already coming in now. It's going to be a bumper year.' Dan set off up the gentle incline, his daughter holding tight to his curly hair.

As the show got started, people were still coming in at the gate, and there was quite a queue building up on the track from the side gates. Pepper drove through the car park and got a prime spot where they could see everything from the car if they wanted to. At least Chelsea wasn't wearing her Jimmy Choos. Now she had sensible brogues on, a necessity if she was to pull off the lame old woman façade.

'It's vital you get as much information as possible. You know your role, don't you?' she nagged Pepper for the umpteenth time.

'You've been prattling on about it all the way here. If Dan isn't with Leah, I follow him. Better if they're together though, and I should record as much conversation as I can without looking suspicious.' Pepper nodded her head. 'Don't get your double-gussets in a twist, Cousin. Everything will be fine.'

'And you, Brioche, what is your role? Remind me or should I say remind yourself.' Chelsea was ready to get out of the car, but not before Brioche understood his job.

Like a schoolboy who was reciting prayers, the tall young man obediently furnished Chelsea with almost word-perfect instructions of what he would be doing.

'Good, now we know what our jobs are, we can get going. Brioche, you'll have to help me out of the car and hand me my stick. I must keep in character.' Chelsea cackled, and once out of the car, the other two followed. They all went in different directions. Chelsea tottered off to the Hall.

AUNT PENNY LOOKED for Leah out of the bedroom window and couldn't see her. The battery in her phone had died because she'd forgotten to plug it in earlier and charge it. Phones like this should be illegal. Why hadn't anyone invented the solar telephone at a reasonable price for old folk? It wasn't natural that people knew your business every minute of the day anyway, but she had to admit the phones were convenient, such as when she had broken down the other day as she was going into Malton to do some shopping. Shrugging, she thought how hard could it be, fitting into a dry suit? She knew it was designed to fit over her clothes. Should be a cinch.

Undoing the colossal box, Penny peered inside. Yes, the suit was there. Not an exciting colour either, just a dull grey - like the lifeless eyes of the Great White shark. She had hoped it would have more pizzazz. However, Penny was as sure as heck she would brighten everyone's day when she came to do her *pièce de résistance*. She tried picking up the dry suit. Oof! It was so heavy.

Trying again, she let it drop back in the box. How did those people in the lake walk in and out so easily? Maybe hers was made of chainmail? She sighed. She was already sweating but managed after a while to heave-ho it out of the brown cardboard box. Slipping her shoes off, she put one leg in and had to lean back against the bed. She put the other leg in, then almost doubled over with the sheer weight of it. How stupid was this? With a mammoth-like effort, she reached both her arms in the sleeves and fell backwards onto the bed. Whilst she was down, she zipped up the top; wondering why the cord was so long, she snipped it off with the scissors. Now to get up. She swung her legs time and time again to get a good grip with her feet on the floor, just enough to get herself up, but each time she fell backwards again. She decided she would have to roll over and try to get up the other way. This was no mean feat either, but with sheer strength and determination, she finally got to her feet, not noticing the knee pads were at the back of her legs. She had the whole thing on the wrong way around.

She tried to look in the box, but if she moved forwards, she felt like she was going to fall; if she so much as leaned over she felt dizzy, so carefully, she reached down and pulled the container up onto the bed. Inside, she could see what could only be described as a helmet. She looked at the brass plates on her neckline and realised that the helmet somehow fixed on. She noted too that she would have to look through the glass window.

With another enormous sigh, she was now wondering whether it was all worth it and also, whether one dog would be enough to pull her in from the lake. They would need ten dogs at least to drag her ashore. Penny tried to pick up the helmet then gave up. First, she would put the boots on, which were easier by far. They were big, so they slid on without effort. She then tried again, lifting the helmet from the box, but it was too heavy.

Funny, she thought she had heard someone coming in downstairs but decided not to bother them. As she picked up the helmet, the weight of it made her topple onto the bed. Struggling, she swore. This thing was not going to beat her. With superhuman strength and effort, she got up and plopped the helmet on her head. Now all she had to do was to negotiate the stairs and get out into the field and down to the lake. Easier said than done.

CHELSEA LOOKED up at the house and limped into the courtyard. Quinn was coming out of the stable yard and was watching the strange old woman tottering with her stick towards the house.

'Excuse me, madam, can I help you?' Quinn asked.

Chelsea baulked; afraid he was going to recognise her, but the make-up saved her and he didn't identify her. 'Yes, young man, you can. Leah said I could use the house toilets. I can't negotiate the steps on the Portaloo.'

'Oh. Well, if Leah said you could use it, then you just need to go through the kitchen door, and the toilet is in the hallway.' Quinn pointed towards the door. 'There's one in the stable block too.'

'Thank you, young man, but I couldn't use *that* one,' Chelsea said with dignity, and walked the length of the courtyard best as she could with Quinn watching her.

The young man frowned then shrugged. He was a little uneasy allowing the woman into the house, but if Leah had given permission, then she must have been happy with it.

CHELSEA WALKED into the kitchen and spied out of the kitchen window to make sure that Quinn had disappeared down to the lake. Then she saw Hero, and just out of spite she deliberately emptied the packet of self-raising flour all over him.

'There, that'll teach you, you ugly brute,' hissed Chelsea, nearly raising her stick at him before thinking the better of it. Then she let him out of the kitchen door into the courtyard. There was no love lost with him as he grumbled at her.

'Get out, you horrible thing,' Chelsea muttered, wishing she dared to kick him, but as she was about to go into the hallway, she heard someone coming downstairs. Whoever it was, they were making such a racket she hung back and watched from the pantry doorway, then quaked as she saw something akin to a sea monster heading towards her, making for the kitchen. She hid behind the door, her heart speeding up. Its gait was like that of Frankenstein: slow, methodical, and almost as if its joints were bolted together.

The monster walked through the kitchen; its breathing laboured. It crossed to the outer door to let itself into the yard with slow, deliberate steps. Chelsea dared not move until the apparition almost fell out of the door, swinging on the door handle then tripping over its enormous boots. It clung to the door handle, swinging on it for several seconds, then it regained its balance, stood like a robot, and walked across the courtyard.

Chelsea ran and stared through the kitchen window to watch its slow walk down towards the lake. She didn't notice she'd walked through the spilt flour.

Coming to her senses, she quickly ran up the stairs and tried to find the master bedroom suite: there might be something in there that would be useful to her. That's when she spotted the safe, or at least the cupboard that held the safe. She couldn't imagine Dan using the same code for the safe as he had used in the office when she was down in London. Opening the door of the cupboard, she was thankful she had gloves on to avoid leaving fingerprints as her palms were sweaty. She started turning the clock to the left and the right, then right again. It wasn't the first set of numbers. Spinning the dial, she tried a second time, and as she heard the familiar clicking whilst twisting the knobs, she knew the second code was the right one. 'Bingo. How lax you are, Dan Ryan.'

The jewellery case staring at her from the top shelf was too irresistible to ignore. She opened it, and a stunning diamond necklace stared back at her, twinkling and screaming for her to remove it from its case. Dan had the same leather pouches where he kept his money in cash. So predictable.

'Gotcha!' she whispered to herself. Rummaging through the safe, she put the necklace and other things of interest into her large old lady's handbag. Then she removed the considerable wads of money from the pouches and stuffed them into her bag too. Closing the safe door, Chelsea spun the knob to lock it. Jumping up from her knees, she caught sight of the dressing table. Ah, this must be the famous engagement ring that was lying there. How careless Leah had been, leaving it out, but the wedding ring she was searching for wasn't there. That was a shame – but then it had been a long shot: most people kept their wedding rings on all the time and never took them off. She would buy a cheap wedding band in Whitby and that would have to suffice. If her plan were to succeed, she would need a wedding ring to convince Dan they were married. Indeed, if the hypnosis sessions were to be her saviour, she needed him caught and put in the top room of that dump Sledborough House to work on him.

CONSIDERING THE CIRCUMSTANCES, Penny was waddling slowly but methodically towards the water. The lake was barely visible through her port hole, and it was all she could do not to pass out. She was so hot in this get-up she couldn't breathe. Sweat was pouring down her brow, her face, her neck and down into her cleavage, but she didn't want to disappoint everyone who had come miles to watch her, so she pressed on.

It would be spectacular. She would be the talk of Whitby and the surrounding coastal villages.

Penny could see why the people in these dry suits wanted to get into the water as soon as they could, just to cool off. Diving in wasn't an option for Penny when each step was excruciating. Trying to clean the glass face, and failing miserably, Penny was by now so steamed up she couldn't see where she was going, and she just hoped she was heading in the right direction for the lake. How on earth did the others cope, she wondered.

As the gentle incline became a little steeper, she picked up speed, only now she couldn't stop. She could hear a dog barking behind her but couldn't turn her head to see who it was. She had tunnel-vision about the size of a baby pea.

LEAH AND DAN were chatting to friends further down the hill. Howard was with them, waiting for Penny's big appearance. No one in the party except Alice saw what she thought was a monster from outer space. Alice pointed, then looked up at her daddy, pulling on his hand as everything unfolded. Hero, covered in flour, was following the monster and barking loudly at it.

'Daddy, Daddy, there's a monster and Hero is chasing it, and it's spitting white stuff on him,' shrieked the little girl, grabbing Dan's hand again and shaking it as hard as she could. She looked across and realised that the monster was heading for the lake at speed and it seemed it couldn't stop. She shook her daddy's arm again.

Dan looked down at his daughter with a small frown on his face. 'I'm talking, Alice.'

Alice frowned herself and put her bottom lip out. This was important! She pointed, and Dan looked around.

'Holy hell on flippin' fire!' Dan unhitched himself from Alice and ran after the space monster for all he was worth.

'Daddy, Daddy, *nooo*, it will eat you up!' But his little daughter's words fell on deaf ears.

Dan ran faster than he had for years as he knew if Penny went into the lake with the deep-sea diving suit on, she would sink, and disaster would soon follow.

Dan was frantic to reach her before she got to the water's edge.

Hero, who was barking loudly as he followed the monster, acted on instinct; he bumped into the back of Aunt Penny's knees. They buckled beneath her and she tumbled into a heap just before she reached the edge of the water. Exhausted, Hero sank to lie at her side.

7

A HERO SAVED THE DAY

Dan reached Penny just as she collapsed. He managed to get the helmet off her head. Long lengths of her hair were saturated in sweat, and her breathing was coming in gasps. She resembled a beetroot in the rain.

Other people were now running down to the lake, Joey in particular shrieking in a high-pitched yell and racing towards the scene at top speed.

'Aunt Penny!' he screeched. 'No, Aunt Penny, hang on in there! Aunt Penny, I'm coming to rescue you.' He was charging so fast he couldn't stop, and with no Hero to save him, with legs akimbo he did a screaming nosedive into the ice-cold water. Getting up from the muddy water, he asked, whilst spitting the murky water out of his mouth, 'Is she alive?'

'Did - Hero - save me?' was all Penny could say, her breathing rapid and laboured.

Dan let out a deep sigh of relief. He nodded. 'Yes, Hero saved you from a horrible accident, Penny.'

'Oh, bless him. The speed I was going I just couldn't stop running, you see. I can't remember when I hit the water. Why, I didn't even hear a splash?'

Leah and Alice reached them. Alice was crying.

'Don't cry, munchkin, the monster didn't eat me.' Dan took Alice into his arms as they were kneeling by Aunt Penny, but Alice tried to shrug him off.

She looked into her father's face in disgust. 'I thought it would eat Hero, not you!' With that, she untangled herself from Dan and went to hug the big dog; she was cross with her daddy for leaving her in the first place. Then she patted Aunt Penny on her back and returned to Hero to stroke him.

Leah and Dan shared a look and a grin at their daughter's anger.

Joey ran up the banking ringing wet-through and joined them, making the drama much worse. 'Does she need the kiss of life? Do I have to punch her chest? I must jump on it because it's so big as you can all see.' As usual, he was playing to the crowds. His gaze roamed over Penny's face. 'Oh. You're OK.'

Aunt Penny looked down at her dry suit. 'No

thanks to you! Well, at least it works. It is a dry suit - look, I'm not even wet.'

It was Leah who started laughing at the hilarity of it all, then biting her lip she smothered her laughter as she knew only too well that Hero had saved the day, but she couldn't stop laughing. This could have turned out far, far worse, but she just couldn't stop the hysterical giggling. She knew it must be due to shock.

'Leah, please! Let's get Aunt Penny to the first-aid tent,' muttered Dan, lifting his eyebrow at her in disgust.

Dan, Joey and several other men helped Penny to her feet. She was so exhausted she collapsed every time they got her upright. They eventually managed to get the huge suit off, revealing her crumpled and sweat-stained clothes, and then gently walked/half carried her to the first-aid tent to be checked over and rehydrated. There was a crowd gathered by now, and Brioche was there with the little dog in his arms.

When Dan came out of the first-aid tent, he reassured everyone: 'Our dear Aunt Penny is fine, I'm delighted to report. Despite the incident, in about an hour, she will re-enact her run to the lake in a proper dry suit. Thank you, everyone.'

'Don't think so. We haven't got one that's a size XXXXL,' said Joey on repeat.

'Like flippin' 'ummer I will be putting a dry suit on again,' said Penny to Howard, who had followed her into the tent. 'Thank you,' she added to the lady who had brought a welcoming cup of tea.

'I believe he was joking, Penny,' reassured Howard. He leaned forward. 'This deep-sea diving suit you were wearing was very sexy.'

Penny was shaking her head. 'No, dear, it's a dry suit.'

'Yes, a deep-sea dry suit at that, but it was still a big turn-on.' Howard looked flushed at the thought of how it might have been, getting it off Penny on his own, in private . . . but then the idea fizzled. He was much too old these days. But he told her of his fantasy all the same.

Much recovered, Penny grinned and said cheek-ily: 'By the time you got it off, It would have disappeared.'

'What would?' Howard looked puzzled.

'You know - *It*. Your thingie.'

Howard laughed. 'My thingie? I said you looked sexy, but it wasn't an invitation. I'm too old for all that malarkey. Give me a splendid dinner any day.'

'Oh, well, thank heavens for that. You can say I'm sexy more often if that's the case. But I could do with a hug.' Penny smiled at Howard. 'You do know they'll laugh about this for years to come.'

Howard willingly hugged this lovely lady. 'At least they will remember you with joy in their hearts. I've no one to remember me.'

'That's sad. Join this family and everyone will remember you, dear Howard.' Penny kissed his cheek, knowing full well she had a soft spot for this man.

LEAH WATCHED as Howard and Aunt Penny, now fresh from the shower and dressed in a pretty tropical summer frock from Ruby's wardrobe, came down from the house hand in hand to sit with Grandad Thomas and Sophie. Joey had taken Alice and the boys to the pink tent to keep Ben company. It was lunchtime, so everything was quiet. Dan and Leah shared a table close to Sophie and Thomas. Ruby joined Dan and Leah.

'When is Sisco coming home?' Ruby asked, stuffing a sandwich in her mouth.

'Sometime later today. This evening I think the train comes into Whitby. I told them to get a taxi up from the town,' Dan said as he bit into his sandwich. 'Mm, this is nice, Leah.'

'Who's "them"?' Ruby enquired, her interest piqued.

Dan gave her a warning look. 'Not a word to Joey, mind, or anyone else. Scouts honour.'

'Dib, dib, dib. I'm intrigued, but you know I can keep secrets.'

'Well, Sisco has tracked down Joey's parents. And, after the first shock of hearing about the marriage they agreed to come home for a week or two. It's a long journey from Australia but of course they want to see their son wed. Sisco will drop them off at their house, then he will come back here. Joey's mum had recovering from a sprained ankle, so she was pleased to come back to Whitby to recover for a rest, and I gave them the use of our private jet and pilot to get here. Then, I believe there's just Scotty to come home. Although we hope that Joey's mum can persuade her daughter and son-in-law to change their minds about coming to the wedding.' Dan seemed rather smug.

'You're a good man, you know, isn't he?' Ruby turned to Leah. 'He's a good-hearted guy, your husband is.'

'If not rather conceited at his triumph. However, I believe it was Sisco who did all the leg work. He's chased halfway around the world. But it was Dan's idea. He'd noticed how depressed Joey has been because he thought his parents wouldn't be able to make the wedding or even agree to come. The stupid thing is, he'd never even asked them because he didn't want rejection again, but he asked his sister, and I thought she was really mean to say no,' Leah said.

'You're right it was my idea - but it was you who

put the thought in my mind,' Dan said fairly. 'One night, you told me, "If only I'd been able to have my parents at our wedding, it would have been perfect".' He smiled at Leah and touched her hand. She had tears in his eyes at his words. 'So, most of us had a part to play.'

'Well, Ethel told me that my mum and dad *were* at our wedding. She had a dream, and she described it so well that I'm inclined to believe her.' Leah looked out to the lake and beyond to the North Sea. She couldn't remember much about her parents, but Thomas had furnished her with so many lovely memories of them both, and some of her dad's friends still went fishing on the trawlers, and they often talked about her father too.

AS THE AFTERNOON WORE ON, Leah saw that the young woman with the dark blonde hair always seemed to be hanging around near to Dan. She watched as the woman offered Alice a sweetie. She saw Dan take it and put it in his pocket. He said something to her and smiled down at her before taking Alice's hand and walking away. The same woman had also been two tables away over lunch, playing with her phone, and Leah noticed she had followed Dan out of the refreshment's marquee with a certain amount of deliberation in her step . . .

Leah was interrupted in her thoughts as Aunt Penny came across to her, followed by Howard.

'Was Dan serious when he said I was to jump in the lake?' asked Penny. 'I'm not sure I could cope with another round of getting another suit on and off.'

'No, not at all, Aunt Penny. That suit was very dangerous in this kind of set-up. Please: you must never wear it again. It's for deep-sea diving, and you need oxygen with it. We shall help you send it back, explain what happened and get your money back. I will get Keira at the dress shop to put another tape on for the zip. I'm so sorry I didn't go with you to get a dry suit. You could have been in deep trouble in that thing without oxygen.' Leah hugged Penny. 'I would never have forgiven myself.'

Penny squeezed her great-niece back. There were tears in both their eyes. 'Nay, it's my fault, Leah. I'm a stubborn old fool, I should have asked. I thought it was a proper one, not a deep-sea diving suit. How foolish was I?'

THERE WAS a lot of crackling and banging on the Tannoy as Joey's voice came through loud and clear.

'Hello, ladies and gentlemen, thank you all for

coming to our marvellous doggie weekend. Beside me is our lovely Alice, who wants to tell you all about what she's been learning in school this past week. Come on, Alice, don't be shy. Wasn't it something about Paula Pig?' Joey prompted, sounding so proud.

'Nope. It was all about vaginas. I have one. Mrs Roberts told us, and she said she has one too. She said it shouldn't be called *down there*. Because *down there* means Australia. Oh, and my mum has a nice one too, because she's very pretty.'

Everyone could hear Joey almost choke, and laughter erupted outside in the field. 'But Alice, hush now, hush, talk about Paula the Pink Pig.'

'Yes, all right. Well, she has one 'cos she's a lady pig.'

'What about Brian the bull?' Joey said desperately, then realised his mistake.

'Mrs Roberts said boys have a penis and Brian has a big one, I've seen it. You have one too - not a Jolly Roger as you call it, Uncle Joey, and Mrs Roberts heard my daddy has a good one . . .' Her voice trailed away as she saw Dan running up to the tent as fast as he could.

He switched the Tannoy off, but of course it was far too late. Everyone outside was laughing their socks off. What a day it was turning out to be!

'Who told you that, Alice?' Dan panted, trying to get his breath back.

'You mean about v-vaginas?' she asked, pushing her cheek out with her tongue.

'Yes,' Dan said, trying to look stern but wanting to laugh.

'Our teacher, Daddy. It was Mrs Roberts. She says little girls have vaginas and boys . . .'

Alice stopped as she saw Dan looking very worried. 'Don't they? Was it a fib? Mrs Roberts says so.'

'I shall be talking to your teachers. All of them.' Dan picked Alice up in his arms, but he couldn't help seeing the funny side of it all. As he moved outside of Priscilla the pink tent everybody cheered, especially other parents who knew how children can show you up. He carefully put Alice back on her feet.

One man cried out, 'It's called plain English, Dan. They've been teaching it a while now in schools.'

As Dan made to reply, Alice tugged at his hand and when he bent down, she whispered in his ear and was pointing at Brioche. 'Daddy, look, it's the man who attacked Mummy in London.'

'No, poppet, that's Brioche. He couldn't hurt a fly - he's Joey's friend.'

'Huh, no one believes me 'cos I'm a little girl,' Alice moaned.

'Let us have no more talk about that man. It disturbs Mummy and Brioche isn't that man. Why look, he's caressing the old woman's puppy.' Right now, Brioche was whispering sweet nothings into the little dog's ear, and the dog's tail was wagging.

'Huh,' Alice groaned.

Dan looked more closely at the older woman; there was something familiar about her. Maybe he'd seen her in Whitby or the village or indeed at the café. Wherever it was, he knew he'd noticed her before. Somewhere deep inside him, an alarm bell rang out but he saw Leah approaching and focused on his wife.

'Isn't it great?' she burst out. 'Everything is going so well, and everyone seems to be enjoying the displays. The grooming demonstration has been a triumph as it's put a few people off. And our naughty Alice is a natural speaker.' Leah giggled. 'And when Quinn's mate Alan was pulled across the field, I believe we helped people to understand the reality of owning a Newfoundland dog. That should save a whole heap of trouble and heartache, shouldn't it? So, I reckon that's a great result.'

'Yes, it is,' confirmed Dan.

'We don't want people acquiring these dogs, just to put them into rescue when they realise they need grooming and are stronger than an ox, pound for pound.' Leah saw where Dan was looking and followed his gaze.

'Who is that woman, Leah, do you know her?' Dan asked.

'The dark blonde?'

'No, I don't know her, but she's been following you about all day long.' Leah was aware her voice sounded jealous.

'No, I don't mean her – I'm talking about the old woman next to her. The grey-haired miserable looking one. There's something off about her, plus I feel I know her from somewhere.' Dan scratched his head. 'You say the dark blonde has been following me. I never noticed it. Probably just a coincidence.'

'The old woman is the bane of Joey's life. She sits and listens to his conversations in the café. She's not very nice to her dog either, plus she complains about the price of the coffee. The fact is, since she started coming in the café, which is often, she has become a constant pest to our lovely Joey. He hates her. Other than that, like you I think I must have come across her before: even her perfume seems familiar. Maybe she's been in Whitby a long time, and we've not noticed or paid any attention to her.' Leah had furnished Dan with what little knowledge she had of the woman.

'No matter, she's friends with Brioche because he's been looking after her pooch this morning.' Dan looked down at his daughter, who was scowling under her little eyebrows, fit to burst with her news about Brioche. Her dad put a finger to his lips, so she released a gigantic sigh. 'Come on, munchkin,' he said kindly. 'I believe you need rescuing by Hero.'

Alice's face lit up. 'Please, Daddy, will you come

in with me? In the boat?'

Dan nodded, then turned to Leah and asked, 'Would you get Hero for me and bring him down to the deep end of the lake, darling?'

'What about Yin and Yang? Can they come too, Daddy?' asked Alice, all animated.

Dan explained to her: 'They are old Pomeranians, not Newfies, besides, Yin is frightened of the lake now, so it wouldn't be fair to him. He only likes the heated swimming pool. I will swim with Hero and help him pull you into shore.'

'And Yang?'

'He gets upset without Yin.'

'You mean since he fell in the cold water?' Alice asked.

'Yes. It's frightened him, and he has arthritis too. So, we will leave the boys in the house. But first, Alice, shall we take them for a short walk?' Dan laughed as Alice jumped excitedly.

'I'll come up with you,' he went on to Alice and Leah. 'I put Hero back into the kitchen, but I've no idea how he got out the first time, have you? Plus, he had flour all over him.'

'They did us a favour, whoever it was who let him out, because Hero saved Aunt Penny's life, with no exaggeration.' Leah shuddered, still shocked by what had so nearly happened.

Dan nodded gravely, then comforted his wife as

they set off together for the big house.

LEAH LOOKED at the shocking mess in the kitchen. 'What on earth has happened in here? This must be why Hero has flour on his coat.' The bag contents were all over the floor, and the flour had travelled everywhere.

At that moment, Tom, Harry and Troy walked in. 'Mum, can I have . . .' began Tom, but before he could finish, Leah said urgently: 'Have you seen anyone in the house, Tom?'

The boy shook his head. 'No. It's the first time we've been in. I was just going to go to the toilet. I'm not keen on those Portaloos.'

'I'm taking Alice to the one down here. You boys pop upstairs,' suggested Leah.

The three of them set off, then suddenly there was a shout from upstairs.

'Mum, Dad, there is a mess up here too!' Tom called down from the top of the landing.

Both Leah and Dan ran up the stairs to investigate. Troy tried to help Alice up the steps, although she shrugged him off as she always did, being an independent little madam. Leah and Dan followed the trail of flour into their bedroom.

'Where did Aunt Penny get changed?' asked Dan.

'In the bedroom Howard is sleeping in tonight. Quinn put her box with the supposed dry suit in it this morning. I think we've been robbed, Dan. But this looks like whoever was in here was searching for something of mine. Your Rolex is still on the night table, and mine has gone missing.' Leah went across to her dressing table. 'Oh no! My diamond and turquoise earrings are missing. My engagement ring has gone too. Oh, God. I suggest we get the police in.'

Dan had gone pale. 'I will ring them now.'

'No,' Leah said hurriedly. 'Wait a bit. Let me just get Alice to the toilet, and you and the boys can take her and Hero down to the lake. We will not let this put our children's enjoyment at risk. I will phone the police, Dan. Until they come, just act as if nothing has happened. Send Joey up, that's all I ask.' Leah searched again for her engagement ring, but she knew in her heart it had been stolen. Then she took hold of Alice's hand, as the little girl had just come into their bedroom with Troy. 'Come on, darling, let's get you ready for your rescue with Hero.'

Dan watched Leah take their daughter into the en-suite. Within minutes she was back and ushering them out of the door. He looked back at her as if he wanted to help, but she indicated he should take their daughter away from this room. It was a crime scene, and the more people who contaminated it, the worse it would be.

8

JEWEL THIEF

Chelsea had stuffed the money and the several items of value that she had stolen and put them in the glove compartment of the car. How Leah could leave things worth thousands of pounds just hanging around their bedroom beggared belief. Was that what being mega-rich did for you? Chelsea slammed the car door, careful to lock the vehicle, and marched off towards Pepper at a brisk pace before remembering she was supposed to be old and lame.

Pepper and Brioche were standing just outside the candy-striped refreshment marquee when Chelsea joined them. Brioche went into the marquee and kindly bought her a cup of tea, then handed it to her as he came out. They stood talking for several minutes, then Chelsea looked across the field and saw

Dan and the boys coming from the house: there was no sign of Leah. Dan stopped to have a quiet word with Joey. She saw Joey put a hand to his mouth and run in the direction of the house. Seeing this, Chelsea threw her tea and the plastic cup on the ground.

'We have to move - sharpish,' she told Pepper. 'I think they've found out we have robbed them. You can stay with the mutt, Brioche, and find out from Joey what is happening.'

'Why, what did you do?' asked Brioche with a growl. He looked at the cup she'd thrown on the floor and bent to pick it up. 'I just bought that, and you shouldn't litter. You must have done something awful.'

'Never mind what I did, you just try to find out from your new bosom-buddy what's going on at the wedding. Pepper, come *on*.' Chelsea almost dragged Pepper up the hill to the car.

'What did you steal?' Pepper asked as they reached the vehicle.

'Just a few things. Leah's engagement ring. A beautiful diamond necklace and some earrings. Oh, and some money. Lots of money. Why should we use ours when I've now got theirs?'

'But the necklace was surely locked away in a safe place?'

Chelsea gloated, 'True, but luckily, I know all three codes that Dan has ever used. The safe is the same make and model he has down in his London office. The necklace must be worth at least a hundred grand trade. That's the last she's seen of that,' Chelsea sneered, the tone of her voice butter-soft, yet laced with steel.

Joey and Leah had a good look around the room, touching nothing else. Leah unlocked the safe. The case that held her diamond necklace was open and empty.

'Oh, no. This is worse than we thought.'

Joey looked at the empty case. 'Don't touch another thing. Ring the police and let them deal with it. Someone knew the code – so who could it be? Who else has the code?'

'Just Dan and me.' Then Leah paused and said thoughtfully, 'However, he hadn't changed the codes since before we got together - and guess who knew the codes too?' As she spoke, she reached for her mobile.

'Chelsea!'

'Precisely.' Leah grimaced.

'But how can she know where you are? I mean, I know she's devious enough to hire a private investigator, but would she really be bothered to do that now, after all this time, and risk another jail sentence?' Joey blew out a breath then repeated: 'Please ring the police, Lee-Lee.'

'Yes, but it will mar a wonderful day.'

'And you think the day isn't spoilt already? We had Aunt Penny almost drown. Then Alice gave everyone a sex education lesson in two or three phrases. Now this. Ring them,' Joey insisted. 'Then we shall walk down to Dan, get Sophie and Grandad Thomas to look after the kids, and we'll come up here to meet the police.'

Leah nodded her head, then tears formed in her eyes. 'She's been in our house - *our house*, Joey. I know it.'

'Or she's given the code to a jewel thief. She knows Dan is worth a bob or two. And just think - I was going to borrow that necklace to wear at my wedding,' Joey said, trying to cheer Leah up. He hugged his cousin. 'Come on, let's do this.'

WHEN DAN SAW Joey and Leah approaching across the grass, he left Alice with Tom to look after her as he went to meet his wife.

'Is there much missing?' he asked, putting an arm around her shoulder.

'Yes, I'm afraid so, and it's worse than you think. They've managed to open the safe, Dan. My diamond necklace has disappeared, and all your money has gone missing. The bracelet is in the jewellers for cleaning. There were other bits of jewellery, some stuff that the kids bought me, but nothing of yours has gone that I can see.'

Dan was shocked. 'That's impossible. You and I are the only ones who know the code.' Dan searched Leah and Joey's faces and he knew what they were thinking. 'Unless . . .'

'. . . that woman has given a jewel thief your codes. Why on earth did you never change them, Dan?' Joey asked.

'I never dreamed she'd follow us here. To be honest, it stunned me when I discovered she was out of jail so early. She must've tricked the authorities, that's all I can think,' Dan surmised.

'Impossible as it is to believe, maybe she came out due to good behaviour.' Joey tried to change the mood, saying, 'At least today is turning out well.' He had seen the older woman getting into her car with a younger woman by her side and moving much faster than she had this morning. 'I heard the old bag with the little dog saying it was a delightful day. So, you're even letting the oldies enjoy themselves, and our lovely Ethel is in her element in the catering marquee. Now, I think you ought to wait for the police up at the house.'

'Yes, we will. Will you please monitor the kids for

me, Joey?' Leah asked, then took Dan's outstretched hand.

Joey watched the couple walk up to the house together then he immediately went to look after the kids. There was still some enjoyment to be had with these dogs. Ruby joined the group and linked arms with him.

'Is everything OK?' she asked in a low voice. 'I know that worried look on Dan's face, and Leah has gone a whiter shade of pale.' Then she was distracted as she saw Tom, Troy and Harry playing with Alice. 'Those boys are so tolerant of Alice. Although it shocked me to hear her version of *The Vagina Monologues*. Maybe Sophie and I should ask her to give us more lessons? Might teach us a thing or two. Or should we just book Alice in with the WI?'

Joey couldn't help himself; he roared with laughter. When Ben walked up and linked his other arm, Joey looked around this beautiful place with the stunning view over the cliff tops to the North Sea. He cuddled into Ben and for a moment, and despite the robbery, he felt supremely happy: however, he knew there was always a 'but' in his life. Where were his parents for his wedding day? Out of contact and doing their own thing again, that's where! He knew that with this man by his side, he would remain strong even though he would be gutted at their absence on his big day. Even his sister and her husband had agreed to come and then cancelled. If that was how it was going to be, he could rely on his proper family, Grandad, Leah, Dan and the kids and Great-aunt Penny. Bless her and thank the heavens that her near-fatal accident in the deep-sea diving suit had been averted by their Hero. Dear old Penny. Even she was more of a family than his own.

Down by the edge of the water, Alice was throwing a green fabric dummy for Hero, and even people who couldn't read a dog's body language could see he was retrieving for Alice to please her as he loved her; poor Hero looked tired. Alice had taken to him from being born, and he'd always protected her, alongside old Goosey Gander who had flown onto the spot a year ago and was found by Leah, tired and exhausted, lying next to her and Alice when both were laid on the sun-lounger together and had fallen asleep. From that day on he never left. Often he would be seen guarding Alice and Scarthingdale Hall. The big bird was a force to reckon with, but Alice had won him around, and he protected her just like Hero did.

Joey nuzzled into Ben and Ruby, thinking, yes, this was his family now.

'Come on then, Alice, give old Hero a rest and let's see if the sweetie tent has something nice for us,' he said indulgently. 'A bit of cinder toffee, maybe. Or some Dolly Mixtures.'

'Give me Dolly Mixtures any day,' returned Ruby. 'I love the Yorkshire Mixtures too, from Whitby town centre.'

Overhearing the offer, all the boys followed them to the tent. It wasn't often Joey got his wallet out, but when he did, he was very generous.

WHEN THE POLICE ARRIVED, they did their best to keep a low profile, but it soon became apparent that quite a few items and all the money Dan had been keeping in the safe were missing. Leah and Dan walked to the stable yard to leave the Crime Scene Investigators to do their thing.

They looked in on some horses as they'd brought them in from their grazing field. They were all busy munching on hay.

'Do you think it really could be Chelsea?' Leah turned in Dan's arms and looked up into his face.

'I'm inclined to believe what Joey has said, that she has given the codes to a jewel thief. I should have listened to you. You wanted me to change the codes, and I fobbed you off. Forgive me, my love.' Dan blamed himself fairly and squarely. 'Let's join the others and leave the police to do their job. We should start the barbecue fires soon, as the people who have been in the lake will be hungry. Let's not allow this to put a dampener on a great day. I believe we've taken a good deal on the gates for charity.' Dan rested his chin on Leah's head and encircled her in his arms. If this was down to Chelsea, he thought privately, he had an awful feeling it would not be the last they had heard of her.

'Come on, let's have a drink and be with our kids.' He turned Leah in his arms and saw tears glistening in her eyes. 'Hey, come on, I can buy you a new necklace.'

Leah nearly wept; he was so generous. 'It's not that. I just feel that our beautiful home has been violated. We've just got it right, and she's spoiled it.'

'She can't spoil what we've got. We won't let her,' Dan said sagely as he tugged her along. He loved Leah so much. Being the resilient type, when adversity hit her, Leah usually bounced back, but this afternoon's ordeal had upset her like he'd not seen before. Maybe he'd give Greg Biggs a call. The man had helped Leah before with her fear of storms, so perhaps he could help her now.

As if reading his mind, Leah interrupted him. 'And before you say it, no I do *not* need another session with Mr Biggs. I will get over this. Things happen, Dan, to everyone and we just have to take one day at a time to get used to the new normal.' She smiled cheekily. 'Promise me one thing.'

'Anything.'

'I want a cuddle tonight.'

Dan laughed. 'Goes without saying, Lee-Lee.'

THE BARBECUE WENT WITHOUT A HITCH. Leah had even sorted things out for the vegetarians and their vegan friends. Brioche had stayed with the little dog, and Yin and Yang were let out to make friends with the new canine. Halley, Stanley's Australian Shepherd, rounded them up if they strayed too near the lake.

They invited Brioche on to Joey's table as their dogs rested and everyone was filling up with new potatoes, salad and different barbecue meats and poultry, with tofu and a special lasagne for the vegans. Beer and wine were flowing, and everyone was having a whale of a time.

Brioche couldn't relax as he knew he was supposed to be asking Joey what was going on. Reluctantly, he tried to approach the subject by saying, 'Mate, why were the police here? Is everything OK?'

Joey screwed his eyes up. The shot he'd just swallowed back in one had made him wince, but it had also loosened his tongue. 'Well, someone has stolen Leah's diamond necklace and some jewellery the kids bought her, and they've pinched all Dan's money.

They also took her engagement ring, so to say she's pissed off is an understatement.'

'Cor blimey. Who did that? One of the visitors here?' Brioche opened his mouth wider than a humpback whale. 'Unbelievable! When did this happen?'

'Well,' Joey leaned in closer, 'this is between you and me. We think it's Dan's ex-PA, Chelsea. She came out of jail not so long ago, but how she found out where Dan lives now is a complete mystery.'

In actual fact it had been dead easy to find Dan, thought Brioche. I came to Whitby, and you were all there in plain sight. But then he had a sad thought: if he hadn't found them, would Chelsea have done so?

'I'm so sorry. I didn't think whilst we were all enjoying ourselves that someone could do that. How awful.' Brioche was shocked by what his horrible, scheming cousin had done.

'The sad thing is that these are all sentimental gifts. I mean, the things the kids bought aren't worth a fortune, but Leah is heartbroken.' Joey decided not to drink any more in case he needed to sort things out for Leah. Plus, he'd like to see if the CSI team needed his help as he'd always thought he'd be a darn good detective.

'I can see why you called the police. So how will they find out - you know, if it was this Chelsea woman?' Brioche enquired, picking the little dog up.

Suddenly changing tack he added, 'I worry for this little dog; that old woman can be cruel.'

'Oh, I thought you were related to her? You're not? Well, thank heavens for that because I hate her, and I think she's unkind,' Joey said frankly. 'So, are you her dog walker?'

'Yes, sort of. The poor thing hasn't even got a name. I call him Billy. I think it's a boy,' Brioche said sadly.

It was Ben who, whilst stroking the poor mite said, 'Well it could be Wilhelmina instead 'cos this little girl is a bitch.'

All three men laughed.

'So, what time is your wedding?' Brioche asked.

'It's on the invite, silly,' Joey replied. 'But in case it's not on yours, be here for noon. We get married at half-past twelve. And we've got the caterers in so everything should work out fine.'

'Nothing can go wrong.' Ben smiled at Brioche and crossed his fingers. 'We hope.'

Brioche returned his smile, thinking that somehow, he would have to do damage limitation. He couldn't let Joey and Ben's big day get ruined by anyone, let alone his crazy cousin, so he would have to foil whatever horrid plan Chelsea had set-up.

As EVERYONE who was staying on the place had settled their dogs down and retired to bed in their campervans, Dan found Leah looking around one of their spare rooms. The police were just cordoning off their bedroom to do more investigating tomorrow.

'I need to make more tea and coffee for the police.' Leah went to pass Dan, but he took hold of her shoulders and made her stop.

'I've organised the drinks and snacks for the CSI people. Joey and Ben will stay until the police finish for the night, then they will walk back to the cottage. So, we can take the spare room in the attic. It's a good thing you insisted on doing that room up.' Dan dropped a kiss on her lips. Five years on and his wife could still make his pulse raise, and he reckoned she always would.

'I'm just so upset,' she cried out.

'Oh Leah, I'm so sorry. This is all my fault. Chelsea has ruined a lot of my life, and I was such a fool. I never realised she could be so cruel . . .'

'Besotted, Dan, she is besotted with you and your money - and she still is! I didn't think she'd go to these lengths, but now I realise that she will never give up.' Leah's voice broke. 'But what gets to me is that she's been in our home, I know she has. The necklace was beautiful, but I didn't wear it often as I was so scared, I'd lose it. Now she's stolen it and taken my engagement ring and the cash too, and the little brooch the kids bought me. It's too much.'

Dan dragged Leah into his chest. 'Babe, I'm so sorry. We will be free of this woman, I promise.'

'We don't have proof. So, what can we do?' Leah felt so helpless as she cuddled into her husband. She stiffened. 'We shall have to sanitise the entire house, now she's been in it.'

'Yes, but not until the police have finished with our room and permitted us to go back in it. However, they have taken shoe prints from the flour. Come on, let's go to our tiny room with the mattress on the floor and be all romantic,' said Dan.

But Leah was shaking her head. 'We can't. Tom's taken it with the boys. We'll have to have his room.'

'You mean he's actually allowing us in his den?' Dan looked doubtful. 'I'm not sure we can make love in his bed. It might have crisps and popcorn in it. Maybe we should carry on in the games room where we left off the other day.'

'With the police still in the house? We'll be arrested for indecency.' Leah softened as a memory came to mind. 'If you remember, we christened that room before Tom moved into it.'

'Ah yes, I do remember - very clearly. I don't suppose you got your basque out of our room before the police came?' Dan watched Leah's eyes as she wrinkled them in a frown.

'You mean, my designer bodies - the blue or the ivory?'

Dan thought for a split second, his eyes full of mischief. 'The ivory. Well, over the past five years you've put a few pounds on since you wore it last, so I must peel you out of it. What fun that will be, inch by inch.'

Leah gasped in outrage. 'Take that back, or I'm going to slug you. You've put at least half a stone on yourself. I saw the scales when you thought I wasn't looking. So there!'

Dan pouted. 'I'm wounded, but maybe you're correct. I've put on double your f . . .'

'Be careful,' she warned with a grin.

'Your four-to-five pounds,' Dan said, then set off running to Tom's room with Leah hot on his heels. He was laughing so much that Leah couldn't help but laugh with him. As he reached the bedroom, he hid.

Leah moved into the darkened room which threw light in from the landing. Her eyes scanned the space. She either ran for the bed or she trapped him behind the door. Maybe she'd do both. She shouldered the door in and fell as he wasn't there. Jumping to her feet, she saw him appear from the other side of the bed to catch her in his arms. She fought, giggling up into his face. He picked her up, tucking an arm under her legs and strode the several paces to the bed.

'Fight me, will you, woman?' She dug him in the

ribs just before he dropped her onto the bed, and before she could cut and run, he'd landed on top of her, taking her breath away in more ways than one. He had her captured.

'Get off me you, big oaf,' she said breathlessly.

'Nah. Now I've caught you I'm going to spank that bottom of yours for trying to flatten me against the wall with the door.'

'Ah, but I didn't, did I, and that's a fact. No spanking for me – but maybe for you. And now I've put on my five pounds, as you say, I can deck you.'

'Oh, you can? Just try it,' Dan jeered as her puny efforts against his superior male strength proved futile. She tried to strike him; he caught her hands in one of his and held them above her head.

She kicked his shins. 'It's turning dirty, is it?'

He pinned her legs down with his, panting, 'Right, let's get this T-shirt off.' With the other hand, he pushed the material off whilst she writhed about trying to stop him.

This was fun. The more she writhed, the higher the T-shirt came.

'Ha! You can't hold my hands and get my T-shirt over my head. Can you?' she said breathlessly.

'Watch me.' The challenge was on. Grabbing the neckline in his free hand he pushed it up and over her head, which made the material tighten at the shoulders.

'Not fair. I'm stuck now.'

He wasn't thinking about what was fair when he looked down at the pretty bra she was wearing. 'Just the way I want you. Kick your shoes off. You're always telling me off for wearing them upstairs. Now kick 'em off.'

'No!'

'Do you dare say no to me, wife?'

'Yes, I dare say no,' confirmed Leah, struggling with her shoulders.

Dan manoeuvred himself, then pulled her into a sitting position.

'Do you like it if I'm your prisoner?' Leah asked with a husky tone.

'Might do.'

'Let go of my arms then I can get my T-shirt off, darling,' she purred, kicking her shoes onto the floor.

Dan finally let go of her arms, and she eased the T-shirt over her head. He watched as she slowly peeled off her tight spangly jeggings. Grabbing him by the arm, she sat him up on the side of the bed then undid the buttons on his shirt, feeling inside at the hairs on his chest and then the rock-hard male nipples. She pushed the shirt off his shoulders and tugged it out of his close-fitting jeans and threw it down on to the bed. 'Hm, promising,' she said as she skimmed her fingers over the front of his jeans. 'You never disappoint, do you?'

Dan lifted his lips in a smile. 'Neither do you.'

'Chelsea will never take this away from us,' Leah whispered fiercely to Dan. 'Never.'

'No, sweetheart, she won't.' Dan pulled his wife into his arms and tucked them both under the covers for cuddles.

Later, much later, as Leah heard her husband's steady breathing, she got out of bed and put the T-shirt and her jegging bottoms back on. She tiptoed out of the room. The police CSI tape was still over their bedroom door, and as much as she would have loved to go in, she knew she mustn't until they'd finished their investigations.

She went down the stairs and into the kitchen and could hear Hero's tail thump a welcome on the floor. The police had even got part of the kitchen taped off.

Leah let the dogs out in case they needed a tinkle. Reaching for the kettle, she filled it and waited for it to boil. Afterwards she sat with a cup of tea, thinking about the past twenty-four hours. She remembered how, when Dan had bought her the diamond necklace with matching bracelet and earrings, he'd told her how he wanted her forever. She didn't realise tears were rolling down her cheeks until she tasted them, nor did she hear Dan until he was taking her into his arms and holding her.

'Come on, Leah, my precious, we can weather this storm.'

'I know, but it's hurt me so much that she's taken things that are so special to me. Our first anniversary present. The things the kids bought me,' Leah sobbed.

'Hey, it could be worse. I'm going to get the dogs back in and then you're coming back to bed, OK?' If she disagreed, he would insist because she looked all in. It was the shock that was just sinking into her.

Leah nodded and blew her nose with some kitchen roll. 'I suppose she can't take the memories, can she?'

'No, she can't, my love.' Dan hugged her. 'Oh look, the dogs have brought themselves in. Come on now. Let's go back to bed.'

'I'll just give them a treat,' Leah said, reaching for the treat box, whilst Dan locked the door again. She gave them all a liver biscuit, and she took Dan's hand as they went back to Tom's room. They got into bed, and Dan held her in his arms until she fell asleep.

Eventually, after making mental notes that he needed to change all his security, he closed his eyes. He wished Chelsea would leave them alone because Dan wanted Whitby to be his forever home. The people here had taken him into their hearts, and he was so freed and happy up here. He went to sleep with his wife wrapped in his arms until he woke up with someone prodding his bare chest.

9

ANNIVERSARY GIFT

'Daddy, Daddy, wake up, there's someone to see you,' Alice said with a cute smile and her hair sticking out all over the place. 'I think it's the police. Grandma says they are here to recheck your room.'

'Thank you, Princess. I will be down in a tick. Is your brother awake?' Dan asked his daughter, who screwed her face up, stroking her chin as she was thinking.

'Yup, everyone is awake. The dogs, the horses, the chickens and the geese and everyone except you and Mummy.' Alice leaned over Dan and poked Leah in her booby. 'Is Mummy awake, Daddy?'

A sleepy Leah opened her eyes and blinked several times. 'Hello, sweetheart. What time is it, Dan?'

'It's just past eight, darling. Alice has come to tell us the police are back, so she's going to ask Tom to put a pot of coffee on for us, isn't that so, Princess?' Dan turned to Alice, who was nodding. 'Off you trot, sweetie-pie, we will be down in two minutes. Who brought you up, Alice?'

'Grandma's waiting outside the door for me,' Alice said, as she went back to the door.

'OK, Princess, hold Grandma's hand on the way down,' Dan ordered gently.

Alice huffed, 'I was going down on my bottom!'

Dan could hear Sophie asking for Alice's hand. He smiled and leaned his head back on the pillow. He felt more loved and more content than he had ever been, and this all came about since he met Leah. She, Tom and now little Alice had come along to make his life complete.

'That told you, Mr Ryan.' Leah smiled at her good-looking husband.

He looked down into her eyes, then dropped a kiss on her lips. 'Come on, Mrs Ryan, we have things to do.'

'I know, I just feel so tired.' Leah stretched and yawned.

'If you want to sleep a bit more, I can deal with the police and the kids,' Dan told her.

'I'm awake now, it's fine.' Leah climbed out of

bed, still yawning. 'I'll try and catch forty winks later but I love you for offering.'

'And I love you for being so stoic,' he murmured against her lips, then added in his best Yorkshire accent: 'What is it Thomas says? You just have to gerron wi' it. Keep buggerin' in.'

BRIOCHE HAD BEEN LISTENING at the door of the living room in their rented house on the moors for some time now, and he quaked to hear Chelsea's plan on how she was going to disrupt Joey and Ben's wedding. Not only was she trying to ruin one part of the wedding but also three integral components. He knew he had to work quickly, but at least he had discovered where she'd stashed the stolen money - so that's where he would go first, and as soon as the girls had left for their fitting for the waitress costumes, he would spring into action.

He knew Chelsea hadn't counted the money because he'd heard her say so to Pepper. Brioche reckoned this was his chance to show Chelsea and Pepper just how clever he could be because they didn't think he had a brain at all. They were oh so wrong, and he would prove it with his damage limitation for the wedding.

Once he was alone, Brioche took several thousand pounds out of the money and hid half of the rest. He'd heard Chelsea on the phone cancelling the buffet and purporting to be Leah. Then she did the same with the cake and the liquor. That was the kind of person she was: unhinged and dangerous. He didn't want to be in her life any more.

Brioche liked Joey and Ben as they made him feel that he belonged. He'd never felt as if he'd belonged to anyone or anywhere, but Joey and Ben had welcomed him with open arms; even Leah had been so kind to him, and he shuddered at what Chelsea had wanted him to do to her in London. He hoped he'd not hurt her too much, because she'd put her own life in danger to save her family. Who wouldn't want to be a part of that?

Fortunately, Brioche knew exactly who to call to get all the arrangements back on track. Joey had told him everything, shared stories and tears about his parents not coming to his wedding and Brioche was upset for him. But now he must focus on the tasks ahead.

Two days later, Leah was busy sorting out the table favours for Saturday's wedding; if she was lucky, she could probably let Tom do a few favours too when he came back from seeing Troy and Harry. The two buddies were always up in Tom's room, so it made a nice change to see Tom going out to their houses. Alice was still asleep as she had been awake during the night with tummy-ache, and Leah had ended up sleeping with her to get her settled.

Dan walked in and looked at his wife, busy with the wedding favours. He went to put on the coffee-maker. 'Fancy a drink, darling?'

'Please, love, but the machine has been playing up. Try the cafetière,' Leah replied. 'Did you enjoy your ride?'

'I did, but I missed you. How is my Princess?'

'Asleep, bless her, her little tummy was hurting. I thought if I could get her back off to sleep, I'd come back to join you.'

'But you fell asleep, and I missed my morning cuddle,' Dan moaned with a cheeky grin. 'Never mind, as long as she's OK now.'

'After we've had a coffee, we can check on her. Want to do some favours?' Leah looked up at him.

Dan put his hand over Leah's shoulder to her right breast and stroked it, saying, 'Nice to know I can still get it perky: isn't that a favour?'

'That's a privilege. Behave! I have to get these finished - only thirty more to do. Make the coffee,

Dan, and I will share this packet of loved-up heart chocolates with you,' Leah said, laughing when he pulled a face.

'What are loved-up heart chocolates? I've never had one,' he said.

'You're looking at one,' Leah told him. 'I'm sweet like one.'

'In that case, I can't get enough of your loved-up heart.'

Leah touched her heart. She then passed him a stick of rock. 'Joey had these mini sticks of rock made. They contain messages of love.'

Dan took the packet with him when he went to make the coffee. 'Hm, a man could get inspired by these messages.' Leah watched him read every one of the messages on the sticks of seaside rock. Their eyes met. 'You do realise that I now have every birthday message for the next ten years,' Dan joked.

'That's a cop-out, buster. I like it when you make things up yourself.' Leah pushed some favour bags in front of him. 'Come on, lend a hand. The sooner we get them done, the sooner we can go back to bed.'

'In that case . . .' Dan grabbed the bags and was filling them so quickly, Leah burst out laughing.

'I've never seen you work so fast,' she said with a huge grin.

'They're nearly finished, you're bound to want a

rest. Besides, that hideout on the hay is beckoning. You told me I had to be inventive, so I have. Stuff these; we can do them later! Come on,' Dan said in such a hurry he'd forgotten his Princess.

Leah gazed across at him, the sultry sparkle in her eyes turning Dan on even more. 'Calm down, have you forgotten Alice?'

Dan gave a big sigh. 'I'll check on her. She's bound to be fast asleep. I can ask Mum to keep an eye on her. I will say there's something we need to do down at the stables, and I'll take my phone.'

Leah was up for that. She watched him stride out of the kitchen to find Sophie and Grandad Thomas. Almost everything was ready for Joey and Ben's forthcoming nuptials, but tonight she was going to take the whole family down to the famous fish restaurant on the harbour. She'd booked the window table, and unbeknown to Scotty, she'd included him. He'd been quiet and preoccupied lately since Dan had suggested he come out of retirement. Leah would have to chat with Scotty and see if she could find out what was bothering him. She had a knack of getting people to talk to her. Amused, she recalled Greg Biggs, who had been Dan's way-out therapist at *The Elixir Therapy Centre* in London's Harley Street. The crazy man had told Dan about his 'big dic', and said he would have to get it out – which had made Dan flee his consulting room before the therapist was able to explain that he'd been talking about *his big dictionary!*

As Leah grinned at the memory, Sophie walked into the kitchen with Dan following her; he looked at Leah as if to say, *Hurry up!*

'She's still asleep, Leah,' Sophie said. 'I've turned the baby monitor on.' She raised the volume on the device in the kitchen and added, 'I'll make Thomas some coffee. You two lovebirds get off to your hide.'

Dan had the decency to smile. 'Thank you, Mother.'

He tugged Leah along as they ran down to the barn. 'Up there, wifey.' He slapped Leah's bottom; she squealed.

Climbing up the hay bales, Leah was touched that he'd put a picnic blanket down on the hay and had champagne cooling in a bucket of ice. It was romantic – and very sexy. Leah looked up at him with a quizzical expression on her face. Was she missing something?

'Don't tell me you've forgotten,' Dan tutted. 'I will let you off now, but later in the sanctuary of our bedroom, you might have to grovel to me, preferably on your hands and knees.'

'What have I forgotten?' Leah looked puzzled. She didn't usually forget anything, although lately she'd been so busy she had been meeting herself coming back.

'It's the anniversary of the day we first met at the Byzantine Hotel – in the King Suite no less, which Scotty had arranged for me. That's when you bungee-jumped into my arms as I was standing on the balcony, almost knocking my block off. I mean - which man could ever forget that?'

Dan started to take off her clothes one by one. Stopping her giggles with a kiss, he finished undressing her and was soon lying naked and proud beside her. Now he was going to make magic with his tongue as an entrée. Dan knew Leah preferred the whole three courses, and his first course was to awaken Leah's body any which way he could and take all her cares away.

JOEY WAS WALKING through the middle of Whitby, listening to his footfall on the pavement as he went past the Harbourside. He always liked looking in the shop windows there, and then gazing out to the fishing boats and yachts gently swaying with the tide, the chinking musical sound reminding him of wind chimes. It was extremely beautiful listening to the different tunes and tones, and one of these days he was going to ask one of those butch fishermen precisely what caused it.

He'd seen fishing boats at high tide when there had been a storm, thrashing about in the water as the waves plundered up the River Esk, often spilling out onto the nearby streets - and that was when the music got louder. When that was happening, the chinking and tinkling became angry - usually when there was a full moon, and the tide was up. He didn't often come down to the seafront when the tide was high. It was too dangerous. He remembered when Ben had come up from Hertford-shire to spend the weekend with him, and how he had brought Ben down to witness the high-water. They had both ended up getting sopping wet when a huge wave came unexpectedly over the harbour wall. They both laughed and made the best of it, but Joey had made sure to warn Ben just how dangerous the tide was at any time, but especially when it was high. Joey said he must always respect the sea; seeing as Ben was a landlubber, he needed it drumming into his skull.

Joey had a look of melancholy on his face when he glanced over at the cabin where the travelling lady was. He reckoned he'd outstayed his welcome last time when she'd read his Tarot cards. Mizelli had tartly reminded him she had a big queue outside and was wanting to crack on with it; after all, she had her overheads to pay just like everyone else. It looked like she was closed now so he wouldn't chance his arm and try to get a free reading; maybe on his way back he would knock on her door.

He glanced across to the swing bridge where, if he didn't know better, he could have sworn that the couple hurrying across the road right now were his parents. However, he knew that was impossible, so he didn't even let his imagination go there. Not even his sister was coming now - what kind of family was that? As he'd decided previously, the only family he had - and it was the best kind - was Grandad Thomas and his Cousin Leah. They shared their kinfolk with him, and he was utterly grateful for that.

Ben had been so accommodating when they were trying to decide who was going to be the bride and wear a dress, but they both knew Joey was by far the more camp of the two. In the end, they'd both chosen to wear smart suits.

Joey's thoughts returned to last night when he'd heard Dan mentioning something about a 'wedding present for Joey'. The thought of Dan and Leah having bought him a wedding present was divine, and he couldn't wait to find out what it was. Joey knew how generous Dan could be, and maybe he was hoping for more than a pair of cufflinks, but even if they were cufflinks, he knew Dan wouldn't be skimping on cost. He wondered if they would give him his present tonight as Leah was taking them all out for fish-and-chips for their evening meal. Joey treasured family occasions and dinners out; sharing Alice's enthusiasm. He loved those kids as his own.

Joey was popping into the supermarket as he'd run out of flour; he had so much on his mind what with the wedding an' all - and besides anything else, he needed to walk around Whitby as a single man because soon he would be married. If it hadn't been for Leah and Dan meeting again, he would have never met his Ben, the love of his life. He had so much to thank them for.

DAN AND LEAH left the hay barn hand in hand and walked back up to the house. When they entered the kitchen, Alice was there with Thomas and Sophie, eating a bowl of chopped-up fruit.

'Hello, Princess, how are you?' Dan leaned down to kiss Alice on her cheek then snuggled into her neck, trying to take a nibble, knowing she'd scream and laugh.

'Naughty Daddy!' Alice hollered, then climbed on his knee as he sat at the table.

'We came back to finish those favours,' said Leah as she saw Sophie put the last one in the big box.

'Done,' Sophie announced. 'Right, are we having

a light lunch? We don't want too much because we're having fish-and-chips for tea, courtesy of Leah.'

'So, why was your tummy upset?' Dan asked Alice. 'Do you have something to tell us, Alice?'

'What do you mean, Dan?' Leah asked.

'Alice . . .' Dan nudged his daughter.

'Because I ate ten chocolate biscuits and that's why my tummy was poorly. Sorry, Mummy.' Alice hid her face in Dan's sleeve.

Leah looked astounded. 'Where did you get all those biscuits from?'

Alice shrugged. 'Don't know.'

'Try harder, darling, because I told you to only take three and *not* to tell your mummy,' Dan said, his eyes scrunching up in humour when Leah was about to say something.

Leah was shocked.

Alice sniffed, 'They were in the stables. In the fridge, because they had lots of chocolate on. Daddy said three, but they were shouting at me. Loud!'

'And you stole them?' Leah asked.

Alice's bottom lip was trembling. 'I didn't mean to steal. They were. . .'

Thomas started laughing. 'Shouting at you, Alice? Tell me here who hasn't stolen a bit of chocolate before now? Well, apart from you, holier than thou Leah.'

'Grandad, it's not funny. OK, Alice, this is what

you will do. You will buy more chocolate biscuits out of your pocket money, and you will put them back, and you will apologise to Quinn, and if you do that, we're all good,' Leah said firmly.

'My pocket money?'

'Yes, Princess, your pocket money,' confirmed Dan.

Alice looked from Dan to Leah. She nodded, seeing that they were united. 'All right. I am sorry, Mummy. It's only because you didn't give me enough supper. Naughty Daddy.' Alice climbed off Dan's knee. 'I've seen Tom and Daddy eat things they shouldn't, but they don't have to pay out of their pocket money.' She went across to Hero, who was laid on the floor and cuddled him. 'I love you, Hero. Mummy and Daddy are mean.'

Leah and Dan shared an amused look.

'Come on, Princess Alice, let's watch some TV,' Sophie said, almost giggling at her granddaughter's outraged face. 'What shall we watch?'

Alice grabbed Sophie's hand. '*Frozen*, please, some of *Frozen*.' She poked her bottom lip out and threw Dan and Leah such a grumpy frown.

As soon as they were out of earshot, Leah and Dan grinned.

'You've no reason to grin, young lady,' Grandad said sternly to Leah. 'You used to pinch carrots and bread for the donkeys, and both you and Joey got in trouble when you took apples from the Vicarage for the horses, so you've no need to be self-righteous.' Grandad Thomas confided in Dan: 'Your young daughter's a chip off the old block.'

'I know, but you are so much more lenient with her than you used to be with me and I'm trying to get her into eating healthy food, not chocolate biscuits,' grumbled Leah.

'That's the pleasure of being a grandad. You leave the tough love to the parents but remember I raised you as if I was your mum and dad, so before you say anything else, I used the tough love on you. And I think I did a good job.' The old fellow patted his beloved Leah comfortingly on the shoulder, then added, 'Oh, by the way, the caterer rang and said you couldn't cancel the catering for the wedding – that it was too late. I told them they must have had a crank caller on because the wedding is still going ahead big-style.' He looked panicked for a moment. 'Bugger, the wedding is still on, isn't it? Yon lad hasn't changed his mind, has he?'

'Yes, the wedding is still on. Hmm, I might call the caterer myself and have a word. It must have been a mistake, but I'll check: we need to make sure every-thing is up to scratch.'

'Oh, I'm sure it will be worth waiting for.' Dan's eyes gleamed with mischief. 'After all, days like weddings and anniversaries are so special when you love someone.'

'That message wasn't on a stick of rock, was it?' laughed Leah, rushing away from the table as Dan scraped back his chair and made chase after her.

'Anyone would think you were the kids around here,' muttered Thomas to himself, but secretly he smiled. They were right for each other, that they were.

10

THE CANCELLATIONS

L eah duly phoned the caterers and was astonished to find out that someone had decided to cancel the wedding food. Her senses on full alert, she emailed everyone again - only to find that other things had been cancelled too. With a firm reservation on everything wedding-related reinstated, Leah checked out her dress for the big occasion at the weekend instead of leaving everything to the last minute.

Being back in their room was lovely. Leah looked around at the bedroom. She flung wide the windows before she changed all the bedlinen and placed two dishes of potpourri on the bedside stands. She'd vacuumed earlier and wiped everything within an inch of its life to eradicate any sign of the intruder. Satisfied that the room had been disinfected and any trace of Chelsea was now banished, she went to her walk-in wardrobe. She'd settled on a cocktail dress in turquoise, cream and apricot with cream sandals for the wedding night. As she made sure everything was ready to put on, she realised that she wasn't going to be able to wear her diamonds. A sick feeling griped in her tummy at the memory of the upset Chelsea had caused at her own wedding to Dan all those years ago and she wasn't even there!

'Oh Lord, I can almost see her in here. Please let this feeling go away,' Leah whispered as she wiped an errant tear from her eye.

Dan stepped in and pulled Leah back into his arms, saying, 'Mmm, I love your perfume. We will replace everything she's taken. I know it's not the same, but we will get through this, darling.'

'I think that must be the potpourri because I've only put deodorant on this morning, no expensive perfume today, I've been too busy. I will shower later before we go for our early supper with our lovely family, and we can forget all about Chelsea Saffer.'

'Yes, let's forget that she even exists. Cheer up, Lee-Lee. She will want to cause this reaction. So, we won't let her,' Dan said firmly.

Leah let out an enormous sigh. 'There's something else worrying me. Do you think Alice is getting nervous being the only bridesmaid?' She turned in Dan's arms and hugged him for comfort. 'I love you, Dan Ryan.'

Dan smiled. 'I love you too, my beautiful Leah.'

Neither heard Alice walk in, but they both saw the face she pulled. 'Eew, soppy, sloshy stuff. Get off her, Daddy. Mummy is mine.'

Dan looked down over Leah's shoulder at his cheeky daughter. 'Not soppy, Princess. Your mummy needs a kiss and cuddle sometimes. She's always so busy.'

'What is the matter, Alice, did you want me?' Leah asked. 'I would like to try on your wedding clothes again, just to make sure they still fit. Are you sure Uncle Joey wants you to wear your dinosaur T-shirt?'

Alice nodded. 'Yes. Please let me put on my T-shirt. Can I wear it all day?'

'No, darling, it's for Saturday, for Uncle Joey and Uncle Ben's big day. I have a nice sundress for you this evening. I think you'll like it,' Leah added with a smile.

Alice beamed. 'Uncle Joey has bought me a present to wear on Saturday too.'

'You are a lucky girl,' said Dan, pointing to 4 p.m. on his Rolex watch and noting that Leah had a brief smile on her face. He bent near her ear, whispering,

'See you in the shower for gymnastics.' Then he walked out of their bedroom, ruffling Alice's hair as he went.

'Right, let's get you in the bath. We'll make your hair look nice for this evening, and let's do some trying on, shall we?' Seeing her daughter's sulky expression at the thought of a shampoo, she added, 'I will be as gentle as possible, and as a reward, you will give Uncle Joey his present as we don't want him sobbing all over the place too many times on his wedding day, do we? So, he can have it today.'

Alice's face lit up; now she was ready for pampering.

LEAH HAD DRIED her own hair, brushed it until it shone, then put it into a loose chignon as she went to get dressed in her dressing room. She slipped on her brown leather trousers and her cream silk blouse; the pearls from her drawer were put in place next as she fastened them around her neck. Luckily, they had not been stolen the other day. She wore her cream leather pumps because Whitby with its pebbled lanes was not suitable for high heels.

As Leah went back into the bedroom, Dan was putting his socks on. He stopped, letting his gaze slide over her. The low neckline revealed a compelling amount of breast, but the pearls covered enough for her to look classy. What was he thinking? She always looked elegant, even in jodhpurs and a T-shirt, and especially when all she wore was stilettos!

'You like?' Leah asked coyly. She could still look innocent after the five years they'd been married. God, he loved that about her, and he prayed that would never stop.

She gave him a quick kiss.

'Eew. Not *again*, Mummy,' Alice stated in apparent disgust.

'Doesn't our daughter look beautiful in her Unicorn T-shirt, Daddy?' Leah said fondly.

Dan resumed putting his socks on. 'She's as stunning as her mummy.'

Alice beamed at him. 'Can I have Uncle Joey's present?'

'Not yet, Princess, but soon. It's all wrapped up.' Dan slipped his feet into his brown leather loafers. 'Let's chase Scotty up, shall we?' He held out his hand to his daughter. 'We need to get him ready. He's been lacking in his duty just lately.'

Leah turned to Dan. 'He's retired, darling, he doesn't have duties.'

'Then why does he keep on asking for them? I need to have a friendly talk to him.' Dan raised his dark eyebrows, a trait of his. 'He just needs to be ready on time. He's arranged for the taxis down into Whitby with Thomas and my mother and Ruby in with him. Joey and Ben are already down in town, and Sisco drove down in the vehicle.

'I can't wait to see Joey's face.' Leah grinned then shooed Dan and Alice out of the bedroom.

WHITBY WAS busy because the sun was shining, and there was nothing like the sun to bring out locals and visitors alike. They'd planned a walk around the town centre, not too far away from the restaurant but far enough so they could work up an appetite.

'I notice there are a few more dog friendly cafés since you opened yours, Leah,' Scotty remarked as he walked with Tom, who dwarfed him now.

'That's as it should be,' Leah replied contentedly. 'Dogs are part of the family and shouldn't be tied up outside. They should enjoy it too.' Then she added, 'Remind me to take our dogs a treat back from the restaurant, Dan.'

He nodded. 'It's a standing order whenever we go there.'

Ruby dragged Sophie across the cobbles to the jewellers. 'I think I need something new for the wedding.'

Joey spun around. 'You've got loads of jewellery. You always look a million dollars. Doesn't she, Ben?'

'So much so that I'd like to raid your stash, Ruby,' agreed Ben as he linked hands with Joey, not caring who saw them. That was a side of Joey he had unleashed. In London, gay men and women could hold hands with no one batting an eye; however, in some Yorkshire villages, folk still looked askance whenever they saw couples in such an intimate connection. Joey said they would just have to get used to it, and the lovely people of Whitby certainly had, because since moving in with Joey, Ben had taught him to accept that he was free to do as he pleased in the town that Ben now called home. Why, even Grandad Thomas didn't react now. In fact, it had surprised the old fellow that Joey wasn't wearing drag at his wedding.

'Can we go on the cinder path?' Alice cried as they walked the cobbles back to the swing-bridge. 'Can we, Mummy? Please!'

Leah was shaking her head. 'Not this evening, sweetie. It's time to eat, but tomorrow I will bring you down, and we can go for a little walk and look for your cinder-path treasures. Maybe Daddy will come too.'

Alice glanced from Dan to Leah. 'Oh. Will I be able to have an ice-cream cornet?'

'Probably,' Dan said, scooping her into his arms

while they crossed the bridge. He did that to keep her safe as he'd once seen a toddler suddenly run off and dive into the traffic; fortunately, Leah had managed to rescue the little boy. He gazed across at her, so precious walking with Tom now, listening to his conversation as she always did. He looked out at the tide as they crossed the bridge without incident. It was a balmy summer's evening, and soon they were passing where Mizelli was perched outside her cabin.

Mizelli saw Leah and beckoned to her with frantic arm movements. When she arrived, the old fortune-teller whispered something in her ear. Leah laughed, then her face fleetingly took on a more guarded expression. Mizelli then bade her goodbye and went back to her cabin, waiting for the next client.

THE QUEUE WASN'T TOO bad outside the restaurant as they all waited to be seated. Dan knew he could have got in sooner, but he also knew that Leah frowned on him using his privileged position in her hometown. He might get away with it in London, but never in Whitby. Leah had booked the window seats as per usual because Thomas loved to sit watching people around the harbour. There were so many of them at the table that it jutted right into the middle of the restaurant.

'Why are there three extra places laid?' Joey asked, glancing around and noticing an empty seat either side of him, and one next to Ruby.

Leah shrugged, pretending ignorance but thinking to herself that in only a few more minutes his first surprise would be here - and what a surprise it would be when his mum and dad turned up! Ruby had saved the seat next to her for a reluctant Sisco. Bang on time, with Joey's back to the door, his mum and dad walked in with Sisco behind them.

His deeply tanned mum, Susan, was wearing a neat shift dress in cream and turquoise with matching shoes. Around her décolletage she wore a beautiful Australian Fire Opal necklace which sat on top of the dress and made her look spectacular. She came around the back of him, putting her hands over his eyes. 'Guess who?' she said fondly and she kissed Joey's cheek.

'Budge up there, Joey lad,' his dad Robbie said, elbowing his son in his side. In contrast he looked like a Yorkshire version of Crocodile Dundee. Hat an' all.

Joey gave a shrill yell and spun around in his seat. Everyone in the restaurant turned to see what the commotion was all about, and Joey being Joey furnished them all with: 'My mum and dad have come home for our wedding, Ben.' He burst into tears, just as Ruby more or less forced Sisco into a seat.

'Stop fighting this,' she hissed at Sisco. The look they shared was electric as he sat next to her.

While all the theatrics were going on, Dan asked for the sparkling wine he'd pre-ordered a few days before, with fruit juice for the kids and beer for the men, himself included. Five years ago, he never thought he'd admit to being a beer man, but Yorkshire had a way of getting into your heart and your belly. As they were drinking a welcome home toast to Joey's parents, Dan confirmed by text the number of people for a round-robin taxi for everyone's return journey home.

Leah watched Grandad Thomas look at the menu. Unlike everyone else who had chosen fish and chips, Thomas and Sophie chose the Four Fish sharing platter which consisted of mouth-watering cod, haddock, plaice and a skate wing served with freshly cooked chips or salad. This was their favourite dish on the menu.

Once they'd all finished their main course, Dan spotted the pink Beetle being parked just a little further up the road. Leah excused herself, saying she needed the loo, and slipped outside to pick up the keys from Keira and her sister Ellie from the retro dress shop. They all knew that if Joey had seen Sisco driving the Beetle, he would have realised what was going on, so Sisco had dropped the car at Keira's just around the corner. Keira waited for Leah to text her, then she had brought the car around the block. Placing the key into a pretty pink bag with a bow, Leah thanked her friend and went back inside the restaurant and surreptitiously passed the bag to Dan.

'Princess, give this to Uncle Joey,' Dan said as he in turn handed the pink bag to Alice.

'Uncle Joey, Happy Birthday,' Alice screamed and clapped her hands.

'Oh, darling, thank you. My birthday is in December though.' Joey kissed her on her cheek, then vibrated his lips against her petal-soft skin until she screamed as she always did.

'Oh, pink knickers, I got it wrong!' Alice exclaimed.

Everyone who heard in the restaurant laughed, and some people said, 'Aw, bless her.'

Joey tutted. 'Stop stealing my sayings, young Alice. Here, this is your gift from me and Uncle Ben-Ben for the wedding.'

Alice passed the box to her daddy to open. Inside was a lovely silver bracelet. 'Ooo, thank you, Joey and Ben-Ben. It's fandabidozi!'

Dan said sadly, 'I have no chance of trying to raise my daughter as a lady, do I?'

'Now, Joey, in this bag is a wedding present, but you must share it with Ben,' said Leah with a beaming smile as she watched Joey and his parents. The love sparkling in her eyes was reserved only for family, but to Leah, Dan knew, most people were family of sorts.

Joey opened the bag and a key fell out. 'A car key? Is it a car key?'

Dan and Leah had big cheesy grins on their faces. They were so happy to be able to do this for him. Joey had worked so hard in the past few years and Ben had helped too. Ben had become part of the family and the café team.

'Tom, point to the car for your Uncle Joey and Ben. I'm afraid you have to share as Leah says,' Dan said, almost embarrassed.

'You see that pink one . . .' Tom pointed out the car, and Joey gave a squeal.

'It's a Penelope Pit-Stop Pink too! I'm going to call her *Thunderbirds* after my favourite TV series. People will see us coming, Ben, and move to make way for the beauty within. Oh. My. God.' Joey looked around. 'I can't drive home. I've had a drink. Look, Ben-Ben. It's beautiful. *Beautiful.*' Joey's eyes filled with tears and his fiancé rushed round to hug him.

'It's all sorted, Joey, we've got a driver coming here to pick it up soon. You two can drive it tomorrow,' Leah insisted. 'And you need to know that everyone here, including your parents and Alice and Tom, contributed.'

'I gave five pounds of my saved-up pocket money,' announced Alice, and everyone laughed.

With tears falling down his face, his arms around his husband-to-be and his longed-for parents at his side, Joey had never felt happier or more loved. He said thank you to everyone at the table, as did Ben.

'If you're happy, Uncle Joey, why are you crying?' Alice asked. 'Look - Uncle Ben is smiling.'

'It's complicated, being a grown-up,' Joey replied.

'Aw, piss-piss,' the little girl said airily. Then, hungry for her dinner that hadn't yet arrived she moaned, 'I'm starving, Mummy. I need a whale to eat.'

'Where did that expression come from, Alice? Piss-piss? Alice?' Leah queried.

'Uncle Joey says it.' Alice grinned at him.

'Oh, you little tattletale. I say psst-psst. *Psst-psst*, not anything else, lady!' Joey huffed.

Dan was sympathetic. 'Whatever pronunciation it is, Joey, whenever you say it, you'll be up to no good.'

'Can a man not say psst-psst without people thinking he is a criminal?' Joey asked, expecting at least one person to back him.

Everyone spoke together. 'No!'

LATER THAT EVENING, walking the dogs down the fields to check on certain mares who were a little late dropping their foals, Dan and Tom enjoyed a comfortable silence until Tom pointed across at one mare.

'Dad, look, oh wow, Rosie is having her foal. Over there.' Tom beamed at his father.

'Let's just watch from here, son. It shouldn't be too long now.' Dan looked carefully to see if Rosie appeared stressed, but she seemed relaxed. They'd thought she was due to foal as she had bagged-up and had waxed udders. Dan had explained to Tom that pregnant mares often had wax on their teats just before giving birth, and their teats were full of colostrum, but it wasn't always a sure-fire way to tell the timing of the foal's imminent birth. Dan saw the spasm in the mare's gut as it ran along her backbone; when she pushed again, he knew with the next push this youngster would be born. 'There you go, son.'

They both witnessed the miracle of birth as the foal slipped to the grassy ground, all wet and covered in afterbirth. Rosie turned and licked to stimulate the baby. Father and son waited until the foal got to unsteady feet, fell and got up again, wobbling like a drunken creature. Its broad white face was very pretty.

'I think you should be responsible for naming her, son,' Dan said, clearing his throat because he was feeling moved.

Tom responded, his voice full of passion, 'Thank you, Dad, thank you so much.'

'Why the thanks, son?' Dan asked as he shot a glance at Tom and squeezed his shoulders.

'I am just so glad we're all together. You, Mum, Alice and me. *This!* You know, I always wondered what you were like, and my mum said she fell in love with you when I was conceived and I knew if she loved you, you'd be great - and you are. I love you so much, and all this, this good that you do, the charities, the animals . . .' Tom wiped a tear from his eyes. 'She kept that stupid phone you bought her, and on pain of death, I wasn't to go near it, but I looked at it several times because I knew you'd bought it for her, and I thought maybe you'd touched it.'

Dan hugged Tom, a little tear in his eye too. 'I know she kept it, you told me when we first met. Never tell your mother this, but when she jumped from the roof onto the hotel balcony that first night, I thought she was a female version of James Bond - until she landed on me. I think she knocked my heart sideways that night, and all over again when you sent her looking for me quite a few years later. Wow, she took my breath away. She was even more beautiful than I remembered. And when I think about all the silly capers that she did, not only when we first met but the way she told me about you, going up onto a crane just so I would speak to her about the son I knew nothing about . . . why, she even brought cakes for me. Yes, I reckon I've loved my flying angel, my

Angel of the North, from the moment we met - but don't you tell her. Promise?'

Dan let go of the lad's shoulders and looked down into his face, wiping a tear from his son's cheek.

'I won't tell her, but I think you ought to, Dad.' Tom grinned, bright-eyed again. 'And when you yourself did that bungee-jump outside the café - were you crazy or what?'

'Yes, crazy. I'd do it again to be a part of all this, Tom, with your mum, you and Alice, and all the rest of our mad big family.' Dan and Tom picked up speed as they walked to the house in a comfortable silence, stopping off to tell Quinn about Rosie's foal so he could check everything was OK.

DAN AND TOM walked into the kitchen just as Leah came down from putting Alice to bed.

'I've read four stories until she went to sleep. She wanted you to regale the story with the monsters you make up, Dan. You are better at making monster faces than I am. And I was getting worried that something might be wrong with one of the horses. I hope not.' Leah moved to switch the kettle on.

'Mum, we saw Rosie having her foal. It was awesome - that's why we were a long time,' Tom assured her.

'In that case, you should be the one to give her or him a stable-name,' Leah smiled at her son.

'That's just what I said,' Dan agreed.

'Fancy a cup of tea?' Leah asked her menfolk.

'Yes, I'd love one. To think I never used to drink tea before I came to Yorkshire,' Dan replied. 'Then it's our bedtime. We've a big day tomorrow.'

'I'm going to bed now. Thank you for dinner, Mum. It was lovely. Night-night,' Tom hugged Leah and kissed her. Then he went to Dan and said, 'Tell her, Dad.'

Dan nodded. 'I will. Night night, Tom.' When the lad had left, he asked Leah if everyone else was in bed.

'Yep, and I'm about all in, so I'm going up as soon as I've had this cup of tea.' Leah took a sip of the weak tea, just how she liked it.

'OK, but first I have something to tell you, and your son insists I must do this.' Dan cleared his throat. 'I think when you appeared like an apparition on the hotel terrace that night, I wasn't sure if you were a fallen angel or 007 reporting for duty. I think I must've hit my head that night, or was it my heart? And then, when you came back to find me, I'd arrived back in the country and it seemed you were standing on a crane offering me cakes! What I have to say is I was touched, Leah, but confused. I wondered if you wanted to start a relationship or if you were just offering yourself on a plate to me.'

Leah drank her tea. 'You should be so lucky,' she mumbled.

Dan said, 'I *was* lucky. Our son masterminded the whole get-together scene. Granted, he'd not considered my stubbornness because I knew I'd used condoms. I didn't know I'd used tampered ones. Chelsea was responsible for that; Sergeant Warke told me she confessed.'

Leah was shaking her head. 'He's a clever boy, our Tom, but he was only eight – well, almost nine - and we now know your mother was his piano teacher. Some ruse they thought up to get us to see each other was planned out while he was learning the piano. There were greater forces at work than me and you, Dan.'

He came across to her and rested his chin on her head, his arms on her arms. 'Ah, yes, but what a brilliant choice they made for us. We are perfect.'

Leah smiled rather sadly. 'As for Chelsea, she has stolen so much; robbed you of not knowing Tom from birth, stopped us from being together. Thank heavens we are together now, but we still have the problem of wondering when Chelsea will strike again. You see, I know she will, Mizelli told me this evening.'

'And you believe her?'

'She's been right before, so don't you dare mock

her, Dan Ryan,' Leah warned, her stubborn expression making him want to laugh.

'I'll reserve judgement. Now, I don't know about you, but I'm dead beat.' Dan went to the treat jar, as all three dogs stared hard at him until he gave in and handed them all a treat or two.

11

THREE DARK FIGURES

The night before the wedding, three people dressed in black with hooded tops could be seen sneaking around the grounds. Two of them were women, and they were loosening the ratchet tie-down locks on the tents and the marquees so that overnight they might collapse - or at least, that was what Brioche had told Chelsea and Pepper would happen. The third was a larger figure in black. Brioche was secretly following them, and stealthily fastening the ratchets back into place.

Chelsea whispered to Pepper, 'That was easy. I thought it would take us a lot longer to sabotage the tents. As long as Farmer Foster opens the gate so we can escape without being seen, if the need should arise.' She gave a shudder. 'Foster was groping my arse - he said he was into older women. Ugh! I almost ran for the hills. Instead I bargained with him, and I paid him enough for the privilege of us getting a quick getaway if need be. I confirmed it earlier today, and he invited me around again. Pervert. Yuk.'

'This is fun. I could get used to sneaking around at night. I wonder if they will invite Farmer Foster to the wedding?' Pepper said, deliberately winding her up, making Chelsea frown.

'We might as well do the pink tent too. I've got a good mind to put a great big hole in it,' Chelsea sulked.

'No, you can't, it's a very nice tent,' Pepper insisted. 'You mustn't be vindictive to a tent.'

'Huh. OK, we leave the pink tent alone altogether. Now let's go home, I've had enough of this.' Chelsea turned on her heel to sneak back the way they came through Farmer Foster's field.

Brioche had been shadowing the women all week, and here he was making everything good again; as they had set up certain things to ruin Joey and Ben's wedding day, he had reversed almost everything. He was shattered. Instead of re-booking most of the things Chelsea had cancelled, he'd sorted out alternative arrangements. He'd managed all the little details. Huh, he would never understand why women wanted to be wedding planners.

THE WEDDING MORNING came around soon enough with the sun shining over the North Sea as Dan walked the dogs down the field with Tom. It was a beautiful day.

'I never thought Joey and Ben would marry,' Tom said, surprising his dad.

'Why not?' Dan enquired. 'They're a match made in heaven, don't you think?'

'Oh, you know, I thought Ben would never move up here. He's a Southerner.'

'So am I, son.'

'No, you are not a Southerner. Mum says you're Cosmopolitan.'

'I suppose. Whatever that is.' Dan laughed. 'Let's make our way back to the house, or your mum will be on the warpath.'

'I wonder what Aunt Penny will have in store for us today?' Tom said, changing the subject. 'She'll probably try to get herself killed or something. She asked me what she should do for the wedding, so I told her to make a cake that looked like the Beetle. Was that a good idea?' Tom had a look of achievement on his face.

'An excellent one, Tom.' Dan clapped him on the back as they turned round and headed home.

Brioche had got his contingency plan organised with Fetch-a-Meal from Charlie's Mobile Chicken Shop. He'd bought lots of cans from the late-night off-licence, and he'd hired a woman to make cakes. What could go wrong? Well, apart from his devious sister and his crazy, cruel cousin. He knew they had got out of bed early so Pepper could do Chelsea's disguise, even making her put coloured contact lenses in her eyes. The two of them had managed to get themselves employed to serve drinks, and they'd already buzzed off to get their wigs in place.

'Here, Penny, I can take the box,' offered Dan as he lifted the cake box out of her arms. He noticed tears in her eyes; she looked devastated. 'What on earth's the matter?'

'I have a wardrobe malfunction. It's my own fault,' she said tearfully.

The big woman followed Dan through to the kitchen. He popped the box down carefully on the table and told her, 'I'll get Leah to come downstairs. I'm sure she can help you. You take a seat. I'll just be a moment.'

Dan ran upstairs and found Leah tying Alice's hair in a low braided plait. 'Leah, your Aunt Penny has a problem and she needs you to help. You look amazing, Princess, just like your beautiful mummy.'

'Any idea what's wrong with Aunt Penny, Alice?' Leah asked as she finished her daughter's hair. 'You just need your diamanté's putting in at 11.45 a.m., sweetie-pie, and your side-saddle habit.'

Alice nodded after looking at herself in the mirror. 'Thank you, Mummy. Aunt Penny was acting like a divvy.'

'You mean a diva, Princess,' Dan told his daughter. 'Uncle Joey calls Penny a divvy because he can be cruel. I don't want you to be cruel.'

'That's just the way he is,' Leah put in gently. 'Aunt Penny doesn't mind; she knows he's just teasing her. Right, let's go and see what the matter is.' Leah put her brush back on her bedside table and took Alice by the hand. 'Lead the way, darling.'

'She looked very stressed - just thought I ought to warn you,' Dan called after them as Leah went downstairs with Alice.

He picked up a phone from under the bed to text someone.

DAN: *Hi, Madness. Is everything arranged for later this evening? We will have to meet up either when Leah is in bed or fast asleep, but that's not late for a*

Madame like you, is it? Or about 9.30 p.m.? Yes, earlier would be better for me too. Who are you bringing this week to our rendezvous?

Madness: *I will bring Love and my Sexy Bum: they will be just what you are looking for.*

Dan*: Hi, LOL. Yes, or just bring yourself, you're sexy too. No need to upset the apple cart just yet. I'm sure I will get to see all the ladies soon enough. See you at 9.30p.m. And remember, this is our secret. XX*

Madness: *Oh, what a romancer! You know I'm married; my husband is one of your best friends. See you then, lover-boy. This is Madness, you do know that? Why don't we just come clean and tell them all? I'm sure they'll be happy for us. I wouldn't do this for any other man in the world. Love, Madness XOX*

Dan: *Ha, ha, funny, funny. I bet you would. D XOXO*

DAN FELT PLEASED WITH HIMSELF. So, his rendezvous was at 9.30 p.m. He could slip out of the wedding reception for fifteen minutes, maybe even half an hour on the pretence of checking the dogs, and that would get the job done. God, he was so excited. It would have to be a quick rendezvous. *Yes!* His plan was coming together well, and Leah was oblivious. He fist-pumped the air. *Love and Sexy Bum, here I*

come. And Madness's husband Lenny didn't suspect a thing. Both Lenny and Leah were clueless.

Hiding his burner phone, he knew he must remember to put it in his jacket pocket. He would do it right now, then he wouldn't forget it in the rush to get ready. Sliding it into his jacket pocket, Dan patted it down. He was all set, and he just couldn't wait. Leaving the bedroom, he ran down the steps to have a last-minute chat with Quinn. Walking through the kitchen, he could see Joey in his dressing-gown laughing his socks off, and Aunt Penny was dabbing tears away. What was going on? When he checked, Penny's tears were of laughter too.

'Something I should know about?' Dan asked, wanting to be in on the joke, but also appearing to be casual. He needed to act normal, or they would find out about this whole fanciful affair, and he didn't want anyone being hurt yet - at least, not until it was time to come clean.

Joey picked up two pieces of sticky material from a generic box. He held them up, flapping them in the air in front of him, not noticing a piece of paper flutter out of the box and onto the floor. They were shaped like a curly speech mark with cellophane over them in a nude colour. 'Here, get your beady eyes around these bad boys, Dan. You won't need glasses as they're big enough but not, it turns out, big *enough*.'

Dan inspected them, his brow creasing. 'What are they? I'm puzzled.'

'It's Penny's hold-up bra. That's what it is,' Joey giggled. 'And what size would you say that is, Dan?'

Dan studied the pieces. He walked over to Leah and put them near her boobs. She slapped him away with her hands. 'Leah's size. Maybe 36b.'

'Nah, and what size are you, Aunt Penny?'

'Humongous: 48F. As one girl said in the department store in York: "Madam, you need scaffolding, and we don't sell that in this store!" Which is why I walked out and bought online,' Penny retorted, disgusted by the false advertising of these things and the rude girl in York.

'The size is XXXXXL and should fit Aunt Penny's boobies,' Joey commented with tongue in cheek, adding more Xs than he should have. He snatched one of the bra bits. 'Excuse me, Aunt Penny.' Joey put one against her left bosom. The material hardly covered a quarter of her generous breast.

'I guess they're made for smaller people.' Penny looked upset but she was a game old bird. 'But I will say, I love all this buying online. LOL.'

Dan bit his bottom lip. He and Joey exchanged glances, and they both burst out laughing. Penny cracked up too. They were soon all crying with laughter.

'Joey, everyone, it's not funny. Poor Aunt Penny has a big problem. Her backless, strapless dress is no good without a bra that will hold her up,' Leah explained. 'What are we going to do?'

'I can run you down to see Keira, if that helps, Penny?' Dan offered. 'Let's take the dress with us and I'm sure she'll know what to do.'

'I will phone her now and tell her the problem, while you take Aunt Penny down into Whitby,' Joey said. 'But first, take a peek at our beautiful wedding cake that Aunt Penny has made us.'

Joey took the lid off the box. Dan bit his lip; he wasn't sure Tom would understand, as what stood before him on the cake stand was utterly beautiful, but not what Tom had meant. It was a beetle, with pink iridescent wings that changed to blue and silver and gold as you moved your eyes over it, and its eyes were so real. In matter of fact, it was breath-taking.

'My God, this is beyond beautiful, Penny. I don't know about you being a head teacher, but maybe you were a head chef at the Ritz or the Belleville. This family I joined is amazing You are so very gifted.' Dan bent to kiss her cheek. Leah was nodding emphatically.

'That's what I said. I'm over the moon and I know Ben will be too.' Joey hugged Penny. 'Thank you. I may tease you an awful lot, but I love you.'

Penny felt her cheeks flush, then falling back into

her native Yorkshire slang, she shoved him away, saying, 'Gerron wi' ya.'

'We're going to Keira's now; if we are lucky her sister will make us a cuppa.' Dan manoeuvred Penny off the chair. 'Oh Leah, can you pop and see Quinn for me about Twinkle? And can you check on Blossom's beautiful baby while you're there?'

'Great idea, darling,' Leah said. She grinned at Dan, and he winked at her with lust in his eyes. Leah was clueless about his rendezvous tonight. Who would he choose, or could he have both? He was looking forward to seeing the girls. He knew he would get lots of kisses. As long as they didn't make a mess of his shirt or his bow tie, and especially not his trousers.

CRISIS WAS AVERTED with Aunt Penny's dress, thanks to Keira's skills and Ellie supplying Penny with coffee and finding a beautiful big retro corset they had in stock in their dress shop. It fitted Penny to a T and gave her a lovely curvaceous outline. Joey asked Leah if he could see the gift she'd bought to wear for Dan from the department store in York. She passed the box across and let him look inside to see the very sexy négligée in pink with cream bows, which tied down the middle with laces. Joey could just imagine it revealing enough silky skin to be the most tempting thing he had ever seen, so imagine what Dan would think of Leah dressed in it?

Joey held the delicate garment up to his chest. His mind was whirling. He pressed the silky material to his cheek and then breathed, 'That's the most beautiful thing I've ever seen, or felt. Oh my God, he's going to rip it off you. I can just imagine the scene now.'

'It's lovely, isn't it? I don't want him to rip it off me, but I just couldn't resist it when I saw it. And there was me buying things with Aunt Penny and concentrating on her wardrobe. I wish she'd told me about the bra-drama. I wasn't with her that day. She said she's doing something with her eyebrows too. I hope it's not extreme.' Leah heard the doorbell. She guessed it would be the woman with the buttonholes.

Joey put the box with the négligée on the side table in the hallway so that Leah could take it back upstairs. Oh, why hadn't he seen it first! He knew Ben would love seeing him in it. Joey then went back into the kitchen and switched on the kettle for the umpteenth time. 'I'd better not have any more coffee,' he reminded himself out loud, 'or I'll be crossing my legs in the Portaloo before I say "I do".'

Ruby walked into the kitchen looking somewhat the worse for wear. 'Stop reciting verse, *Portaloo* and *do,* it's too early. Is the make-up artist arriving soon?

God, I forget her name. Anyway, she's supposed to be coming to titivate Sophie and me. I'd better tell those bodybuilders who Dan has hired to let her in. Apparently she's also serving drinks.'

'I'm doing my own make-up, darling,' Joey told her. 'I've no idea about anyone coming to tart you up, but by the looks of it, you'll need plaster of Paris for all your dips and crevices.' He chuckled while Ruby swiped him, then said wistfully, 'I just wonder how Ben is getting on down at the cottage. I left him there all alone, as I didn't want him to see me last night. You know I'm superstitious, but he's not, so I came hiking up here in the middle of the night and slept in one of the many attic rooms Leah has had done out. We were trying to stay away from each other. Me in one room, him in the other and it just wasn't working so I came up here, but the strangest thing was, I thought I saw three people in black running around the marquees. They were following each other, and then I realised they must be the extra security Dan had hired.' Joey poured boiling water into the cafetière. 'There's something wrong with the coffee machine too. I'm sure since that break-in, we have had more things go wrong, and Mizelli has refused to do me a reading today. I mean, I even invited her to the wedding.'

Leah looked thoughtful. Mizelli had warned her

about people acting strangely. She glanced up as her grandad walked in.

'How many readings do you expect her to do?' Thomas asked. 'I think you've been to see her five times in the last month. The poor woman doesn't know whether she's coming or going. First, she can't predict if you want her reading from the Tarot cards or in the role of the psychic medium or that of a spiritualist from the people she says are standing behind you, and who you can never see.' Grandad Thomas walked further into the kitchen with Sophie following. He thought to himself, All that mumbo-jumbo! How was it possible, and yet . . .

'They're standing behind you. One hundred per cent guaranteed!' Joey exclaimed.

'And you believe him, Ruby?' Thomas asked with a resigned shake of his head.

Ruby nodded. 'I do, Thomas.'

'Me too, darling,' Sophie said.

'Well, I'm not so sure,' Thomas mumbled. But as they outnumbered him, silence was the best option.

LEAH WALKED BACK in from the stable yard with Tom and clapped her hands. 'Right, come on, everyone, we all need to get changed, but before we do, look at these photos of this beautiful foal Tom is going to name.' Without thinking, she passed the phone to Tom to pick up a clothes tag off the floor. Glancing down at it, it had "XS" printed in feint letters with, "*Made somewhere in the world.*" written in black. Slipping it into her gilet pocket she leaned against Tom to look at the photo of the foal and completely forgot about it.

To the cries of 'she is beautiful,' from everyone in the kitchen, Tom grinned and said, 'I'm naming her Petal.'

'What a great name and fitting too. Her nose is as soft as a petal,' Leah smiled, kissing her son on his cheek.

Then she soon got the gang going again. 'Time is moving on. Check the flowers, Joey, they've just arrived. It's a good thing I confirmed what colour they were as someone had written it down wrong.'

'What do you mean?' Joey's eyes were on stalks.

'Nothing to worry about, I've sorted it.' Leah tutted. 'I hope nothing else goes wrong. Someone had ordered *black* flowers - would you believe it? Fortunately the head florist rang to double-check the colour before ordering them in. She said she remembered you'd ordered a symphony of different shades.'

Joey gave a loud sigh of relief, before asking: 'Any idea where my mum and dad have got to?'

'Looking at the foals. They'll be up in a minute,' Tom replied.

'And where's our Penny?' asked Thomas. Then he saw the cake. 'By 'eck, she's excelled herself here.'

'Wardrobe malfunction, wardrobe malfunction,' mimicked Joey in his best effeminate Dalek voice. 'She went to buy something she thought would hold her dragons up.'

Thomas raised his eyebrows. 'Who would ever know she was an intelligent head teacher at one point in her life? She shouldn't use that flamin' tinternet. Was it you who got her onto it, Joey? She got the wrong size, I bet.'

'We just told her she could look online for a dry suit.' Joey shrugged, making his way to the door. 'Right, I'm off. The bride must get ready.'

'Penny almost killed herself with that dry suit, my lad,' Thomas shot back. 'Aye, get thissen ready, lad.'

'Hero saved her, Grandad.' Leah stroked Hero's head as he ambled in from the garden.

'Well, let's hope that's all she's bought off that there tinternet,' Thomas muttered darkly to himself, as Tom strode over to look at the cake and quietly giggled to himself. Great-aunt Penny had done it again.

12

SHENANIGANS GALORE

Earlier that morning
Chelsea and Pepper had arrived at the wedding marquee to find it still standing. In fact, all the marquees were all still upright. They stared at each other in shock! They'd been met and were being ordered about by a frumpy older woman named Ethel and told to report for duty in the kitchen tent.

'No way. We are here to serve the drinks when the wedding party come in. That's all they have hired us to do and all we are going to do,' Chelsea qualified as she and Pepper marched off.

Ethel listened to their insolent cackle of laughter as they left the marquee, and she shouted after them: 'Huh, you two ought to have been born when my dad was alive; he'd a sorted you out! Lazy louts!'

'Do you think you can get into the house again, Chelsea?' Pepper whispered to her cousin, who was still sniggering at the older woman's words.

'No, I can't. Dan will have proper security on by now,' Chelsea scowled. 'Not that little double-crossing man who went behind my back, because if he hadn't turned up to the police station in Whitby with the Bot thing that Tom gave Dan, which showed me handling his precious Faberge we would have been married by now, I am certain! So, if you see him - his name is Scotty. If he walks past you, trip him up. By the way, I love that black wig on you. You look so pretty and completely different from your usual self.'

'I am getting into the house too, to do Ruby and Sophie's make-up, but you won't be allowed in. I saw the little man ordering the beefcake security guys around this morning. They didn't flinch a muscle.' Pepper seemed as pleased as punch.

'I know that - I'm not a fool. As I was saying, Scotty is retired now, according to Joey, but I believe he's coming to the wedding. I've noticed Dan still orders him about.' Chelsea stalked off towards another tent. Pepper followed and listened to her cousin moaning and grumbling even more. 'When we slipped in here last night, the night-watchman succumbed to my new sleeping tablets. I swapped his tea, and he didn't even know, but we won't let our guard down, Like I said, Dan will have even more security staff by now, maybe even ex-SAS.'

'Oooh! Yes, and that stable-hand fellow was hanging around. He almost caught us and then Dan came out with the dogs. My God, there was no air in my lungs.' Pepper gleamed with excitement. 'I felt like I was in the movies. At least we cut some ties on the marquee. I did the catering marquee too. We'd better make sure they haven't had deliveries. OK, let's split. It gets the job done quicker.' Pepper grinned at Chelsea. 'I've got to go on up to the house soon. So, you check the catering marquee, and I will do the make-up. I thought Brioche was coming, and yet I've not seen him. I will send him a message. You, Chelsea, text me when you need me out here.'

'Don't call me Chelsea here, you fool, someone will suspect! And get that lazy article here pronto,' Chelsea demanded, shimmying off towards the catering marquee.

'What should I call you?' Pepper shouted after her.

'Amy.'

'And you can call me Sienna,' Pepper snapped.

'No bugger knows you, you idiot.' Chelsea watched her cousin march off. 'You are Pepper!'

*B*ACK TO THE *present*

Pepper went around to the front door with her cosmetics box in her hand. She sashayed towards the front entrance as she saw a big burly man guarding the impressive front door. He watched her walk down the path with her little hips swinging and her breasts jiggling. She looked up into his eyes and fluttered her extra-long lashes. 'I'm doing make-up for the old ladies, but I forgot my cement, that's why I'm late. Hahaha.'

The security guard grinned, then he pointed to the front doorbell and went back to his sentry duty, watching her wiggle her bottom at him.

Ruby answered the door. 'Ah, you're here at last. We just need a little touch-up. Sophie, the make-up lady is here. Come on in, dear. We'll go to your quarters, Sophie.' Ruby let her in and closed the front door but ogled the big, security man with interest, staring at his muscles bulging under his T-shirt.

'Oh, wow. This is a lovely house,' Pepper commented as she followed Ruby off to the left to walk down a corridor.

'Yes, it is, but it hasn't always been this impressive. It's been a work-in-progress and still is. Just in here, we have got a chair in front of Sophie's dressing-table. You set up there, darling. You might as well do me first. I'm grateful to you for taking this job with such little notice, and I do hope you have the right shade of cosmetics for my colour.' Ruby sat on the chair and closed her eyes. 'What is your name again?'

'Pepper,' the young woman said, 'and I have all the different shades I require.' As she mixed her palette of colourings and put in the secret ingredient, Pepper thought spitefully to herself, You conspired against my cousin, so now you will get what you deserve.

'Mm, what an unusual name. The quicker we get done, darlin', the faster you get to trowel the foundation onto Sophie and the sooner we can all get out and enjoy ourselves. I'm going cocktail crazy soon,' Ruby rattled on.

Pepper stopped what she was doing and looked at Ruby in the mirror, saying 'Would you mind if I quickly used the toilet? Sorry, I should never have had that second cup of coffee.'

Ruby nodded as she sat at the dressing table. Tonight, she was going to make a play for her man.

Pepper took the air-freshener from her bag and put it onto the windowsill. She flushed the loo, washed her hands and went back out. No one would know the air freshener was a camera. Chelsea had asked her to put it into a frequently used room, but that was impossible. The en suite would have to do.

She was moisturising Ruby's face when the door flung open and in walked Alice.

'Wot are you doin', me old cock-sparrer?' Alice asked in a cockney voice as Sophie followed her in. Sophie was a picture in a beautiful floaty lemon dress.

Pepper couldn't help herself; she laughed at the cute little girl.

'Ignore Alice, she copies anything anyone tells her lately,' Ruby said. 'This cockney lark is a new one though.'

Sophie dabbed at her dress. 'I love those Newfoundland dogs, but boy do some of them slobber all over you. This is my third change of clothes. And you, my sweetheart, who taught you that saying, Alice?' Sophie then turned to Pepper. 'Hello, dear. Oh, what are you mixing? Not too thick, eh. We need to look like we're growing old gracefully, not like tarts, so use a light touch, won't you. You think you can do that?'

Pepper smiled and nodded, thinking, Oh, I can do it all right. You just watch me.

Alice looked smug. 'Uncle Joey sez it all the time, Grandma.'

Just then, Scotty marched in, breathless and looking good in his navy pin-stripe suit. 'Has she passed security?' he demanded, pointing at Pepper.

'Why? Does she look a threat?' asked Ruby, pulling an ogre-type face.

Alice giggled.

Scotty scowled twice as badly. 'Can't be too careful. Those Arnie look-a-likes won't even speak to me, so I have to co-ordinate with you lot. See you at the marquee, ladies. You are all so stunning. Even you, make-up lady. I have a thing about uniforms.' And he leered.

'Don't most men, but it's a tabard, not a uniform,' muttered Ruby, remembering back a lot of years ago when one good-looking client who was a doctor had asked her to dress as a nurse. When she asked him why, he told her his girlfriend was a maternity nurse, and she wouldn't wear her uniform for him. Ruby had obliged, of course, and enjoyed posing for him and seeing how excited he got. His silly girlfriend had left him not long after that, announcing he was weird in her eyes. After all, what harm was a little role play, if you loved someone? Hmm, maybe that's what she herself needed to do tonight, thought Ruby.

Pepper's phone dinged with a text message. 'Excuse me.'

CHELSEA: *Brioche has just said we can't have followed his instructions properly with the Marquees because they're all still standing. NOT what I expected at all! We did unfasten them all, didn't we?'*

Pepper: *Yes we did. That's very strange.*

Chelsea: *We can only hope something else goes*

wrong. We've still got the food and drink stunts. Where are you?

Pepper: *In the house doing make-up. I have planted the you-know-what.*

Chelsea: *Brilliant! Let's hope everything else goes wrong.*

SOPHIE LOOKED at Pepper over her reading glasses. 'Time is money, and we don't pay for the internet, young lady.'

There was a rap on the door. 'Fort Knox, come in!' trilled Ruby.

It was Leah, with one of the security men. Pepper raised her eyes and caught the latter's piercing navy-blue-eyed gaze.

'Do I know you?' Leah asked Pepper, who was busy going all gaga inside about the blue-eyed hunk next to her.

'I'll wait outside, ma'am,' the guy said politely and left, after giving a sneaky wink at Pepper.

'Thank you. This make-up lady won't be long - sorry, what was your name?' asked Leah, thinking, I'm sure I know those eyes . . . now where was it I saw you?

'Erm, my name is Pepper,' Pepper said, caught off-guard.

'I could have sworn I've met you before.' Leah tutted in annoyance. She was usually very good at remembering faces and knew she'd definitely seen this woman's face before. She checked a text and said hurriedly, 'Sorry, I have to dash. Alice, come with me. We have to saddle up Twinkle as she's the only pony Uncle Joey wanted at his wedding.'

'Aw, that's nice. Will your daughter be wearing a hard hat?' Pepper asked.

'Sorry?' Leah turned, staring at the woman again. She'd heard her voice too, somewhere.

'I asked if she would wear a riding hat. I'm sure you know that horses can fear things, and get startled. I wouldn't want someone so cute to fall off and get hurt,' Pepper added, her words genuine as she'd taken a shine to the little girl. It would be a shame for such a precious mite to get hurt, all because of her cousin's grudge.

'We'll be looking after her, don't you worry,' Leah assured as she took Alice's hand. 'Come on, baby.' And she walked out of the room and down the corridor with Alice in tow.

'Mummy,' Alice said. She pulled her hand out of Leah's palm and pointed back to the room. 'That lady in there was at the doggy weekend when Aunt Penny was a monster.'

'Was she, darling?'

'Yep, she followed Daddy around. Her hair was

mucky blonde then,' Alice said. 'She tried to give me a sweetie, that's why I remember.'

'Did you take it?'

'I think Daddy took it and put it in his pocket. He said it was very kind.' Alice smiled.

'Oh well. Let's get down to the stables. I shall talk to your father about that. He told me he hadn't noticed her.' Leah bit her lip. Why was Pepper wearing a black wig? Oh well, she didn't have time to worry about it now, but she would ask Dan because something was a bit off in the way he was acting.

BRIOCHE SAW Charlie's Chicken van arrive. He waved like crazy, guiding the van to where it should be parked, right up next to the catering marquee. He'd seen waiters taking crystal glasses in, and he'd noticed that the tables and the chairs were dressed for the occasion in classic cream satin with pink ties. Hah, he thought - he would get to sit down at a table, and Chelsea and Pepper would have to serve him.

Going into the tent, Brioche stopped and gaped in amazement. All the food Leah had ordered was there, being brought in for the buffet. How did that happen? He was sure he'd heard Chelsea cancel it. Brioche shrugged. Oh well, they could have Charlie's Chicken too. It was a delicious treat.

'There are seventy guests, Charlie, what do you think, two or three portions per person? Oh, and I'm sure Leah would want one piece each for the staff. Plus, we need some mini-fillet things, can you do those?' Brioche asked as Charlie walked into the tent.

The man shrugged. 'I'll cook the lot. I'd better start now - is there a free coffee going?'

Brioche nodded. 'Thank you for coming at such short notice. We both know Joey and Ben love your chicken. I'll get you that coffee, Charlie - two minutes.' Brioche dodged into the booze tent to check if his order had arrived, but there was a huge consignment of drink there already. The bar was well-stocked, in fact it was overflowing with booze. Surprised but pleased, he went to get Charlie his much-needed coffee, fetching one for himself at the same time.

THE BEST MAN, Dan, turned and watched Joey walk down the aisle in the huge marquee. In his exquisite pale grey suit, pink silk shirt and pink tie, and his shiny leather shoes, he looked very much like a film-star on set. Then Leah entered, leading the pony by her side. Dan looked at his wife; today she wore a pale cream broderie anglaise blouse, showing a hint of cleavage, coupled with a beige leather skirt which ended just above her knees. She looked like a sexy cowgirl - and as usual with Leah, she took his breath away.

Then his eyes went to his daughter, sitting side-saddle and beautiful on Twinkle, the sweetest grey Welsh Mountain pony Dan had ever purchased. Alice was sporting a little bowler hat, her dinosaur T-shirt and smart trousers, and a long-line, pale-pink riding habit which finished the outfit off to perfection. Tom walked at the other side of Twinkle; he was so hand-some in his own smart light grey suit, and Dan thought how much his son resembled himself at the same age. Both Tom and Leah had lead reins on Twinkle. Dan was a proud, proud man, having such a wonderful family. So why was he risking it all by meeting Madness and the girls? He prayed he would get away with it. Could you have your cake and eat it? He hoped so.

Leah glanced up and met his eyes. She pointed to Joey and put her thumb up. Dan nodded. He knew what she thought; Joey looked sensational.

ALICE WAS FIDDLING about in the saddle as they reached Ben. Dan had been surprised when he realised how creative Ben was, once he'd had time to get to know him. Now the two men were firm friends.

'Alice, whatever is the matter? You are fidgeting – do you need the toilet?' Then without waiting for an answer, Dan moved back for Joey to take his place next to Ben. 'You are a million-dollar man today, Joey. Go get your man,' Dan whispered to him.

Dan put an arm around Leah as he took over the rein duty. He stroked Twinkle, whilst holding the lead-rein and murmuring soft words into the pony's ear. Then he turned to Leah and said softly, 'You are ravishing, darling.'

Leah smiled at him, but if she were honest, something didn't feel quite right.

AS THE WEDDING PROGRESSED, Alice kept moving in the saddle, and her little face was scrunching up as if something was bothering her.

'Who gives this man to this man?' asked the vicar.

'I wish everyone would 'urry up,' Alice fretted.

'I do.' Joey's dad stepped forward.

Then Dan placed the rings onto a pink cushion.

As the vicar announced, 'I now pronounce you man and man,' Joey interrupted, 'Oh, no, Vicar, I'm most definitely the wifey. Can I kiss my Ben-Ben?'

The vicar nodded, and Alice shrieked out, 'Thank God for that, my arse is killing me!'

The entire congregation burst out laughing as Joey and Ben kissed, and Dan frowned at his daughter.

'What's wrong with the saddle, Princess?' Dan lifted her off Twinkle to examine it, and to his dismay he noticed deep indentation marks in the seat. He looked at Alice's behind and saw a pinecone stuck to her riding habit with Velcro attached. He pulled it off and noticed it had a sticky substance on one surface too, to ensure it didn't come off. Wrapping it in a tissue, he slipped it in his pocket. This was no accident.

Picking up his daughter and giving her a cuddle, he whispered, 'Brave girl for putting up with the pain. It must have hurt. Did you see anyone before you came into the marquee, Alice?'

'Yes, I saw a waitwess, but no one else, Daddy. Am I in trouble for saying arse?' Alice looked into Dan's eyes. 'I love you, Daddy.'

'No, you're not in trouble, baby. Something was stuck to your coat and it was poking into your bottom. That's why it was hurting. In fact, I believe you are a star, and I love you too for being so brave at Uncle Joey's wedding.' Dan kissed his daughter's cheek.

'Phew,' she said as she snuggled into him.

As THEY ALL walked out of the wedding tent and headed towards the catering marquee, Joey squealed and turned to Leah. 'Oh, Lee-Lee, you ordered Charlie's Chicken just for Ben and me. Thank you so much.'

Leah looked surprised. True enough, Charlie's Chicken van was parked next to the catering marquee, and the most delicious aroma of fried chicken was coming out of it.

'Yes,' she fibbed. 'But you can't eat all of it.'

Charlie shouted, 'It'll be ready soon, Joey. I will bring it into the big tent.'

Leah walked up to Charlie's van as the others went into the marquee. 'Charlie, who ordered you?'

'You did, Leah - well that big bloke did so on your behalf. He's already paid me,' Charlie confirmed.

'Well, just make sure you come to the celebrations too. Thank you for being here at such brief notice, we appreciate it.' Leah saw Dan coming out to find her. 'I'm just coming,' she called.

'Something has gone wrong with the arrangements,' Dan said with a frown.

'What's wrong?' Leah asked, feeling trepidation run through her blood.

'We have enough food to feed the five thousand and enough booze to sink a battleship. I feel Chelsea

is behind this too. Did **you** book Charlie's Chicken?'
Dan asked.

Leah shook her head. 'From what I can gather,
Brioche booked it on my behalf, but I'm wondering if
he did it for Joey and Ben. The three of them have
become firm friends.'

'Brioche?' Dan put his arms around Leah. 'Ah
OK. Let's worry about this later.'

'Or not at all. It's delighted Joey. I don't know
why he didn't book Charlie himself. Let's go in.'
Leah took Dan's outstretched hand and they walked
into the marquee, where she saw all the food being
brought out. 'Wow, you weren't kidding. I think all
the helpers can eat too for a week. There'll be enough
to send to the shelter too.'

'You should see the booze,' Dan hissed. 'My God,
they're all going to have a good time tonight,' then he
added softly, 'just like me.'

Leah's hearing was sharp. 'Why, are you getting
drunk?' she asked as they sat down at their table with
its name-places prettily arranged. She made a mental
note to move her riding boots from the bedroom and
to leave the en-suite door open with a light on, as
once when in his cups, he'd almost mistaken her
riding boot for the loo.

'I am not getting drunk. I need my wits about me.
Someone sabotaged Alice's riding habit.' Dan showed
Leah the pinecone.

'My God. How? I was with her all the time!' Leah exclaimed.

'Alice said a waitress was near her, other than that I've no idea, but I'm going to get more security men in here and maybe even call the police. Chelsea will not beat us at this. We will deal with her once and for all,' Dan promised, with a comforting squeeze of his wife's knee.

AFTER THE MOUNTAIN of food was served - and eaten - and the speeches had been made, Joey and Ben started off the dancing. Joey's style of moves was making people chuckle and Thomas hold his head in his hands in despair. When Joey's dad got up, put his tie around his forehead and danced around like an Indian Chief circling a campfire, the guests roared and clapped.

'I don't believe it! My eldest son has been travelling the world and he comes home to dance at his son's wedding as if he's Chief Sitting Bull.' Thomas took a lengthy swig of good Yorkshire ale, adding philosophically, 'I suppose as long as he is enjoying himself.'

13

A LOAD OF OLD GREEK

E ros Savidis, the good-looking Greek who was Sophie's nephew, drove down the country lane on the top of the Yorkshire Moors. He was driving his vehicle on the right-hand side of the road and getting hooted at and sworn at by every driver who passed him. His Cousin Dan had told him Yorkshire folk were friendly, but they weren't so friendly to a Greek Prince. Why the hell he wasn't able to hire a chauffeur-driven limousine in York he didn't know. It was his first visit up north, and Eros had alighted from his First-Class seat on the train from King's Cross in London hoping to get a limousine ordered. Instead, when that proved impossible, he had hired a Mercedes.

London was easy to navigate because his driver did it for him. Alas, his driver was on holiday. He guessed he'd be able to get to Scarthingdale Hall and was hoping to do it well before dark, but this driving on the wrong side of the road was making him bewildered.

As Eros drove past a car smouldering at the side of the road with smoke coming out of its engine, he shook his head. It reminded him of the cars on the Greek mainland. What was his friend Christos's business name again? Ah, that was it, Dead-A-Loss (after the Greek myth of Dedalus) Rent-A-Car. Christos himself admitted the cars were all bangers. Eros laughed to himself, but then decided he must concentrate as he'd almost written this car off several times already.

Tootling down the country lane, singing at the top of his voice in Greek, he came across a mirage, a beautiful woman walking in the road without a care in the world - and on high stilettos. Wow, she had killer legs. He bibbed his horn, swerving to miss her as she dived out of the way into a muddy puddle that turned out to be deeper than it seemed. The water splashed up into her face and made her gasp with shock and annoyance. The ground had not dried out from the heavy rain a few days ago.

'Stupid woman,' Eros swore out loud, not realising how condescending he sounded because his window was already wound down to give him the benefit of the country air.

'Friggin' hellfire, you bloody stupid lunatic, don't you know we drive on the left?' The drop-dead gorgeous redhead swore as she looked down at her muddied dress and shoes, then she raised her head to scowl at the most handsome man she'd ever seen, getting out of a Mercedes car. He wore an expensive-cut grey suit, white shirt, plum tie and polished, designer brown lace-up shoes. He screamed style and sophistication, and as he marched towards her, she could smell heavenly aftershave.

'Do you always walk in the middle of the road?' demanded the Greek heartthrob. His dark brown eyes were travelling down from her mud-splashed face to her feet.

'And do *you* always drive on the wrong side of the road? Just look at my dress - you've bloody ruined it - and here am I, going to a wedding reception. How can I turn up there now, looking like this?' Angel was very upset. Her cousin Joey would be devastated if she turned up dirty to his wedding. Huh, and men say women can't drive!

To her utter consternation, the stranger started laughing, a full out-and-out belly laugh.

'Think it's funny, do you? Well, I don't.' Angel was in a red-hot rage. Suddenly she picked up some mud in her dirtied hands and threw it in his face. 'Laugh at that instead, you imbecile.'

Still, he was chuckling as he walked back to the

car and climbed in. Angel stormed off up the road with tears of anger in her eyes. She glanced down at the ruined white dress. It was expensive too - had cost her fifty quid in the sale. All that effort wasted.

She heard the Mercedes idling behind her; it was still on the wrong side of the road. Angel whirled round and shouted, 'Do you have a death wish? You'll be in an accident if you don't get to the right side of the road. Never mind killing me.'

'I am on the right side of the road,' mused Eros. He knew it was wrong, but he was enjoying playing with this woman. He loved a fight.

'The right side of the road *is the left*!' Angel muttered.

Eros grimaced. 'The right side is the left? I do not understand this saying. Is it because I'm in Yorkshire?' He deliberately pronounced the word 'Yorkshyerrrrr' to irritate her.

'Try harder, mate. We drive on the left here in the UK. So, therefore, the right side to drive is the left-hand side.'

'Ah, I understand now, beautiful lady. Did you say you are going to a wedding?' Eros asked, drawing the car to a halt and getting out once more, still with that smug smile on his face. He brushed the mud off his shirt and walked towards the woman who had the most beautiful green eyes and luscious red lips, not to mention the head of gorgeous red hair that he would like to run his fingers through. 'Maybe you would like to drive? I too am going to a wedding reception; surely it must be the same one?'

'Why would anyone want to invite you?' Angel said rudely. The guy was so pleased with himself. What an idiot!

'I am the cousin of the man whose land the wedding reception is on. I too know the groom, Joey - or is he the bride?' Eros wondered to himself. 'Who has invited you?'

'My cousin who is getting married invited me, and Dan's wife Leah is my cousin too, she invited me, so I am invited *twice*. Do you mind, I have a long way to walk with a ruined dress thanks to you,' Angel snapped at him and turned to go, but he had the audacity to grab her upper arm.

'Maybe we could help each other? Do you drive?' Eros asked, trying to get the mud off his tie. He wasn't used to women turning away from him. What's more, her touch was electrifying!

'Why? Or how?' Angel asked, her eyes flashing nastily.

'Isn't it obvious? You could drive my expensive car, as you know where you are going, I presume? It would save me from crashing this hire car,' Eros said. Even caked in mud, this woman was taking his breath away. He pushed a hand through his dark head of hair. 'What do you say?'

Angel had to admit he was a sight to behold, with his dark brown eyes, thick dark lashes and his olive skin, his jet-black hair a little longer than the norm. She guessed he was a rake. He was very smart even if his tie and jacket had mud on them, thanks to her. She felt bad now because she guessed he had come all the way from Greece. She knew Dan was half-Greek, and she was also aware that they drove on the right over there in Alonnisos.

'Yes, I can drive us there,' she said. She would love to drive this baby. A Mercedes no less. Poor Marvin, her own car, she'd just left him smoking. She knew the breakdown truck would suggest she scrap him.

'And I can buy you a new dress,' he said, adding, 'Pity, you are beautiful in this dress even if you have mud all over you.'

Both pairs of eyes crinkled up in laughter, and Eros snorted his laugh as Angel giggled.

'Beautiful?' she echoed.

He moved in closer, cupping her cheeks, 'Beautiful.'

'Ah, gerron wi' yer,' Angel laughed and nudged him.

'Pardon?'

'Never mind, it's lost in translation. Keys?' She held her hand out.

He dropped a quick kiss to her startled lips,

'Thank you. I was afraid I wouldn't get there in how you say?'

'One piece.' Angel dashed to the car. 'Come on. We need to get there before the dancing finishes.'

'Of course.' Eros ran to the passenger side of the car, whilst Angel got into the driver's side.

'Hecky thump,' she said, 'this is nice.'

Eros frowned. 'I know, lost in translation.'

'It's a very nice car,' Angel said happily and set off down the winding road. As she drove safely on the left, no other cars were tooting their horns.

Now the left-hand side made sense, thought Eros. It was easy coming from the station in York. He just listened to the SatNav and followed the cars but as soon as he hit the moors, did he get confused!

'It drives lovely,' Angel sighed.

'You are easily pleased,' Eros said. Now he had the chance to take her in properly he liked what he saw.

'Yeah, well, my own car broke down just up the road.'

'You mean that beat-up old buggy thing which seemed abandoned at the side of the road?'

'Don't you dare call Marvin a beat-up old buggy, he is neither,' Angel warned. 'He just blew up. No warning cough or fart - he just blew up.'

'I saw him.' Eros shuddered. 'You have a love of your car named Marvin?' he asked. 'I have heard of this affliction before. How can one get attached to a car? What did you say your name was?'

'I didn't, but my name is Angel. And yes, my heart is broken because I think Marvin has died,' Angel said. 'Smoke was coming out of his engine.'

'If you dance with me all night long, I will buy you another more reliable car,' Eros offered.

'Just for dancing with you? Are you crazy?'

'Yes.'

'Without kissing? Or sex?'

'Just dancing all night long,' Eros promised, then added with a shrug, 'Unless you find me irresistible. Then who knows what the night might bring?'

'OK to dancing.' Angel mused to herself, I can just get him drunk. He won't even remember when I'm finished with him.

'Good, I like a wager that is a certainty for me,' Eros confirmed, straightening the leg of his trousers. It was a movement that caught Angel's attention as she pulled up at the main gates of Scarthingdale Hall. He was a stuck-up bloke, thinking he could beat her!

'Why the cavalry?' Angel asked the gateman, looking around at the many guards.

'Just a precaution, madam. Your name, please?' The security man held up his list.

'Angel and my plus one,' she confirmed, showing him her invite.

Eros leaned over. 'But I am already invited on my invitation.' He passed the man the snazzy card and saw the security man's eyebrows raise as he studied it. It was a standing joke between him and Leah because Eros had always believed he should be the King of Greece, so Leah and Joey had ensured that *Prince Eros* was embossed on the invite. Eros loved his invitation.

'Very well, Your Royal Highness, you can go in. Park on the right in the field, someone will direct you,' the security man said, glancing over Angel's muddied outfit. 'Pity about the dress, miss.'

'What did he say to you?' Angel asked as she drove towards the field.

'He gave me a title, Angel. I am Prince Eros of Alonissos.'

'Huh,' she said, unimpressed. 'I will have to borrow a new outfit from Leah. I think yours will clean up. I only threw one bit of mud. What's your name again?' she asked.

'Eros Savidis. I rarely use my title; it is too . . .'

'Pretentious? Dan's cousin, you said?' Angel smiled. 'Ah, I know - you're the fellow who thinks he's a prince. I remember Leah telling me about you, mister!'

As she parked the car, Eros said, 'Angel, what a beautiful name for a beautiful woman.'

'Cheesy,' Angel scoffed. Then: 'You don't mind if

I get changed before this mammoth dancing session?' she asked with her sweetest smile.

'No. I may get changed too,' he said. 'I need to be presentable to dance with a beautiful woman all night long.'

'What if I lose? What do I give you?' Angel enquired with no intention of losing.

Eros glanced across at her. 'A kiss.'

'Just a kiss?'

'Not just any but a proper kiss, Angel.' The way he said it sounded so sexy, so inviting.

She shrugged, not showing her feelings. 'Deal.'

'Which we need to seal right here, with another kiss,' Eros added as he watched her eyes scrunch up. 'The deal was struck here on this property. Therefore, the kiss must be engaged here.'

Angel gave up. She leaned over. 'Go on then, Prince Eros. One quick kiss.'

Eros reached over, took her face in his hands and gently ran his thumbs down her cheekbones. Angel's eyes opened wide in surprise; she hadn't expected this. Eros took her lips in a tender kiss, sneaking his tongue into her mouth. As the kiss deepened, instead of pushing him off, Angel found she was clinging to his jacket lapels. Her breathing had sped up, her eyes dilated as he pulled away.

'That's called a Greek god's kiss,' Eros murmured against her lips.

Clipping him around the ear, she hissed, 'God, you're so up yourself!' She climbed out of the car and passed him the keys. 'Come on, lock the car and let's find Leah. I need a new dress.'

Eros retrieved his case from the car boot. Brushing himself down, pleased with the effect he'd had on her, he said: 'Let the challenge begin.'

As ANGEL and Eros walked towards the house, she noted with surprise that her mum Sylvie and her dad Andrew had arrived as their car was already parked up. She was amazed her mum had managed to persuade him to move from his armchair and actually go to the wedding. He usually arrived late and left early but for some reason he had agreed to come. Amazing! She knew Leah would be so delighted to see them both as they very rarely ventured out of the village after work. Her mum Sylvie was Grandad Thomas's only daughter. Oh well, Angel was pleased they were here, as it would do her mum good. Her parents both worked very hard at the local stately home and a party was just what her mum needed.

LEAH SOON FOUND Angel something to wear. 'It has to make me drop-dead gorgeous, Leah,' Angel urged her, 'because that man is so far up his own backside that I need to teach him a lesson. I'm going to try to make him fall in love with me.' She giggled.

'I get the picture. You *are* drop-dead gorgeous, Angel. Look in the mirror, even in the muddied dress. Here, try this dress on, in fact, keep it. I've been meaning to go through my wardrobe and get some things out for you.'

Leah had dug out an emerald-green dress which highlighted Angel's eyes and her rich red hair. She handed it over and said, 'Come on now, let's get back to the dancing because everyone seems legless.'

'I need a vodka,' Angel said, taking off her soiled white dress and being helped on with the green one. 'Hmm, I might try two vodkas. I could do with them.'

'Well, Joey is legless without even trying, Ben isn't faring much better, and it's only a quarter past five. So, do you fancy Eros?' Leah asked, interestedly.

'Maybe, but he loves himself so much, doesn't he?' Angel then confessed. 'We might have had a bet.'

'A bet?'

'Yes. You see, Marvin broke down over the moors. I think he's had it: gone to car heaven and all. So, Eros was driving on the wrong side of the road in his fancy Merc. Almost killed me. I leaped out of the way, straight into a puddle, hence the muddy face and dress. Don't worry, though - I chucked some mud at him too, smug git, as he was laughing at me. I explained my car had died so we had a bet: if I can dance with him all night, he will buy me a new car.' Angel scoffed. 'Easy-peasy, lemon-squeezy.'

'Not so fast, young lady. I've seen him drink Scotty and Sisco under the table, and that man can dance all night long.' Leah's eyes sparkled. 'This should be fun – but it's got to be a fair fight. You cannot let Yorkshire down. You *cannot* - you hear me, Angel? And you must play fair.'

'Oh, what have I got myself into?' Angel moaned. 'Come on then, lead me to my doom.'

'All I said was, you have to play fair. I said nothing about anyone else. I'm sure Joey will help you in whatever way you want. I am with you, Angel: I agree that Eros needs taking down a peg or two. I thought Dan was arrogant, but Eros is much worse, and only you can do it. So, are you going to beat him?' Leah pulled back her shoulders and watched Angel do the same. 'This way, Angel. All of Whitby – no, all of *Great Britain* is behind you.'

DAN AND EROS watched Leah and Angel shimmy across the dance floor, both dressed up to the nines.

'Wow,' Eros muttered to himself. Had he kissed *that* woman?

'Angel, how lovely to see you, you look stunning,' Dan said politely. 'I'm so pleased Leah could help you out.' He stood up and kissed her cheek. 'I believe you know my cousin, Eros?'

Angel grinned. 'Yes, we've met.' Turning to the Greek, she asked, 'So, Eros, what time do we start the clock?'

Eros studied her in the green dress. She was his idea of gorgeous. 'I was thinking around nine o'clock.'

'Good, I can eat my dinner first. I'm starving. Remember, I've been walking on the tops of the moor.' Angel looked at Eros's glass. 'What are you drinking?'

'*Neró*,' Eros said with a grin, his Greek accent sending Angel's pulse skyrocketing.

'Water, he's drinking water, Angel,' Dan explained with a laugh.

'Oh, don't you drink?' Angel asked, and shared glances with Leah.

'Not when there is a car at stake. But we will see. I believe I could out-drink you, Angel. You are just a woman,' Eros challenged, then he saw Dan flicking his hand across his throat.

'I'm up for a drinking competition. Yes, instead of dancing, what do you say?' confirmed Angel with a sly grin.

Dan leaned in. 'Watch out, Eros. I've been through this with her and believe it or not, I had to give up before she'd even got really started.'

'I'm not a Greek man for nothing, Dan.' Eros stood up, his pride to the fore. 'Let's go to the bar, Angel. Where you will meet your doom.'

'I thought you were in a dancing competition?' Leah muttered. 'Grandad is going to go mad if you end up helplessly drunk, Angel. You will make yourself ill. It's not good for you, and we are not teenagers.'

'You practise drinking often, Angel?' Eros held his arm out for her.

'She certainly does,' Dan intervened. 'She has recently been banned from riding horses under the influence of alcohol by the local police constabulary. Her charge was for drinking with a local farmer then recklessly racing his horses down the beach at two o'clock in the morning.' Dan knew all about it because he'd been woken up and asked to stable the two horses overnight.

'Bring it on,' Eros said airily. 'Come, Angel, let us take a seat at the bar.'

When they'd gone, Dan asked his wife, 'What was all *that* about?'

'He almost killed her by driving on the right side of the road, or in his case the wrong side. Her car had broken down. Long story short, he bet her if she could dance with him all night, he'd buy her a new car. I think the stakes have just escalated.' Leah looked a bit apprehensive.

'It will be interesting to see it play out, but I don't like the idea of a drinking competition.' Dan moved next to Leah, murmuring into her neck, 'You are so beautiful in that dress, my gorgeous wife.'

'I think you're biased.' Leah planted a kiss to his lips.

A squeal was heard coming from the dance floor. It was Joey who, having spotted Eros, had flung himself into the man's arms, causing him to stagger back. 'My hero, Eros! You missed my nuptials, you naughty man, but you are here now and that means a lot to me.'

Eros's eyes were out on stalks. He liked Joey, but he was not altogether comfortable around gay men. 'Joey, good to see you. Congratulations, and I'm so sorry I missed the big moment. I see your husband is waiting over there. I'm with Angel tonight.'

'Oh yes, you're my hubbie now, Ben.' Joey turned around and sashayed across the dance floor to his husband as if he was Zsa Zsa Gabor.

Alice came and scrambled up on Dan's knee. 'Will you dance with me, Daddy? Please, Daddy?'

'I thought you were dancing with Tom and his gang?' Dan asked, sparing a glance in the crowd of people in the marquee.

Alice shook her head. 'He's dancing with that Floozy girl.'

'Oh, you mean the Floozy girl has cornered him,' Leah beamed.

'Leah, that's not very nice, calling her a floozy.' Dan scowled, his wife wasn't normally so insensitive.

'That's what I've heard about her, Dan. That she is an out-an-out Floozy, and our son is dancing with her.' Leah gave him a cheeky look.

'In that case, we need to get Tom away from her, whatever her name is.' Dan got up and strode over to Tom and his partner, but when he reached them on the dance floor, he stopped. He'd recognise a Greek girl anywhere.

Beautiful brown eyes looked up at him as if to say, 'Who are you?'

'Introduce me, son,' Dan ordered, smiling down into the pretty girl's face.

Tom grinned. 'Ferrara, this is my dad. Dad, this is Ferrara, or Floozy.'

'Floozy?' Dan looked across at Leah and Alice, to see his wife was laughing like mad. 'Nice to meet you. What a lovely name. What does your father do?'

'He owns a chain of Greek restaurants in this area, but he has a passion for our pet Flop-Eared rabbit. He calls me Floozy sometimes after the rabbit but my real name is Ferrara.' She sniffed. 'Dads can be really annoying sometimes, can't they?'

'True, yes, very true,' Dan coughed. 'Right, great job, carry on dancing, kids. Treat her well, Tom. I need to speak to your mother,' and he strode off after Leah as she fled the marquee laughing to herself. He caught up with her on the steps of Charlie's Chicken van. 'Hey, you! You tried to set me up, woman.'

'I did not, he does call her Floozy,' Leah countered with a huge grin.

'I will exact my revenge on you, right now.' Scooping up Leah and putting her over his shoulder, he said, 'Try to trick me, will you, wife? I agree her father is an imbecile calling the poor child that, but . . . well, you need punishment!'

As he strode off towards the house, Leah struggled to get down but had nothing to hold on to. Since he didn't have his jacket on, she pulled his shirt out of his trousers.

'I wouldn't do that if I were you,' he warned. 'Your backside is right in my line of fire.'

Leah carried on wriggling and received a slap to her posterior. 'I'm not frightened of your paltry threats, Dan Ryan.'

'And I, Mrs Ryan-Savidis, am not used to you setting me up like that.' He opened the door, striding past his security men as they looked on with interest.

'My wife needs putting in her place. Any objections?' The men shook their heads with a grin.

Leah was laughing. She didn't know how he was managing it, carrying her up two steps at a time. Adrenalin, she guessed. He plonked down on the bed and dragged her face-down over his knee.

'Don't you dare, Dan Ryan,' Leah warned him.

'Oh, for that trick I think I ought to.'

'Stop it, Dan. I was just having a laugh,' squeaked Leah.

'And I'm just checking out the underwear, so shut up, woman.'

'Don't you dare tell me to shut up.'

He hauled her onto the bed and lay on top of her. 'That's better. I can see the fire in your eyes now. I love to see you burn up for me.' With that, he kissed her.

Clothes fell in a heap around the floor, and soon they were moving together as if they'd been missing from each other for years. Their lovemaking was always passionate and fulfilling. In the aftermath, they cuddled.

Then Dan saw the time on his watch. 'Come on, we have to get back to the party and I need to take the dogs out. You go back, and I will be with you as soon as I can.'

'OK, darling.'

She dressed herself hastily and had almost

finished when he growled, 'Set me up again like that and I will take it out on your backside.'

'Yeah, yeah.' But then Leah raced off so fast she didn't have time to put her shoes on, she just grabbed them and ran. She heard his laughter and grinned happily. Bring it on lover-boy, she thought.

CHELSEA HERSELF WASN'T happy at all. Why, when she had put all the elements in place for utter chaos to ensue, had it not gone wrong? She'd have to find another way to ruin it all. Pepper and Chelsea were outside the bar by now and that was when she saw the cases of Polish vodka. Elbowing Pepper, she muttered, 'Collect all the water jugs. I'm going to doctor the water.'

Pepper stared at the bottle of vodka Chelsea had just picked up. 'You can't do it with that - those who drink it won't be able to stand for a week!'

'Oh yes I can, and I will. Come on, get a move on. I want the water jugs from every table - even the one at the bar. Eros made a fool out of me on several occasions so now it's payback for him too,' Chelsea ranted.

Pepper shrugged and went to collect the water carriers. Her eyes roved over the tall Greek at the bar. He was good-looking, but not as attractive as the big hulk who was now watching her from the door of the marquee. His eyes held a definite promise, and before the night was out, Pepper knew he would be hers.

Fetching the water jugs, Pepper watched Chelsea putting in two-thirds vodka and one-third water. Swaying her hips at the big man at the entrance, Pepper flirted with him as she went to place the water jugs on the table beside him.

'Fancy a glass of water, gentlemen?' Pepper asked.

Blue Eyes shook his head. 'No, thank you.'

'Well, it's here if you need it and I'm just through there if you want me, big man,' she said as she walked back past the bar, throwing a smouldering look over her shoulder at him to see he was watching her every move. She curled her finger towards him, encouraging him to come to her, which he did.

'Do you need help with those jugs?' asked Mr Blue Eyes.

'Yes, please. And then I'm going to take a break. When is your break due?'

'Oh, right after we've finished doling out these water jugs,' he smirked.

Pepper couldn't wait, but where could she take him? Maybe to the barn, just down the lane.

When she'd finished the last table Pepper said to Chelsea, 'I'm taking my break now.'

Chelsea glanced across at the pair. 'Don't take too long.'

'Lighten up, lady.' Mr Blue Eyes pointed to his friend. 'He's available, just tell him I sent you.'

But Chelsea didn't seem interested in sex with his friend or any other man. She wanted to see the downfall of the bitch who stole Dan away from her.

14

THE RENDEZVOUS

Dan raced through the woods to his rendezvous with Madness and the girls, but his energy was depleted. Madness had just sent the text when she saw Dan doubled over, getting his breath.

'At last, I just texted you!' she called.

Dan caught his breath then winked at the woman who had made his dream come true. Somewhere, back in the marquee, his phone beeped with the text.

Madness: *Where are you? You should be here by now. Please don't tell me Leah has discovered what we are up to. The girls are waiting for you, and they are getting anxious. Hurry up, gorgeous man, they need your kisses as you promised. XOX*

Would he be able to match all their kisses? Still, she was only bringing two of her girls. Or so she said when she had slipped away from the party because her husband had gone for a lie-down. He was already as drunk as a skunk. However, when Dan arrived in the clearing, five girls were sitting in the van, all with pretty ribbons in their hair.

Kissing Madness on the cheek, he exclaimed, 'Goodness, you brought all your girls! I haven't got the energy for all five, Madness.'

'Really? I don't believe you.' Madness went to the van. He couldn't tell her he'd just been having nooky with Leah only minutes earlier - she'd be green with envy as her husband was probably fast asleep by now. And they had their agenda to complete.

'I'll take two, then three,' he said. 'I see you've got a blanket down for me. That's so considerate of you.'

'We don't want you to get dirty, do we?'

'I will have Miss Pink and Miss Yellow for now.' Dan searched their pretty faces. Wow. These girls were *so* beautiful.

'Mummy, Daddy's phone is beepin' in his jacket pocket. I fink someone needs him.' Alice pointed to his jacket on the back of the chair in the marquee.

Leah reached in and took the little payphone out of his inside pocket. She frowned. This wasn't Dan's phone. She typed in her birthday as the code and the phone opened, so he was as predictable as ever, but she didn't understand. There, in big, bold letters, was a message from someone called Madness, and the words made no sense.

Leah put the phone face down on the table. She felt utterly sick to her stomach. Was this Chelsea's doing? The atmosphere from the party had been sucked out of the room like an evil force for Leah, although the reception was going well for everyone else. Even Aunt Penny was dancing. She pushed the little burner phone away as if it was something evil. Then she picked it up again. Those words made her think her marriage was over – but how could that be when they'd just made love?

Raising her eyes to look around the room, she realised there was something badly wrong. Everyone seemed out of their tree. Sophie and Grandad Thomas were slinging things which resembled chicken nuggets at a dartboard. Charlie from the chicken van was encouraging them, guffawing. She looked at the wine carafe then the water jug on everyone's table. Picking one carafe up, she poured a drop into her glass and took a sip of the wine first. That was OK. She then poured from the water jug, sipped and coughed violently. Lord, it was pure alcohol.

The story was the same on each table: someone had doctored the jugs. Collecting them up, she placed them on the bar, asking a nearby security man to empty, rinse and refill the water jugs with fresh water before returning to her table. She didn't trust anyone else behind the bar.

'Let's get you to bed, baby,' Leah whispered to Alice. She wanted to cry, to sob her heart out. Not that she had a heart left as it was in tatters.

Sophie was boss-eyed as she dumped down a massive plate of nuggets and sandwiches, slurring, 'Your grandfather and I can do that, Leah my darling. We can put our granddaughter to bed and then go to bed ourselves because I feel very tipsy and I've only drunk two glasses of wine and three glasses of water.'

Leah glanced at her grandad. He was looking a bit green - and then she saw Ruby and Sisco on their hands and knees, laughing their heads off, playing some kind of game. What on earth was going on? Over at the bar, Eros and Angel were leaning against each other to remain upright on their bar stools. Let them get on with it! But then she noticed the bar staff were lurching around too, obviously drunk. And where was Dan when she needed him? With his girls, no doubt - and who the hell was Madness?

Aunt Penny stumbled over to the table accompanied by Howard. The pair were intoxicated, and Aunt Penny had something akin to sticking plasters flapping off her face.

'What's that on your face?' Leah found she could

barely form words.

'My stick-on eye . . . eye . . . eye . . .'

'Eyebrows,' Leah finished, checking the plastic eyebrows. They were ridiculous. Why hadn't she noticed them earlier?

'They're lovely, I'm falling in love with thish woman,' Howard managed. He sat down heavily on the chair, burped noisily and fell fast asleep.

Leah put the burner phone in her jacket pocket. She had to get away to read all these messages to understand what was going on. For her, the party was most definitely over. 'Come on, let's get you all back to the house and put the coffee on.'

Tom came and sat with them. 'Is it me, Mum, or is everyone drunk? Well, everyone except Uncle Andrew. He's not moved all night.'

Leah had to laugh. 'Uncle Andrew always looks like rigor mortis has set in.' She ruffled her son's hair. 'No, Tom, the more pressing matter is the water jugs have been tampered with. Right, everyone on this table, let's get back to the house. Aunt Penny, let me take those false eyebrows off your face.' Leah looked twice at Sophie now she was close up, and frowned. 'Sophie, your skin is so blotchy. What on earth's happened?'

'I thought my face was itching after that woman put foundation on me. I wonder if Ruby's make-up is OK?' Sophie started clawing at her face.

On the dance floor, Ruby and Sisco were now happily doing the Cha-cha-cha, with Ben and Joey competing.

DAN WAS in his seventh heaven. He'd had more kisses than he could deal with. If he'd been the one wearing the lipstick, it would have long since worn off. Thankfully he wasn't. The girls had got back into the van. Miss Baby-Pink was luscious, he thought dreamily. Her curves, her beautiful arse and those breathtaking dark brown eyes with ultra-long lashes were spectacular. She was a great kisser too. He'd left Madness, but he knew he must get back to the wedding. Leah would miss him, and he needed to act cool as if nothing had happened.

MR BLUE EYES and Pepper had just got their naked bodies dressed again when he received a text message.

'So, did you just get hired to do the waitressing?' the big man asked as he glanced down at his phone.

Pepper nodded, feeling on top of the world after the amazing sex. 'I did the make-up for the old ladies too.'

'Are you free tomorrow?'

Pepper gazed up at him. 'I am, do you want to meet up?'

'Yes, down near the harbour swing bridge, but right now I need to get back. It seems everyone is falling about, off their trollies, and I need to know why.' Mr Blue Eyes kissed Pepper again, lingeringly, with the promise of more pleasant things to come. 'I can book us into a hotel if you like?'

Pepper smiled. 'I'd like that a lot.'

Taking her hand, they strolled back up to the marquee and saw Dan running up the path as fast as he could.

'Now, he looks like a man who's been up to something,' the security man noted.

'He does, doesn't he?' Pepper mused. 'I wonder what?' Had Chelsea got through to him?

ALICE WAS TUCKED up in bed, asleep the moment her head touched the pillow. Tom was on coffee duty, and Leah went to find Dan by way of the marquee, where she saw drunken people everywhere. Then she noticed him, looking around the marquee, confused because everyone was falling around. He strode across to Leah.

'What has happened here?' he asked, wincing

guiltily as he saw his wife's face looking back emotionlessly at him.

'How should I know?' Leah snapped. 'I've been trying to sober up your mother and my grandad and tons more of the guests. The water jugs had been doctored with vodka! Everyone has been drinking at least some of what seems like pure vodka to me. And we know who'll be responsible for that. Don't we?'

'Why are you angry with me?' he said defensively, his sexual after-glow fading fast.

'Because you were swanning off somewhere. Where have you been? You said you were taking the dogs for a walk but I found them ready to pee on the floor!'

'Look, I can explain.' Never before had he felt so shifty and wretched. While he'd been sneaking away, cheating on his wife, all hell had broken loose.

'Not now, Dan!' she burst out. 'We need to get coffee down these people or proper water, and keep a close eye on them. They've been drinking neat vodka. It's downright dangerous!'

Dan felt a hot rage. 'Chelsea is behind this, without any doubt. We have to stop everyone from leaving in their cars.'

'Oh God, I'd not thought about that.' Leah didn't know if there was anyone sober, only herself and Dan. 'You'd better tell security. No one leaves.'

'I will arrange for some taxis to come and take people home. Thank God most of them have their Campers with them. Where can Eros and Angel sleep?'

'Together, by the looks of it. We'll worry about that later.' Leah jerked when Dan leaned down to kiss her. She could smell a feminine perfume on him. She pushed him away. 'Go, go. I will try to get Angel and Eros sobered up.'

She had never spurned him like this. Dan could understand why she was so upset. He walked out to stop anyone leaving, but they were all in such a state, he didn't even think they'd try.

'YOU ARE A NAUGHTY GIRL, ANGEL,' Eros said incoherently. God, this woman could drink. He nearly fell off the barstool, his balance going again. The barman, he noticed, was slumped against a barrel: was he part of the competition too? Eros could barely think straight.

'Ah, Leah,' he said blearily, as she came over. 'I think your cousin has wine herself a car.'

'Angel *won* a car, Eros, and I shall remind you of that tomorrow morning when you will have forgotten,' Leah confirmed. 'I've seen you in action before, remember, but you'd not met my cousin then. Her dad drinks home-brew, so she's what we call here in York-shire "a seasoned drinker".'

'What is this home brew?' Eros asked, his words not forming properly.

'The local name for it is "Wasted". Right, no more to drink, the pair of you,' Leah ordered.

'Not yet, we are having another drink,' Angel slurred.

'Oh no, you're not! Someone has been doctoring the drinks. We'll be lucky if we get out of this wedding without a fatality.' Leah watched Eros frowning.

'That's terrible, isn't it?' Eros managed, his eyes looking in two different directions as he finally fell off the barstool.

Leah tried to catch him, but he was a tall and muscular man and she had no chance. He collapsed on to the ground, a snore escaping him.

'Aha! I won a car. I won a car.' Angel was ecstatic until Leah explained.

'You have - *if* he can remember. Now, I need you to serve coffee to everyone. Eros, wake up and get up, you drunken sod. Angel, first get some coffee down Eros and yourself. I will make some up in the flasks over there. I'll be back in a few ticks.'

Charlie the chicken man was comatose on a chair as she ran past him. Thankfully, the guests on the dance floor were flagging now. Leah threw instant coffee into the flasks and ran around, placing them onto tables where people were sitting, and where cups and saucers were laid out. At the bar, she poured three cups out, saying strongly, 'Barman, wake up. Drink this coffee.'

Eros had managed to hoist himself back on the barstool now. 'Is that coffee? I need some as I have a competition to win.'

'You've already surrendered, Eros. She's won, and you owe her a new car.'.

'Never take on a Yorkshire woman at a drinking competition when she's beaten a Yorkshire farmer at the same game,' Angel said, poking Eros in the chest and nearly sending him off the barstool again.

'Huh. I'm sure you cheated.' Eros was not magnanimous in defeat. He groaned and clutched his head. 'Have you got any headache tablets?'

'A bet is a bet.' Angel was still speaking indistinctly but slurping the strong coffee and grimacing.

'You were down each other's throats not half an hour ago, so play nicely, make friends and drink your coffee. I will get you some tablets, Eros,' Leah confirmed, then she turned and stopped as she saw Dan watching her fondly. He was the image of a Greek god himself, standing all proud and handsome, but she had to remember he'd just been meeting someone called Madness and her girls.

Dan strode over and took her in his arms, whispering, 'We can sort this, Leah. Joey and Ben are just as paralytic as the rest of them. I've ordered taxis for the people who live away from us, but most have their campervans to crash in. I'm going to get the security team to help our friends to their beds.'

Leah nodded, then she pulled out of his arms, saying tersely, 'I need to get Eros some headache tablets.'

'Forget about that. Look, he has forgotten about it already. He's cuddling up to Angel on the dance floor for their marathon dancing session.' Dan grinned.

'She's already won the car. He changed the bet to a drinking one, and he conceded about ten minutes ago,' Leah explained. 'I'd better make some more coffee.'

'I'll help.' Dan took her hand in his and walked with her back to the urn. 'I'll get more water.'

'Where have you been?' Leah asked outright, and he had the decency to blush right up to his neck.

'Erm, I went to check on the girls to see if they'd dropped any more foals. Why?' Dan asked, avoiding her gaze.

'Because Alice wanted you to tuck her in.' Leah went to see if any of the flasks needed refilling. She patted the phone in her jacket pocket. She would read all the messages later. By now, people were vomiting outside on the grass, and moaning; it was deeply worrying. Then she saw the two waitresses scuttling around in the back of the marquee. 'Hey, you two!' she called. 'What are you doing here? Come and help these people.'

Leah marched after them, but by the time she reached the back of the marquee and was out in the open air they had disappeared - and that was when she saw Ethel lying on the ground. Leah immediately raced back inside, calling, 'Dan, Dan! Phone for an ambulance, quick! Ethel is collapsed out here.' She ran back outside to put her jacket around Ethel, then began stroking her hair and talking to her. 'Come on, Ethel. You're going to be OK. Talk to me, Ethel.'

BY THE TIME they crawled into bed, it was 4 a.m. Eros and Angel had said they were sharing a room. They were two consenting adults, even if they were very drunk. Leah shrugged. 'I've put clean sheets on in the bedroom just down the hallway on your right.'

Even though Eros could see two Angels in front of him giggling, he managed to say, 'Are you still game, Angel, for a marathon night?'

Angel laughed out loud, staggering and bumping into Dan as she pointed a finger at Eros, saying, 'Let's see who passes out first.'

Eros grabbed Leah and kissed her full on the mouth. 'Thank you, Leah, for the most amazing wedding party ever.' Leering at Dan, he added, 'I always wondered why you chose him over me. I'm just as rich you know.'

Leah pushed him off. 'Money wasn't a factor, Eros. Love was.'

'Please tell me you are kidding. Don't I stand a chance?' Eros grunted. Leah could smell the alcohol on his breath.

'Angel,' she said, 'take him off to bed, for heaven's sake. Make him sleep on the chaise if you want to. You'll find extra bedding in the wardrobe. I'm sorry, I need go and lie down.' Leah wanted to add 'alone', but she didn't; she was way too tired and worried about their guests for a big confrontation and maybe, just maybe, there was an explanation about all this.

She had hidden the burner phone to read it when she didn't have a migraine. Her headache had started after the paramedics arrived and taken to hospital not just Ethel but several more people who were suffering from alcoholic poisoning. She would have to phone the hospital tomorrow to check on Ethel and the others, then she must find out what had gone so wrong and who was behind it. This was an extremely serious situation, for which she and Dan, as hosts, were responsible.

CHELSEA WAS FUMING; not everything had gone to plan because some dozy trollop named Leah had mucked it up by being too clever. Sitting at the kitchen table, she slurped her coffee and switched to the remote camera Pepper had placed in a strategic location. Lines danced across the phone and then the picture got clearer. Then it happened. The man had sat down to wee. He then stood up and turned to flush, his 'bits' and bum fleetingly on display. He pressed the flush, and the noise almost deafened her.

'Ugh. *Ugh!*' She threw the phone on the table as the door opened and Brioche and Pepper walked in.

'You imbecile!' she roared at him. 'You should have kidnapped Dan when he was drunk. What went wrong? I ordered you to stick him in the van and bring him back here. He should have been in the tower by now. Why didn't you do it, Brioche? I mean, why did we bother to swap all the water for extra-strong Polish vodka so you could let Dan escape, hmm - and why were all my plans scuppered?' Chelsea thumped his chest, causing him to fold-up in pain.

'He'd disappeared, all right? I searched for him everywhere. I mean, that was a good ploy, wasn't it? Getting Dan and Leah drunk when they were the only two who were sober,' he muttered. 'Besides, I heard Leah saying the caterers phoned her and the flower people too. That was nothing to do with me.'

'What about the marquees? They should have been flat by morning. You said they would collapse if we did what you said. Me and Pepper undid all the ratchets, but it seemed someone else fastened them up again. So, what went wrong?' Or should I say *who*?' Chelsea was almost steaming with rage when she rounded on Pepper. 'Everything ran smoothly for the family until my last-minute brainwave of doctoring the water. And then you, Pepper, you were to get a discreet camera into the kitchen, the hub of the house - and all I saw this morning was some man sitting bare-arsed on the toilet! Ugh, I'm damaged for life. All I've got are buffoons, no - baboons - surrounding me.'

'I just read the instructions wrong. The ratchets stop it from falling down in a storm, so I assumed with them undone the marquees would collapse. You should have checked yourself if it was so important to spoil someone's wedding day,' Brioche muttered.

Chelsea prodded Brioche's chest again. 'Today, you will figure out how to kidnap Dan. Last night should have been the perfect opportunity. And why didn't the pony go berserk when you put the pinecone under the saddle? Come on, Pepper, can you tell me why?'

'The answer is simple: because I'm not hurting a child, that's why. For God's sake, Chelsea, why don't you stop obsessing about this man and leave these people alone. They are a nice family and you should have forgotten about them long ago. I'm done with this stupid vendetta.' Pepper stormed out of the room, throwing in her wake, 'I have a date with one of the security men. See you later.'

Chelsea turned back to Brioche, who was just sidling out of the room. 'Stay put, you. You need to find a way of kidnapping Dan. So, get your thinking cap on, or else. I'm going into York by myself, and I won't be back until late morning or early afternoon. He needs kidnapping today and to be in the tower when I get home.' Chelsea tottered into the other room, going after Pepper. Hmm, she thought, if only Dan had drunk some of the vodka-water, he would have been ready for her hypnosis.

'The tower' as she had named it, was the attic rooms in which they had put down an old bed, a chair, a desk and a speaker system. They'd already placed a rope up there to tie him up, and Brioche had put a bolt on the door to the smaller room where Dan would be held, and then she could go to work on him. All was ready for when they kidnapped Dan, which she hoped would be soon. She had been practising her hypnosis. He would soon be hers.

15

AN ACHING HEART

W hen Leah opened her eyes, the first thing she remembered was the burner phone and the messages from Madness and the girls; it felt all-consuming. She glanced to her side; Dan had already left. There was a note on the pillowcase: *Gone out for a ride onto the moors with Galahad. I didn't wake you as you looked tired out. Love you, Dan X0X.*

Leah put the note to her heart and held it there for what seemed like an age. Could she save her marriage? First things first, she must read the full extent of the text messages on the phone, no matter how much they hurt. Taking the phone out of the hiding place she'd put it in last night, she read and re-read the messages, trying to understand what was going on. She needed to forward these messages to her phone, so she had a copy of them, and maybe sometime later today she could text Madness on the pretence that Dan wanted to meet Love and Sexy Bum, or maybe Baby Pink again.

First, she must get a shower and see if Alice was OK. By the sounds of it, people were milling about in the kitchen making breakfast and drinking juice for their sore heads. She wondered if Eros and Angel had woken up yet. They'd both be in for a big surprise, but even that couldn't bring a smile to her face. She must try to get a grip, then get back to reality, even if it was the last place she wanted to be right now.

DAN HAD BEEN out riding for about an hour. Galahad had enjoyed a good gallop over the track on the top of the moors to let off steam, and both horse and rider had exalted in the warm breeze rushing past them. Now they were trotting their way back down. More often than not Leah went with him, but she'd looked so pale and exhausted that he'd left her to sleep and him to ponder what to do. Dan reckoned he should come clean to his wife about what was going on. Then, spotting Brian the Hereford bull quite a way down the fields, standing guard on the track, he changed course, a trail that would take him through the grounds of Sledborough House. His whole point was to avoid Brian because Brian fancied Galahad something wicked. Maybe the bull thought Galahad was a cow?

Dan laughed out loud to himself, making Galahad whicker. Alice had taken a liking to old Brian when they'd been at the local auction mart, and Eric the farmer who owned him had put her onto the big bull's back. She had begged Eric to take the old Hereford bull home and not sell him, so Eric had brought him back to the hill farm. Dan smiled at the thought of his cute four-year-old convincing a hardened farmer like Eric to save the bull's life. Somehow Dan thought Brian might be joining them at their farm soon if Alice had anything to do with it.

As Dan rode down the side of the heather track, he didn't see the adder moving through the grass until it darted at Galahad, sinking its fangs into his front fetlock. The stallion squealed and struck out with his hoof. He reared, throwing Dan out of the saddle and onto the ground with a thud. The adder hissed and attacked again, causing the horse to bolt across the moors towards home. Dan lay unconscious on the ground, and there was blood trickling down his face. The snake disappeared into the heather.

By chance, Brioche had watched the incident from the front door, where he was standing breathing in the fresh morning air; the panicked horse galloped close by him on its way up the track. He saw Dan lying on the ground and ran up to him. At first, he thought Dan was dead. Then, noting that he was still breathing, Brioche lifted Dan over his shoulder and walked towards the house. It was hard getting up two lots of stairs, but he was thankful he'd not been amongst the people with the killer hangovers. Soon he had got Dan up in the tower, and laid him gently down on the bed.

He then ran back downstairs to get a first-aid kit and decided that once he'd cleaned Dan's head wound, he would make his mind up what to do. One thing he knew, his mobile signal was rubbish up here so he hoped someone would come looking for Dan before Chelsea got back, but just to make sure, he rang Dan's home, then Joey's home and mobile. Unfortunately, there was no answer on any of them.

EROS OPENED HIS EYES, putting a hand to his splitting head. *Bang, bang, bang,* his head was thumping, his mouth tasted like a cesspit on fire, and that's when he realised someone was lying next to him, breathing loudly. He couldn't think straight. Where was he? Who was in his bed? Oh, for heaven's sake, he prayed it wasn't Joey. He'd never live it down. He was a man who loved women. So as not to wake the person at his side, he turned to see long red hair sprawled out all over the pillow. Wow, not Joey, thank goodness.

He glanced down over the young woman's bare body where she'd pushed the covers back, his eyes roving over the luscious breasts to her shapely hips. Despite his horrendous hangover, his body reacted. No, no, no, he couldn't afford to get smitten with this girl. Did he remember her name? No, not yet. His banging head refused to work.

First, Eros knew he urgently needed to clean his teeth and gargle with mouthwash, or he might knock her out with his alcohol breath. Respect grew for this woman who had won the drinking competition - he remembered that much. Twice, to his recollection, he'd fallen off the barstool, only to find those incredible green eyes laughing at him. Creeping out of the very comfortable bed, he tiptoed to the en-suite bathroom. After having a wee and cleaning his teeth, a long shower would sort him out.

Eros felt much better after brushing his teeth and gargling, as was his daily routine. He noticed some effervescent stuff in a tin, mixed it with water and swallowed the lot, almost choking on the bubbles. Then he walked into the shower cubicle, feeling exalted under the refreshing hot water. What was he going to do about the girl? Then her name came to him from nowhere. She was Angel, she was Leah and Joey's cousin. Oh God, way to go, Eros. Busy thinking about this apparent problem, he didn't hear Angel come into the bathroom. She too did a wee, brushed her teeth, then opened the shower door.

'Is there room for a small one?' Angel asked as she dropped her towel.

Eros groaned. How could a man resist such an invitation? He scooped her up into his arms and placed her next to the wall in the large shower. 'Enough room for you, Angel.' Because now Eros knew he wasn't thinking with the right *nor* the left side of his brain; he was thinking with his dick, and any self-recrimination would come after raunchy shower sex. He was a Greek god, after all. Or was that a Prince?

QUINN WAS JUST CLEANING out a stable when he heard a horse gallop into the fold yard. Galahad was careering into the yard, slipping and sliding on the dry cobbles. There was blood on his fetlock; his nostrils were deep-red and his eyes wild. The horse was wet through with sweat, panicked and snorting.

'Steady, fella, steady, Galahad.' Quinn grabbed the broken rein. He saw one stirrup was missing. Going down the stallion's leg with a gentle hand, he could see where the small amount of blood was coming from. Galahad stamped his foot. Quinn called for help from one of the stable hands, then phoned the local vet on happenchance he was in the area, but he also urgently needed to tell Leah about Dan because as sure as eggs were eggs, his employer had taken a tumble from the big horse.

He phoned Leah's mobile and got through to her straight away. Within half an hour, people were out searching for Dan. Ruby was looking after Alice while Tom went with his Grandad Thomas and Grandma Sophie to help in the search.

Sisco and Scotty joined in too, Scotty grumbling, 'Why on earth did he have to ride out this morning when we're all so ruddy hungover?'

LEAH WAS busy organising search parties when Eros and Angel strolled into the kitchen. Eros dropped his hand from Angel's then he moved it to the small of her back to guide her inside.

'What's all the commotion? I heard Aunt Sophie saying she was going to search for Dan,' Eros asked in his broken English. He knew Leah well, and she seemed so distraught, her eyes full of tears.

'Dan is missing. He was out on his horse Galahad early this morning, riding across the moors. Galahad has had a snake bite, and he has galloped home without Dan. Could you and Angel go to Joey and

Ben's cottage and ask them to call me on my mobile?' Leah pleaded. 'I can't get through, both phones are off the hook. We need everyone's help, and I mean everyone. Stanley, the lovely old customer from the café had a terrible fall and died up there. I can't bear it if Dan is injured and no one can find him. There's only me and Joey who know the far part of the moors to search.'

Eros held out his hand again to Angel. 'Can you lend Angel a pair of jeans and a T-shirt?'

'And a coat, Leah, I know how cold those moors can be,' Angel added, also having local knowledge.

'Just go to my wardrobe, Angel,' Leah said distractedly. 'You'll find something in there, and the wellies are down here in the boot room.'

Ruby thrust a take-away coffee into Eros's hands. 'I'd let Angel drive your car. She knows the back way through the estate, Eros.'

The tall, good-looking Greek nodded sagely. 'We are on our way soon. Come, lovely Leah. He will be fine.' Eros cuddled Leah to him. 'Cry on my shoulder if you must.' He drank the coffee while keeping a good hold of the distraught woman.

Leah pushed out of his arms. He was a kind man, but no amount of hugging would help her at the moment. 'I will be fine, Eros, thank you.'

'The drink's still talking,' Ruby whispered as he walked out to find Angel.

'You've got some room to talk, you and Sisco were crawling about on your hands and knees, looking for a loo,' Sophie said on her way in, picking up a coffee, and then she made to go back out.

'Yes, but Grandma,' Tom told her, 'you and Grandad were throwing sandwiches at my dartboard. Charlie was helping you too. It was well weird, the whole evening. Now can we look for Dad please, I'm getting worried.' Sensible Tom urged them out of the house and sent the security personnel into the kitchen.

Many of the security team were ex-Special Air Service elite soldiers. Leah gave them the maps she had printed off, advising them of their usual riding route up on the moors and soon the men were off and out, having organised themselves with expert precision.

Leah went out to the Land Rover with a hot flask of tea, her phone charged up, a blanket and a first-aid kit. Swiping away the tears from her eyes and her cheeks, a sob caught in her throat as she prayed, 'Please, please don't let him die. Please, God, he's such a lovely husband and dad. I wouldn't be able to bear it if I lost him, if I knew he had fallen out of love with me, and I hadn't had the chance to save our marriage.'

Eros had drunk all of his coffee and some of Angel's, but she was still on cloud nine from the sensational sex they'd shared, even while they were both off their heads. Now, she was singing at the top of her voice to 'Mamma Mia'. They'd made love four times in total. Once on the dance floor when everyone else had deserted them. She remembered that. Twice in bed and once in the shower, and she recalled those times well. Now she knew how Leah felt with Dan. *Wow.*

Pulling the Mercedes up outside the quaint cottage, Angel put the hand-brake on and turned to Eros. 'Just bang on the door, please?' she asked, knowing that Joey would go berserk if it was her waking him up on the first day of his married life, but not so much with Eros.

'Why?' Eros couldn't understand her reluctance.

'Well, Joey won't shout at you. They both have the hots for you, Eros.' Angel walked her fingers up his leg to his groin and they exchanged steamy glances. 'It will be worth your while. Promise.'

'More reason for you to wake them, he's your cousin. I don't want to be caught up in men's embraces.' Eros stopped her hand and grasped it with his own. 'Behave, Angel, or at least tell me how it will be worth my while.'

Angel leaned across and whispered something into his ear which made him groan.

'OK, I will go.' Jumping out of the car, he strode up to the cottage, thinking, It can't be that bad. But it was. He knocked on the quaint chocolate-box cottage door, and on hearing an angry shout from inside, took an involuntary step back.

'It's our effing honeymoon. Leave us alone!' bawled Joey, sounding chalked off.

Eros knocked again, a little louder, and took another step backwards. Then another step as someone was swearing inside the cottage at the top of his voice.

The door was wrenched open, almost rived off the hinges. Eros fell backwards onto the ground in shock because what greeted him was something he'd never seen before and hoped he never would again.

Standing with hands-on-hips in all his gay glory, Joey had some kind of pink and cream woman's sexy lingerie top on. It was open wide showing his hairy chest, the little ribbons hanging loose, whilst on the bottom half he was wearing such skimpy matching knickers, leaving nothing to the imagination.

While Eros's eyes were wide open, the same as his mouth with the shock of what confronted him, in contrast, Angel was in hysterics.

Eros scrambled up, averting his eyes. He wondered if it was a Yorkshire ritual or maybe coun-trywide, although he hadn't come across it in London. Avoiding Joey's wild eyes, he gave the grave message: 'Dan is missing. Fallen from his horse and there is a search party going on. Sorry to disturb you both on your honeymoon. Leah wants to know if you'll help?'

Joey shrieked, and Eros flinched. Joey stared at him as if he had two heads. Then he took a deep breath and seemed to calm and collect himself.

'Angel, please get hold of Leah and tell her I will meet her near the bridle path on the top of the moors, she knows where, near Sledborough. You two search by the farm, on the backtracks. All of us must keep in radio contact, so charge your phones up or ask Quinn for a radio-controlled unit. Ben,' he called behind him, 'get out of bed, sweetie. They need us to search for Dan. Poor Lee-Lee will be worried sick.' Joey looked down at his attire. 'Tell no one you saw me in this today, Eros, as it belongs to Leah, and she doesn't know I've got it.'

'Your secret is safe with me, Joey.' Eros got back into the passenger seat of the car and wiped his beaded brow. 'I'm traumatised, Angel. That sight has been branded into my brain.'

'Don't you have gay men in Greece?' Angel asked as she started the car.

'Yes, but not prancing around in little bits of material like that!'

'Sexist. I bet you'd like it if Leah or me wore it, flaunting around your bedroom dressed in that,'

Angel pouted, annoyed that he feared lovable Joey, even though the newly-wed did look like a wild beast on steroids in that silky two-piece set. She shot a side-ways glance at Eros, then concentrated on the road again.

Eros cast an appreciative look over her. This woman was something special, so strong. 'I will buy you one,' he promised. 'Yes, I would like to see you in that. I am a hot-blooded man who loves women, especially women like you, Angel.'

'Flattery gets you everywhere,' Angel said as she pulled the car over to the side of the track.

'Here?' Eros liked where her thoughts were going. 'What about my cousin?'

'How about we have a quickie?' Angel purred.

Eros grinned and reached across for her, but she jumped out and got into the back seat,

saying, 'Leah gave me some nice new underwear. Come and look.'

Eros leaped out of the car and raced into the back seat. 'On my knee, Angel.'

AFTER A ZILLIONTH COFFEE, Joey and Ben climbed into the pink Beetle because Joey had had to recharge his phone before they set off to the moors. They'd been driving only minutes when it started raining.

Joey pulled the wiper knob on the dashboard, and it came out in his hand.

'Look, we're driving into sunshine now,' he said. 'Bloody weather - it'll be snowing in Whitby, just you watch. How do I switch the wipers off?'

Ben tried his best to slot the knob back in, but he just couldn't secure it and by this time, the wipers were squeaking something chronic against the glass. Joey stopped the vehicle and pushed the wipers up away from the windscreen; they were just dancing back and forth, still squeaking, but not as bad as when they were scraping on the dry glass.

'Oh, great. You never see a police car on this road, and now he wants me to stop,' Joey muttered. He wound his window down. 'Yes, officer, how can I help you?'

The young policeman watched the wiper blades going back and forth, back, and forth in front of the windscreen. 'Is there a problem?'

'Yes, you could say so, Officer. My knob has broken off, and no amount of pushing will get it back in, and we are against the clock looking for a missing man who went out riding on the moors this morning and his horse came back alone.' Joey was frustrated; he held the knob in his hand, his knuckles going white.

'I see. Would you like me to get your knob back in?' the young policeman asked.

'Oh, yes, please do, Officer. Do you have any experience with knobs? I mean, has *your* knob ever dropped off like this? It's most inconvenient.' Joey got out of the car while the constable climbed into the driver's seat. 'Maybe if you plunge it in because it is long and thin,' Joey suggested. 'What size is yours?'

'Well, my dip-stick is very similar to this, but my police truncheon is fatter and longer; as for my wind-screen-wiper knob, it's on the steering column.' The young police officer grinned. 'There we go. Done.' He switched the wipers off, reached for a card and put his mobile number on it. 'If I give you my number, you can keep in touch while we help in the search. We have helicopters these days, you know, and I will call it in now.'

'Thank you,' Joey said, rubbing his temples. 'I'm so grateful because the noise the wipers were making was causing my head to spin. If you want to visit us at The Amazing Dog Friendly Café, you can have free coffee and home-made cakes on us.'

The young policeman glanced at the cans and ribbons on the car. 'I hope you find your friend well, and if I were you, I'd follow your own advice and have a bucket-full of coffee on your next stop. Luckily this track is not a public highway. When you get to your honeymoon, have a great time. Keep me informed about Mr Ryan-Savidis.'

'You know him?'

'Yes, Tom has just texted. My much younger brother is Tom's best friend. His name is Troy. Off you go – drive safely now.' He smiled and waved them onwards.

As Joey drove away, he said, 'I think he was very kind and at least he will radio Dan's disappearance in.'

'Do you think that gorgeous Greek man will tell Leah about her lingerie?' Ben asked, still much the worse for wear. 'He was shocked seeing you in her creation for Dan. I mean, he fell over, twice.'

They both giggled, then became very serious as they saw Leah's Land Rover parked up on the side of the track because the gate was locked.

WORRYING about her marriage and the possibility she might find Dan dead on the moors or injured at the very least, was giving Leah's heart jolts of fear; she had to force her legs to move up the rough weather-beaten road. Great, she saw Brian grazing in front of her on the path. Would he be in a good mood? She wasn't sure. He was the most unpredictable creature the moors had seen in fifty years, or so Eric kept saying. Brian had a booming voice like his namesake, the stentorian Shakespearian actor, Brian Blessed.

Only the actor had a gentler expression and disposition.

The big bull saw her coming at fifty yards and called, his *moo* deafening. Still, it wasn't an aggressive sound, and Leah hoped she could sweet-talk him with her dehydrated apple and molasses horse treats. Brian was always roaming the moors and when in a good mood, he was a gentle soul, but if anyone or anything had crossed him at all, he could be a foul-tempered beast, Eric had warned her.

'Hi, Brian.' Leah motioned into her pocket to make a crunching noise with the treat bag, taking care not to give him any eye contact. 'I have your favourite treat here.'

Brian's big bulk blocked the path. He was a huge red and white Hereford bull. As usual, Leah wished Eric the farmer had better-fenced areas to keep Brian in, but treats should do the trick. She just wanted to go past him and look for Dan without having to climb the enormous dry-stone wall to her right because on the other side was an even deeper drop.

Brian stood stock-still, eyeing her up and sniffing the air as if he could smell the sweetness of the apple treats. Leah knew she must not show any fear, and he would keep busy and out of her way if she placed a handful of goodies on the ground.

'I don't believe you know you are a Hereford Bull, do you, Brian?' she went on. 'Your ancestors have a reputation for being so chilled-out.' She held her hand out with a treat in it. 'I think you believe you are a Spanish Fighting Bull, don't you, boy?' She touched his face and scratched behind his ear. Then she dropped the pile of treats at the side of the track. When he trotted over and began nudging and gobbling up the treats, Leah heaved a sigh of relief. He was in a good mood, to judge from by the look of bliss on his face. She crept past in a sideways stance, keeping her eyes on him all the while.

Reaching the gate, Leah climbed over, feeling relieved, but she then felt sick when she arrived at Sledborough House to see drops of blood on the ground and pathway leading up to the main entrance. It had to be Dan's. Her eyes scanned around. Yes, he'd been here, she'd already found his stirrup and stirrup leather. And now there was his wand, or as she called it his 'posh riding crop' lying on the tiled path. He almost never used it on Galahad, but she'd take it in case she needed to defend herself. Picking it up, she slid it down her riding boot for safekeeping.

Approaching the house, she could see a light on in a room right at the top of the building. Fortunately she'd come prepared with her climbing rope with the grappling hook on it I her backpack, just in case he'd fallen down a gully. First, however, she needed to knock on the door . . . but when she did so, it pushed inwards. Leah walked into the house calling, 'Hello!' Moving further into the hallway, she felt tempted to put the lights on as the place was so dark. She had a quick scan downstairs. Then, with trepidation, she climbed the steps to the top floor.

Leah had seen the light on in the top room, so it made sense for her to go there first. Opening the door, she could see Brioche bending over Dan with a wet cloth, tending his cut forehead.

'Brioche,' Leah breathed, 'it's you. Sorry for coming in without you knowing. I did knock. Oh God, Dan.' She ran to her husband, fussing over the unconscious man. She touched his face, his lips, his eyes and the gash on his temple.

'I found him on the track up by the gate,' Brioche explained. 'I saw the horse bolt, but Leah, you can't be here, it's too dangerous. If she finds you here, I think she will try to kill you. She's deranged.' The tall man had such an apologetic expression on his face.

'Who are you talking about?'

'My horrible cousin Chelsea, she's due back very soon from York. I intended on leaving, but I've made such grand friends in Whitby that I'm finding it hard. I want to stay here.' He blew out a sigh, wanted to get everything off his chest. 'She tried to sabotage the marquees,' he went on. 'I followed her and my sister Pepper as they loosened the ties; I tightened them all up again. She changed the food order for the wedding and. . .' Brioche stopped and went back to gently cleaning the blood from Dan's head with a special medicated wipe. 'Don't worry,' he said kindly. 'He's not dead. He is still breathing.'

Leah took the cloth from Brioche. 'Has he broken any bones; do you know?'

Brioche shook his head. 'I don't think so. I used to be a First Aider at school, and I'm sure his bones are OK. He was still conscious when I saw him fall. The horse bolted, and he got up and seemed disoriented, then he collapsed to the ground. This was the nearest place to fetch him, but I'm scared that Chelsea will be back soon, so if you can both get away now, it would be best.'

Leah glanced dubiously at Brioche, hoping he was telling the truth. He held out his phone, 'I've been trying to get hold of all of you, lots of times, but the signal is rubbish up here.' Leah saw the long list of times he'd tried to contact anyone at the house, and Joey's and Ben's numbers were included in those he'd rung.

'Joey's on his way up the moors,' Leah told him. 'He should be here soon. The signals up here are diabolical, I know.'

Part of her wanted to slap Dan awake when she thought of Love and Sexy-Bum, but when she saw his deathly white face and his cut head, she couldn't. She stroked his cheek, and her thumb ran across his bottom lip. At first, there was nothing, then the slightest moan.

'My head hurts,' Dan whispered in a ragged breath. He raised his eyes to see Leah bending over him. He winced, putting a hand to his head.

'Is the house phone working?' Leah looked back to ask Brioche.

'No – Chelsea didn't pay the reconnection fee. So, at first, we had it on, and then they cut it off again because her cheque bounced.'

'She paid by cheque, in this day and age?' Leah smiled at Dan. 'Can you move, darling?'

Dan tried, but it was too painful.

Hearing a sound, Brioche went to the window. 'Oh God, she's here. She just parked the car up. Lock the door behind me and keep him as quiet as possible. I will try to send her on an errand. I put the lock on the inside so he could keep away from her.'

Leah raised her eyes, 'Be careful, Brioche, she's unhinged.'

'Don't I know it, but I had to join her plan in order to keep my sister safe. Pepper is so easily led, and besides, Chelsea has been practising her hypnosis skills on her, that's what I reckon.' He closed the door behind him as Leah got up, switched off the light and slid the bolt to. She returned to Dan, who was still ghostly pale. He whimpered.

'Darling, we have to stay quiet. Is there anything you'd like to do, where we don't talk?'

He blinked at her. 'Who are you?' He looked down at his wedding ring. 'Sorry,' he sighed. 'You look nice, but I'm married, and I will never cheat on my wife.'

Leah closed her eyes; her heart bled. She got her phone out. There was one bar only, so she called home.

'Hello.'

'It's Leah here. Dan is injured; we are up at Sledboro . . .' The phone died.

16

SOMETHING'S AMISS

'Penny, something's not right,' Ruby told her urgently. They were both in the kitchen with Alice, having a cup of tea and a chat when Ruby's phone rang, then cut off. 'That was Leah, phoning from Sledborough saying Dan is injured, but the signal up there is poor and she was cut off. Problem is, all the vehicles have gone. We must take Alice and get there somehow, as quick as we can.'

'Well, the cherry picker is outside, and I know how to drive it. Let's use that,' Penny suggested confidently. 'I'll just visit the loo before we set off,' and she popped into the downstairs toilet.

Seeing that little Alice had her eyes out on stalks, and tears welling up, Ruby consoled her: 'Don't cry, baby. Your daddy will be fine, I'm sure.'

'I'm cwying 'cos Aunt Penny is cwazy in the cherry picker, she's a lunaticky.'

But Ruby didn't hear her. She was reaching for their coats, helping Alice on with hers. 'Come on, baby, let's go. Girl power it is.'

'OH, fuck! Brian is on the path - the warpath by the looks of it,' cried Joey, having fallen foul of Brian's temper once before when he'd been out riding with Leah and Dan. The bull eyed the matching pink shirts on the two newly wed men and started trotting towards them, bellowing as he approached.

Ben screeched, 'He's chasing us, what do we do now?'

'We jump over the dry-stone wall,' yelled Joey. 'I'll give you a hitch up. Quick, Ben.'

Ben reached the wall, putting his hands on the top stone and scrambling to get higher.

'Hurry, Ben, he's coming fast now, and this bull can motor. I don't want you to be a widow before our honeymoon has even started.' Joey grabbed Ben's bent leg and hitched him up way above the wall, and then he listened as Ben screamed as he soared high up and over the wall to the considerable drop beyond.

'Aaarrrggghhh!' Joey heard a thud as Ben landed. 'Ouch.'

Joey scrambled up the wall as he heard Brian thundering towards him and heaved himself over to scream louder than Ben had, when he realised the drop was massive. Falling almost on top of Ben, they both heard the scratching of the front hooves of the bovine as Brian charged at the wall, bashing it several times with his broad skull.

Joey and Ben scrambled to their feet, then watched frozen to the spot as the first stone fell.

'Quick, let's run, fast as you can, Ben-Ben. He's a little bit gay, this bull is, and I don't fancy my chances with *that!*' Joey panted as they legged it across the field, wailing and keening across the paddock like two big banshees, their legs pumping like chickens being chased in an abattoir. Neither realised they were going the wrong way, nor that the bull was now following them at a cracking pace.

EROS CLIMBED out of the back of the Mercedes with Angel following. He was spent. Now he knew why Dan loved these Yorkshire women. He was almost bow-legged after the last session when Angel had driven them further into the woods, and she'd demanded another kiss and cuddle. Suddenly, Angel screamed in terror and ran to him. There was so much caterwauling going on – and it was coming from the next field. They both peeked over the wall to see Ben and Joey sprinting across the pasture with a bull bellowing after them.

'It's terrific fun around here,' Eros commented. 'I can understand why Dan never wants to leave Yorkshire for business in London. But should we look for my cousin now?'

'Let's wait for Joey and Ben, looks like it's safety in numbers,' Angel muttered, wondering what the hell was going on. She held out her hand. If they were walking now, she knew Eros wouldn't want his Gucci shoes getting caked-up with cowpat, so that meant she would have to lead him through the paddocks.

Old Brian gave up the chase with one last call. Even nice apple and molasses treats weren't worth this much effort. He ambled back to his sentry post on the path, clambering over the pile of stones from the dry-stone wall he'd butted down minutes earlier. The next lot who came past his patch was going to get it bad; he was in a frustrated mood now.

AUNT PENNY WAS DRIVING the cherry picker up the main road when they came across Grandad Thomas's old friend Cyril and his tractor and trailer full of steaming horse manure.

'Cyril, we need you! Follow us to Sledborough

House, please. Dan is injured up on the moors, so it's all hands to the plough,' cried Penny, turning off the main road down the rough track towards Sledborough.

'Oh, no!' Ruby cried out as she saw the huge bull scratching the ground. 'That doesn't look good.'

'Hello, Brian, hello, my Brian, you've come to the rescue, to help my daddy. It's me, Alice, remember from the cattle sale?' cried Alice. The bull raised his head, and his whole demeanour changed at the sight of this little girl.

Penny stopped the cherry picker and Alice was off at a run. 'Alice, come here,' Penny cried, terrified for the little girl's life. 'He can be a mettlesome beast.'

Ruby was panicking, shouting, 'Alice, come back!'

But naughty Alice ignored her. She reached Brian, standing before him, staring at his front legs as he towered over her. 'Oh Brian, my daddy is hurt, and I need you to let us through. We have to get him to safety. Follow me, and I will put you in that field near the ladies.'

The bull licked his lips as if he was going to eat her. He sniffed the air; he knew this little girl. She'd saved his life once by begging Farmer Eric to spare him from the cattle mart. Following her, he plodded into the open gateway like a docile donkey. Penny got out as fast as she could from the cherry picker, and closed the gate behind him with hands that shook.

The bull looked back as Alice waved; he'd love to live on her farm.

'I'm going to ask Daddy if I can have Brian. I love him. Bye, Brian, thank you. I love you. Yes, Brian is coming home,' Alice said to herself as she got back into the cherry picker.

DAN WATCHED as Leah put a finger to her lips. She could hear Chelsea shouting orders at Brioche and tearing a strip off him from the ground floor. She sat on the old bed, touching her husband's face as if he was someone holy.

'I feel I know you,' he whispered, 'but my head hurts, and I can't think right now.'

'Look at our rings, they match. That is because you and I are married, Dan. We have two children, Tom, almost fourteen and Alice four, and we've just celebrated five years of marriage.' Leah leaned forward and kissed him. 'How is your head, darling?'

'Sore, it hurts a lot. What happened?' He linked hands with Leah, checking their rings. 'I know that I love you so much.'

'Someone is trying to kidnap you, Dan, so we must be quiet as church mice because she's downstairs,' Leah advised, pointing downwards while she was trying to think how they would get out of this house. She had her climbing rope with her only because if the worst came to the worst, they could climb out of the window and abseil the three floors to the ground, but with Brioche's help maybe they'd be able to walk out of the front door. It would all depend on how bad Dan's concussion was.

Dan knew he loved this woman. He also knew they had a priceless connection, and an agenda to fulfil; he just didn't know what it was.

'How is Galahad?' Dan asked suddenly. 'He squealed and reared.' Now he remembered: he'd been on his horse, and his best equine friend had been stung or bitten because Galahad had reared up and as Dan fell, his horse had bolted.

'He will be OK; I'm sure of that,' Leah comforted him, glad to see that her husband was coming back to himself. But inside, she was very worried. They had such dangerous times ahead, because Leah knew Chelsea would never give up. Not even a prison sentence had cured her of her obsession. Plus, there was the other matter of Madness, but now was not the time nor the place.

Suddenly, they heard someone coming upstairs and hid, holding their breath.

'I can't let you into the room, Chelsea, I've been cleaning it out,' they heard Brioche trying to explain.

'Besides, I think I locked it and the key is downstairs.'

'Get me the key then. Come on, Brioche, get a move on.'

'I'll fetch it for you,' Brioche said, running noisily down the stairs. When he arrived back up, he unlocked the door and walked inside.

'The light, Brioche, put the flaming light on!' Chelsea screamed.

Switching on the light, Brioche scanned the room and heaved a sigh of relief. Chelsea entered the room after him; the bed was neat, but the cover stained. 'You will have to change the bedding again. There is blood on the cover. How did this happen? How can I get him to succumb to me when there is disgusting blood lying around?'

'I - I had a nosebleed. It was a bad one too.' Brioche furnished his alibi. His eyes were out on sticks, wondering just how the pair had got out of the room.

'Get on with it then. We need him in here by tomorrow, and he's so filthy-rich he won't want dirty sheets, although I ought to make him suffer.' Chelsea turned and walked out; then she ran down the stairs.

'Hello, hello,' Brioche whispered.

'We're here, Brioche.' Dan slid out from under the bed, as did Leah. She gave him her hand to help him as he was feeling dizzy, and the bleeding had started again.

'I don't think she's going out again. I will let you know when she goes to bed.' Brioche turned and watched the door.

'Stuff that for a lark,' Leah said, getting her backpack from under the bed. 'I've brought my rope. Are you game, Dan? We are a bit high up.'

Dan was looking out of the window and suddenly hissed: 'I don't believe it. Am I seeing things?' Ruby was opening the front gate so that Penny could drive the cherry picker in. Cyril was driving his tractor and trailer around the back too. Leah couldn't believe her eyes when she could see that Aunt Penny, Ruby and little Alice had come to their rescue. Joey, Ben, Eros and Angel were all marching down the next field too and some security teams were circling the property. It brought tears to Leah's eyes.

She waved, then put her finger over her lips. 'Can you lift the basket?' she mouthed to Penny, but her auntie couldn't hear.

Ruby understood. 'You need to lift the basket, Penny. Carefully,' she told her.

'Piece of cake,' Penny said, studying the controls. 'Oh, thank you, Alice. Glasses would help, I suppose.'

'You don't trust her, do you? Remember last time,' Dan said, his head aching. He saw the cherry-picker bucket sway from one side to the other and told Leah, 'I'd rather walk down the stairs and take my chances with the madwoman.'

'We have to decide, rope or cherry picker?' Leah asked.

'Or stairs,' Dan reiterated.

Brioche was solemn. 'If you love your wife, Dan, you'll leave by the window. Chelsea has totally lost the plot. She is deranged and dangerous. The only reason I stay is because of my sister. Let me convince you: if it had been up to Chelsea, she would have made your daughter's pony bolt at the wedding. She will stop at nothing, even the attempted death of your child. Now do you understand? You must get out of here!'

'Brioche, a stupid woman is saying she is our landlady, and she's here to clean the gutters. Get rid of her!' Chelsea screamed from the lower floor.

'I'm coming.' Brioche left the bedroom.

Leah slid the bolt, locking the door from the inside. 'Shall we?' She held her hand out to Dan.

Dan nodded then regretted it, since his head hurt a great deal. Measuring the gap between the window and the top reach of the picker basket, he said, 'We'll have to use both the rope and the basket, as the reach of the cherry picker is not high enough.' As he was talking, he watched Leah search for a place to anchor the rope; fastening the claw around one sturdy bed leg, she then wrapped it around all four legs.

'You first,' Leah said, handing him one of the two harnesses.

'Nope – you first. She needs to catch me, and she wants to kill you. Out!' Dan insisted, his weak voice brooking no argument.

Penny had got the picker basket as near as she could, but it was still a good foot and a half away from the wall. Leah saw her daughter looking up. She waved her hand for her to hide because if Chelsea saw her, she would cotton on immediately.

'I will hold the rope steady,' Dan whispered, then he kissed her. 'You can do this.'

'Put the other harness on first. Be ready to come down as soon as I'm in the basket.' Leah clipped the rope on to her harness.

Climbing out of the window, she made the mistake of looking down. She closed her eyes, feeling quite shaken. What on earth was the matter with her? Heights didn't normally have this effect. She had lowered herself almost into the basket when a window opened and Chelsea's head appeared. A manic expression of triumph was on her face.

Chelsea grabbed the rope to shake it. She pushed Leah away from the picker basket.

Leah still had the rope attached to her harness.

'I'm going to kill you this time,' Chelsea hollered.

She slung the window open again, and it crashed against Leah, breaking the pane of glass into smithereens. 'Where is Dan?'

Watching down below, Penny was infuriated at the wanton damage. 'I will add that onto the rent you haven't paid me yet, you horrible woman,' she called up.

'Who are you? Ugh - some raving old idiot.' Chelsea disappeared inside to reach for a sweeping brush.

'Someone you shouldn't mess with, lady,' Penny growled.

Leah had climbed into the basket while Chelsea was busy sparring with Penny. 'Now, Dan, now!' she called up.

Dan clipped the rope onto his harness. As he climbed out, his intention was to abseil down the wall . . . but that was when all hell let loose.

Joey, Ben, Eros and Angel all began screaming in excitement as the rotor blades of not one helicopter but two were slowly lowered into the field. The scene was one of utter chaos. Both the enormous yellow Search and Rescue helicopter and the Police Interceptor helicopter had come in to land. Joey and the gang were being blown away, all four hanging onto their shirts. Dan was swaying from side to side on the rope, swinging from the down-blast of the choppers.

Alice squealed in delight, thinking her daddy was

acting the fool. While, in contrast, Chelsea was crying with frustration, and still striking out at Leah with the broom. Dan managed to get low enough to reach out for the basket. He swung himself into it and caught Leah in his arms.

Chelsea reached further out with the brush and almost fell as Dan grabbed the broom and yanked it out of her hands; her howl of outrage was deafening.

'Don't you get it, Chelsea?' he bellowed. 'I will always love my family, always. Your next stretch in prison will be much longer: everyone heard you threaten Leah.'

Dan was angrier than Leah had ever seen him.

'You tried to kill my daughter, my wife, and you stole from my family again. This time when they put you away, I hope it will be for good!'

As Penny lowered the picker basket down, little Alice popped her head up.

'Hello, Daddy, Brian helped us get to you so we could rescue you. I'm going to ask Eric if I can have him. Will he be able to come into the house?'

'No, no, and no. Bulls do not come into the kitchen nor anywhere in the house,' Dan shouted down to her above the noise of the helicopter blades. He saw her little angelic face frown then appear incredibly sad. 'But I will buy him for you.'

'Yes!' Alice pumped the air with her little fist.

Chelsea had gone back into the house. There was

a commotion out the back, and everyone, including the ambulance and police officers, ran around the end of the building just as Chelsea was trying to get away in her car.

Almost in slow motion, a trailer load of horse manure driven by Cyril landed on the bonnet of her vehicle. When she opened the window of her car, the horse poo fell inwards onto Chelsea.

'I've always wanted to do sommat like that,' Cyril grinned happily.

Chelsea flew into hysterics as a policeman arrested and cuffed her. Brioche watched on as they dragged his cousin away.

The supervising officer turned to Dan and asked, 'Is anyone else involved?'

Dan glanced at Brioche. He knew now that Alice had been correct when she had told him he was responsible for attacking Leah in London.

Leah piped up, 'No, Officer, only that crazy woman. Brioche and his sister are our friends.'

Brioche raised his head. Tears filled his eyes. 'I think I know where she's stashed your jewellery, Leah. When Pepper comes back from Whitby we will check the house top to bottom.'

'Mr Ryan-Savidis, we want you to go to the hospital to be checked out,' said the ambulanceman. 'Or at least let me check you over to see if your concussion is still a factor.'

ALICE HAD INSISTED that she go in the helicopter to the hospital with Dan and Leah. Once there, Dan received treatment, was advised to rest and was discharged home. Before they left, they stopped by the ward where Ethel was recovering.

'Hewo, Effel,' Alice chimed up, running to greet the old lady.

'By 'eck, Leah, that's the best wedding reception I've ever been to,' smiled the old woman. 'But I had an 'ell of an 'eadache t'next morning.'

IN THE CHAUFFEUR-DRIVEN car on the way home, Dan held tightly onto Leah's hand. He was wondering what was going on in her head because at one point he'd seen tears on her face.

'What's the matter, my love?' He'd looked into her eyes and seen such profound sadness. 'It's over. This time I'm sure she's gone for good. Chelsea will no longer be a thorn in our sides.'

'It's not that,' Leah said, her voice sad.

'Mummy is upset since she wed your message on your phone,' said Alice, looking out of the window as the car travelled across the moors. Their little daughter was so perceptive. 'It was wingin' all

Saturday night when you were out wiv the dogs.'
Then she put on her music and started singing along
with it. The adults were able to talk.

'Ah.' Dan had the decency to blush.

'If our marriage is at risk, I need to know,' Leah
mumbled.

Dan gasped. 'Why would our marriage be at
risk?'

'Who are Love and Sexy Bum?' Tears brimmed
over her eyes. 'And Madness?'

'It's not what you think, Leah, I can assure you. I
promise.' Dan held her hand and brought it to his lips.

'If you need to move out until you decide who
you want to be with, I understand, but I don't want
our children being disrupted.' Leah had decided to
give him his freedom. How could she keep him, if his
heart was with not one woman, but several?

'Do you have my little phone with you?' Dan
asked. How could she believe he wanted to leave her?
He felt sick himself now; he loved his wife with all
his heart. Leah handed the small phone over to him.
He rang the number for Madness and spoke to
someone on the other end.

'Hi, it's me. Are you busy? Can you bring the
girls over? We've been rumbled, and I think it's only
fair we come clean now. Yes, bring him with you too.
See you this evening, Madness, and thanks.' Dan
clicked the phone off. 'I can see why you might have

misinterpreted these messages as something devious, but I can assure you there is a simple explanation, darling.'

'Please don't darling me,' Leah sniffed again, and despite her struggles, Dan dragged her into his arms, kissing her forehead.

Alice had taken out her ear buds. 'Pwease don't darwing me,' she said, mimicking.

'So, you don't deny when you met them you kissed them?' Leah asked.

'Oh, I had so many kisses. I couldn't get enough, but you'll understand, I promise,' Dan said with a cheeky grin. He would not spoil the surprise, although Leah had threatened to leave before when he had suggested the same situation. Even Madness's husband had hit the roof.

The moment the car pulled into the drive, Leah pushed out of his arms and ran down towards the stables. She needed to ride on the beach to blow the cobwebs away, both after their terrifying imprisonment, with all its drama, and also from the terrible heartache she was feeling. What did he mean, he had so many kisses, he couldn't get enough? How could she ever deal with knowing that he preferred kissing girls to his wife?

Dan let her go; he knew she needed to let off steam but once he'd explained, he hoped she would weigh up all the facts and forgive him. He lifted Alice out of her car seat and went to answer the many questions thrown at him by the family. He'd told Maggie (aka Madness) to bring her husband Lenny along with the girls. It would spoil the surprise he'd had for Leah's birthday, but she was always going to know early, so it didn't matter in the grand scheme of things.

GRANDAD THOMAS FROWNED as Dan arrived home with Alice in tow. She leaned across for Eros to take her into his arms.

'Where's our Leah, Dan?' Thomas asked outright.

It was Alice who answered. 'Mummy has gone widing because she wants to leave us.'

'Alice, that's not the reason, she doesn't want to leave us. She's gone for a ride, Thomas, because I think all the trauma with Chelsea has caused a storm inside of her. If you all go into Whitby for your supper, I can speak with Leah. We need some space.'

'What will happen to that bitch Chelsea?' Joey queried. 'I saw her being hauled away by the police. Good riddance to bad rubbish.'

'I saw the bitch too,' Alice chirped up, becoming naughty now because she knew Brian was coming home soon.

For once Dan didn't pick his daughter up on her

copycat behaviour. 'Yes, she was behind everyone getting drunk at the wedding. She doctored the water with strong vodka,' he explained. 'It would seem she tried a lot more things, but as she was causing chaos, Brioche was sorting it out. I think we'll get to know everything in the court case.'

'She was the old woman in the café, wasn't she?' Joey stated, his mouth opening wide. 'Unbelievable.'

Dan nodded. 'She was behind the thefts too.'

Ruby snorted. 'You should have got rid of her ten years ago. She was nothing but trouble.'

'Nuffin' but twubble,' Alice repeated.

THE GALLOP across the beach on Ebby was exhilarating, with the wind in her hair, and as she cantered the rest of the way along the bay towards the road, Leah joined the main highway in an extended trot. She slowed up on the farm track. As rider and horse made their way back up the trail, she saw Brioche walking Chelsea's little dog that had been christened Billy. She tried to wipe her tears away, but they kept on flowing. Even Ebby knew there something wrong with her beloved mistress.

'Hello, Brioche. Thank you so much for today. Am I correct in thinking Chelsea was the old woman in the café?' Leah asked, slowing Ebby down to a walk. 'It was her perfume. I knew I remembered it from somewhere.'

Brioche nodded. 'At least this little one won't be frightened any more, but I'm worried this puppy will get upset when Pepper and I have to go to jail. Would you look after her until we get out of prison? Or maybe Joey would?'

'Why are you going to jail, Brioche?' Leah asked.

Brioche swallowed and took a deep breath. 'It was me in London who attacked you. I never meant to hurt you that day but the scooter wobbled - and then as I got to know you, I realised what a good person you are. Chelsea had told me so many horrible lies about you.' He glanced across at the bay, wiping his own eyes. 'Pepper and I are going to give ourselves up, but before we do, like I said, I think I know where Chelsea has stashed the things she stole. We are not blameless, Leah, but she's lied so much to us and she tried to use her hypnosis on both of us. Good thing she was rubbish at it, but then I realised that Billy had chewed the wires on the speakers last night. Even the dog knew she was trouble.'

Leah looked down from the saddle into his sad face. 'Get me my things back, and I won't press charges for you nor Pepper. Chelsea has mistreated you too.'

'I can't ask that of you.'

'You are not asking, I'm telling you. Get me my stuff back, and we're quits.'

'You have a lovely family, and your husband loves you so much,' Brioche reflected emotionally. 'Everything I've seen with you all is so special, and I know you fall out, but you have each other's backs and that's just amazing. We will search the house tonight for your things, and I will be in touch, Leah. Stay happy, and you're so lucky to have a close-knit family.' Brioche waved as he and Billy carried on up the higher path towards the moors.

Leah squeezed Ebby on into a trot, as now she'd got rid of her cobwebs and wanted some answers. In particular, she wanted to know all about Love and Sexy Bum. No more excuses. As she rode into the yard, Quinn took Ebby from Leah after she'd dismounted.

'Thank you, Quinn,' she said sincerely, hugging him, 'for everything you did this morning and everything else you do for us. Dan seems to have recovered after his fall – just has to rest, according to the hospital. What did the vet say about Galahad?'

Quinn said cheerfully, 'That horse is tough, he'll survive. He had an anti-venom injection, but he was sweating for a while. He's just started eating, and that's always a good sign. Come on, I'll rub Ebby down.' He led Ebby into the stable, calling over his shoulder, 'I'm so glad the boss is OK.'

Leah nodded as she walked towards the house, gathering her courage – but oh no. Lenny and Maggie were here. How could she confront Dan now?

LEAH BYPASSED the kitchen and ran upstairs to get a quick shower and change of clothes. Ten minutes later, she went downstairs, took a deep breath and walked into the kitchen.

Dan looked up and smiled. 'Ah, Leah, I've sent everyone out for tea. We four need to talk.'

Maggie watched Leah's tense face and said, 'We didn't mean to do it, Leah, nor to you, Lenny.'

'Do what?' Lenny asked casually; he seemed so chilled.

'Well, it's my fault,' Dan admitted. 'I wanted a surprise for your birthday, Leah.'

'My birthday isn't for weeks,' she said suspiciously.

'Fetch the girls in for me, Maggie and Lenny, please,' Dan requested.

'Girls?' Lenny frowned. 'What's going on? Even I'm confused now.'

'Come with me, Lenny, quick, we need the girls to help Leah understand.' Maggie dragged her husband outside.

'I know you said Hero was too old,' Dan was

explaining to Leah in the kitchen, shrugging his big-muscled shoulders.

'Too old?' Leah asked, bemused. 'Too old for what?'

Dan put the dogs through into the utility room and closed the door. 'Too old to be a stud dog.'

Maggie and Lenny came in with five Newfoundland puppies. 'They're going to pee all over the place, I reckon,' Maggie said doubtfully.

Dan cleared his throat. 'These are Hero's puppies, darling. I was unsure which one you'd choose, so last night Maggie and I met secretly. Instead of bringing the two puppies, she brought all five girls, which was why it took me ages to get back to you. I had to give them all kisses and cuddles. You know me, Leah, I love puppy kisses. So, you can choose your birthday present.'

Leah watched the five robust puppies running around the kitchen. She smiled, catching a sob in her throat. Relief flooded through her like a raging river. 'Who is who?'

Dan pointed to Miss Baby Pink who was Sexy Bum and Miss Yellow was Love. They had coloured collars on. 'The other three are booked.'

'Who is Sexy Bum and Love, and why did you call them those names?' Leah asked, still bewildered.

Maggie turned to Dan. 'This is your remit, sunshine. You named them, but to make it easy on you, Dan, I will tell Leah. He has a thing about your sexy bum, you see - Lenny, please don't listen to this and get any ideas about my bottom - and he's so in love with you. The names were all about you, pet. The man's besotted with you.'

Dan grinned at Leah. 'Shall I open the champagne?'

'Excuse us just a minute, Maggie and Lenny.' Leah pulled Dan through into the hall.

'What is it? Don't you want a puppy?' Dan asked, worried.

'Yes, I do - but I also want to tell you we are having a baby,' she said with a huge smile.

Dan looked at her, and for a moment he stood stock still in glorious shock. 'Really?' he said finally. 'A baby? *A baby!*' He picked her up and swung her around the hall. 'Let's go and tell Maggie and Lenny.'

Leah nodded. 'I've just taken a test. It was positive. So, I will have a cup of tea. Ring Grandad, Dan, and please ask him to bring pizza back for us four. I'm starving.'

Dan and Leah walked back in, hand in hand. It was Dan who announced: 'Guys, we want you to be the first to know we are pregnant.'

'Congratulations to both of you,' their dear friends said immediately.

Then Maggie said hesitantly, 'Dan, a puppy and a new baby, won't it be too much?'

Dan shot a look at Leah. 'What do you think, darling?'

'We want both, Maggie,' Leah confirmed. 'Sexy Bum and Love.'

Dan laughed, 'I don't suppose you want all five. Hmm?'

'No, but I'll give you five, Dan Ryan. Come on, text Grandad - we need pizza.' Leah watched Dan texting.

She turned to Maggie. 'So, you were sworn to secrecy, Maggie?'

'We knew that you and Lenny thought Hero was past it. As a matter of fact, he was an excellent match on paper. He'd had all his health tests and X-rays done. We didn't tell you in case the mating with Dolly didn't work, but it did. Hero's just as good a stud as his dad, so it seems.' Maggie laughed.

'Mm,' Leah mused.

'Congratulations. You were trying, I take it?' Maggie grinned.

'Yes, we were, but I think Alice is going to be put out,' Dan said ruefully, then he appealed to Leah. 'How could you think I was being unfaithful with two girls at one time?'

It was Maggie who answered. 'Have you read those messages? They have a double meaning: read them again, Dan.'

Dan took Maggie's phone from her and scrolled

through the messages. 'Well, I suppose you have a point.'

Leah glanced out of the window and saw Alice perched on Eros's shoulder as the family returned from their meal and started piling back into the kitchen. 'Looks like we must invite Eros up here more often.' She was watching Angel, who seemed to have taken a shine to his wonderful Greek charm.

'He's in London quite a lot. Maybe we can entice him up to Yorkshire, or the equestrian events, and we can take Angel with us to be groom,' Dan suggested.

'In your dreams! That girl wouldn't shovel anything up. She aims to be a Princess, like Alice, and I believe your cousin has met his match because he thinks he's a Prince or at the very least a Greek god. Now, isn't it time we ate?'

As the others began playing with the puppies, Leah made an announcement. 'Just in case you think I'm greedy,' she said, lifting a large piece of pizza to her mouth, 'I want you to know we are not only welcoming the patter of tiny paws into the house, but we are also expecting another baby.' She said it so matter-of-factly that it took a second or two to register.

Joey and Ben squawked and did a dance together around the kitchen. Eros almost fell over, and then he caught Angel's expression. Maybe there was something about having a loving family that he should explore.

'It's going to be madness in this house,' Joey said, cuddling Leah.

'I don't know about madness, nor even about two moments of madness. I predict there'll be a whole lot more,' Leah said.

EPILOGUE

Joey and Ben couldn't contain themselves.

'What time is Dan fetching Ethel home? We have a surprise for her in the hall,' Joey announced and clapped his hands.

'What kind of surprise?' Leah asked as Ruby walked in with the expensive cat basket Joey had bought in London.

'Must be this cutie. Who is this for?' Ruby asked, placing the basket up high so that Hero didn't frighten the tiny kitten inside.

Just then, Dan walked Ethel in and sat her by the table. 'We've brought you here for lunch, Ethel, because the boys have a surprise for you,' Dan said, helping her to a chair.

Ethel looked up at Joey. 'What surprise?'

'I remember you said how lonely you were since

Katkins died, so we have brought you KittyKat,' Joey said, taking the tortoiseshell kitten out of the basket.

'Oh, Joey,' Ethel breathed and held her arms out for the kitten.

'And if you peg it, you've no reason to worry because Halley, our Aussie Shepherd likes her too, despite being twenty times her size, and we can adopt her,' Joey said self-importantly.

'Joey,' Leah complained.

'I'm just being practical. *How* old are you, Ethel?' Joey teased her.

Ethel took it in good part and was so happy and excited. 'I can stay home now,' she said. 'The house has felt so empty since Katkins died that I never wanted to stay there. Thank you, boys, thank you so much.

Just then, Eros walked into the kitchen, holding Angel's hand. 'I suppose I will have to return to London soon,' he murmured regretfully, squeezing her hand.

'I think you must,' Angel agreed.

'How long are you staying, Eros?' Dan asked. 'You know you are always welcome here. Leah wondered if you'd like to explore Yorkshire with us. Heaven knows, we could all do with a break after what's happened.'

'I'm staying long enough to buy Angel a new car, then it's back to the big city, but I could return in two weeks. I have to say, I find visiting Yorkshire fun.' Eros rather shyly watched Angel's face. It was a new experience for him, wanting to please instead of being so spoilt.

'It's OK, Eros, I'll have Marvin towed away to be mended,' Angel said, letting him off the hook.

'A bet is a bet, Angel, and you won it fair and square,' Dan objected. 'You were both trying to drink the water to keep yourselves sober but alas, you didn't know how sneaky my ex-PA was, and you were already so drunk you couldn't tell water from vodka. The same thing must have happened to a lot of folks.'

'This makes the whole thing disqualified,' Angel stated. 'How can I take a car from someone when your ex-PA doctored the drinks? I play fair, Dan.' With that, she walked to the door to let some fresh air in, but both Eros and Dan had seen the sparkle of tears in her eyes.

'Marvin was on his last legs, you said yourself he was smoking,' Leah remarked as she finished loading the dishwasher. 'Take what the man's offering. He's a lot of things, Eros, but he is not a shirk.'

'You didn't fall off your stool either, and I passed out twice that I know of - and that was before we started on the tainted water.' Eros moved over to Angel and sneaked a hand around her waist, pulling her back to him. 'Come on, don't get upset, Angel. If you don't want a brand-new car, I can get you a second-hand car that will be reliable. What do you say?'

'How about we go looking for a vehicle now?' Dan asked.

But Eros was shaking his head. 'I already bought the car.' He glanced at his watch. 'It will arrive any minute now.'

'What?' Angel spun around. 'What if I don't like it?'

'Then I'll be in serious trouble, won't I?' Eros declared calmly.

'I hope you haven't bought it from Dead-A-Loss?' asked Dan with a grin.

Eros beamed at the private joke, then suggested, 'Let's have a cup of coffee and wait for the transporter to come. That will let me see if I've learned anything about you Yorkshire folk and what kind of car you need to help you traverse these moors in safety. One thing is for definite, Angel. I want nothing happening to my beautiful Yorkshire girlfriend.'

Angel stared at him. 'What do you mean?'

'What I'm trying to say is that I'm falling for you, Angel, and I would like to see where our relationship goes.' Eros smiled at her wide- open mouth. He was praying she'd say yes.

'Does that mean I get to come to London?' Angel asked, breathless.

'Oh, yes, without a doubt. I will travel up here to

see you too. I am assuming Dan and Leah will allow me to use their house as a base.' He watched as they both nodded. 'There, we have an agreement. You will stay with me in my apartment in London, and I will stay here when I come to Yorkshire to spend time with you, and if you like - and assuming Dan will allow me to take his jet - I can show you Alonissos too.'

This almost overwhelmed Angel; she threw her arms around his neck.

Alice pulled a face. 'Don't kiss. Eww.'

Eros ruffled Alice's hair. 'Can I kiss Angel if I promise to come and see you more often?'

Alice was thoughtful for a moment, then nodded. 'If I'm allowed more sweeties fwom London, yes.'

Dan tutted. 'We don't hold people to ransom, Alice. If Eros is kind enough to come and see us, then the only thing he has to bring is himself. Oh look, the transporter has arrived! Let's see what kind of car Uncle Eros has bought Angel . . .'

EVERYONE WATCHED the first car come off the transporter. Eros was scrutinising Angel's reaction with a big grin on his face.

Her face was a picture of disappointment. 'I'm not

driving that around,' she spluttered. 'It only has three wheels, and it's purple!'

Everyone seemed to be laughing at Angel's reaction to the Reliant Robin, and she was so caught up with the purple car in front of her, she didn't see the other vehicle slowly coming down the transporter ramp. It was a Land Rover Discovery Evoke in a lovely silver colour with cream leather upholstered seats.

'Would I be so cruel as to let you drive around in a car as humiliating to your ego as that?' Eros questioned. 'The silver one is yours, Angel.'

Even Leah gawped at it. Wow, she thought, Eros must be serious about my cousin.

Dan shared Leah's surprised gasp.

'No, no, no, that is too expensive for me, Eros,' Angel said in disbelief. 'I'm just a country girl.'

'Yes – a country girl in need of a decent, reliable vehicle.' Eros held his hand out to her. He'd known this woman only two days, and it pleased him so much that he could at least get her in a quandary. She'd been doing it to him from the moment he almost collided with her. Gently pulling her towards the vehicle, he opened the driver's side door. 'Come on, get in. Try it out for size.'

'This is too much.' Angel felt so emotional. 'This is really mine?'

Eros nodded. 'It is, but you may have to collect

me from York station when I visit.' He ushered her into the vehicle. 'Shall we all go for a short drive? I am fancying those fish and chips with . . . with . . .'

'Mushy peas,' Angel laughed. 'I mustn't drive – I don't have insurance for it yet.'

Eros said sweetly, 'Oh yes, you do. Forgive me. I took your licence from your handbag. You can drive us down into Whitby, and maybe we could walk around the Abbey ruins before we eat. It's my treat.'

'We won't all get in, but I can drive the rest of us down,' offered Leah. It was nice seeing Angel so happy; the young woman had had it rough over the past few years.

Angel herself felt giddy. She knew she was falling for this man, and the vodka hadn't helped any, but this was way beyond her wildest dreams. She said a little shakily, 'OK, let's all go. Thank you so much, Eros.' Taking his face in her hands, she kissed him on the lips, and it felt so right.

LATER THAT AFTERNOON while Tom and Alice were playing with the puppies, Alice asked, 'Are we keeping these two puppies and having a baby brother or sister?'

Leah cuddled her close. 'Yes, darling, we are.'

'And Brian is arriving this afternoon too, but he

will be living in the far field away from the house,
Alice.' Dan studied his daughter's face.

'Can I introduce my baby sister or brother to
Brian?' Alice asked, but she wasn't surprised when
everyone chimed in with a resounding, *'No.'*

ACKNOWLEDGMENTS

Thank you to Joan Deitch. Your words inspire me.

Thank you to James for your expert website design, advice and help. Feel Design.

Thank you Michelle Morrow. Publishing Executive.

Thank you, John, Jess and my family.

ABOUT THE AUTHOR

About the author . . .

Gracie Bond loves a good romantic comedy, either to read or to watch on Netflix. Her favourite go-to novel is *Pride and Prejudice* - and she's happy to watch one of the Bridget Jones movies or her latest love *Something Borrowed 2019* any time of the day. Among Gracie's interests are Newfoundland dogs, horses - and handsome Yorkshire men. Her idea of fun would be to ride a spirited horse along a Northumberland beach, followed by a pack of her favourite dogs.

Gracie lives in Yorkshire with her partner John and their Newfoundland Jess, and she has close connections with Whitby, the setting for this novel. *Two Moments of Madness* is the second volume in a planned trilogy about a Yorkshire family. The first, called *Anything for Love*, introduced the main characters and described the unorthodox method in which they first met . . . Join them now, five years later, for more big laughs, fresh country air and darker dramas.

You can follow Gracie on:

Visit her website: www.graciebondauthor.co.uk

TikTok: @graciebondauthor

THANK YOU AND FREE EXCERPT IF YOU SIGN UP TO MY NEWSLETTER.

To my readers, truly and gratefully, I thank you.
Indie authors are always grateful for **honest reviews**.
Writers work very hard, many, many hours a day to
bring you new stories and characters.
You are the reason why I am here writing.

SIGN UP TO MY FREE NEWSLETTER
GET FREE EXCERPT OF MY 3RD IN SERIES.
Chance to become an ARC reader.
Some bonus excerpts too.
Click on the link below.
https://graciebondauthor.co.uk

Printed in Poland
by Amazon Fulfillment
Poland Sp. z o.o., Wrocław

25618619R00210